My Best Rival
Dougie K. Powell

Spectrum Books

Copyright © by Dougie K. Powell

Artwork: Adobe Stock – © tong2530, Aliaksei.

Cover designed by Spectrum Books.

All rights reserved.

Paperback ISBN: 978-1-915905-27-7

No part of this book may be used or reproduced in any manner whatsoever without written permission of the author or Spectrum Books, except for brief quotations used for promotion or in reviews.

This book is a work of fiction. Names, characters, places and events are fictitious.

First edition, Spectrum Books, 2023

Discover more LGBTQ+ books at www.spectrum-books.com

Contents

1. Chapter 1 — 1
2. Chapter 2 — 19
3. Chapter 3 — 29
4. Chapter 4 — 53
5. Chapter 5 — 66
6. Chapter 6 — 79
7. Chapter 7 — 95
8. Chapter 8 — 110
9. Chapter 9 — 120
10. Chapter 10 — 133
11. Chapter 11 — 160
12. Chapter 12 — 181
13. Chapter 13 — 204
14. Chapter 14 — 216
15. Chapter 15 — 228
16. Chapter 16 — 239
17. Chapter 17 — 246
18. Chapter 18 — 259
19. Chapter 19 — 270

Chapter One

Ru

It never takes much for something to escalate; at least that's what I've noticed. Like if you were at a job interview and doing really well. Then at the end, you get a twitch in your eye while looking at one of the interviewers. All your hard work goes to waste and they send you away, deciding you have an 'attitude problem.'

When I was a toddler, I used to run around the house in manic circles, clapping my hands stupidly at our terrified cat. All it took was for Riki to stop once suddenly, and intentionally, in my opinion, to send me flying towards the screen doors. Now I have scars on my right palm and left ear for the rest of my life.

It's like when you throw a pebble into a pond. We sit back and watch the pretty ripples while the fish freak out in the water. One small thing literally shakes their world apart. I don't even remember exactly what I said that afternoon, only that I might as well have set a Gandalf-level firework off in the field. All I remember is that whatever I said changed everything forever.

I remember people walking in groups or lying on the fresh green grass, despite it being still damp from the morning. Everyone's uniforms were still clean, crisp and orderly; home repairs from the summer holidays still holding up. It was a rare few hours of sunshine, a teaser of joy before the monotonous rhythm of the school year set in. It was topped off with a clear blue sky, only offset by a few wispy cirrus clouds.

I had been lying on my back, my hands on my stomach, with my backpack serving as an unsatisfying pillow. There was giggling, a twirl, and a gasp over something. I sighed, barely paying attention, before muttering something dumb.

Then there was a foot in my side.

I rolled a few inches down the incline. Fire flashed in my eyes as I scrambled to my feet. My head shook until I spotted a smug grin. I saw blonde hair scraped back into an impossibly tight ponytail, a tiny blue vein throbbing on his brow. His tie was pulled right up against his long neck, even though it was lunch time and no teachers were watching. I made sure of that.

I grabbed the tie and pulled hard. There was barely a flash. A moment of stunned confusion before I was shoved straight back.

"Fight! Fight! Fight! Fight!"

The sharp, ringing sound of a body hitting the metal, chain-linked fence was like a calling beacon to everyone else on the field. Books and balls were dropped as everyone swarmed towards us in a thunderous stampede. Fights had a funny way of doing that. All social pretence and cliques were swiftly abandoned for the communal lust for disruption. Cheers echoed around the synchronised chanting within seconds, encouraging our declared battle. A battle growing steadily more intense by the second.

I coughed as I pulled myself off the fence. My eyes honed in on the smug smile in front of me. I clicked my neck.

"You bitch!" I charged at Ocean, my hands outstretched, ready to rugby tackle my opponent to the ground.

Ocean dodged to the side.

"Learn to keep your dumb mouth shut, shithead!" Ocean spat back. The side of his hand smacked against my shoulder.

"Learn to not be such a tool about your shitty hair!" I grabbed his thick blonde ponytail and yanked so hard his neck snapped back.

Ocean hissed through his teeth. Long, wispy strands of hair fell over his blazer. His broken hairband curled up like a squashed caterpillar as it blew away.

"Screw you!" Ocean threw a roundhouse kick at me, his shoe slamming into my hip.

I stumbled backwards. I threw my arms out, waving them frantically like a young bird trying to fly. My ears grew hot at the crowd's laughter. My fists clenched. I locked my rage onto Ocean. Before throwing a punch at his stomach.

Ocean dropped to the ground. He choked as all the air inside him shot out of his lungs. I didn't pause. I kicked him hard, taking advantage of my rival's incapacitated state. He shoved my ankle suddenly, making me lose my balance.

Ocean got to his feet. He wheezed like a haunted steam engine. He jerked his elbow and caught me on my side hard enough to leave a substantial bruise. I grunted, taking half a step to the side. Ocean winced as he straightened up, grabbing hold of the chain-linked fence with his long fingers. He flicked his hair out of his eyes. I puffed out my chest, my thick arms hanging either side of me with my head bowed forward. I scuffed my shoe on the ground before charging at Ocean like an angry rhinoceros.

He barely flinched.

Acting quickly, I grabbed Ocean by his collar and butted our heads together. The hasty move ended up causing more damage to me than Ocean. I saw the blood spurt from my nose before I felt it. I sniffed, my mouth instantly filling with a tangy metallic taste. Ocean looked both amazed and horrified.

I raised my fist. Ocean grabbed my wrist, yanking it away as he stamped on my toes.

The rest of our group stood with the crowd circling us, their bags and books at their feet. Noah shuddered; gagging in sympathy when I punched Ocean's stomach. He always looked green whenever these fights broke out, especially when there was blood. He swore later that he heard something click when I smashed my nose against Ocean's forehead, but given the roar of the crowd, I think he imagined it.

Enzo was right at the front, cheering the loudest, and throwing his gangly arms up in the air with a huge grin on his face. We had given up questioning why Enzo got so keyed-up at his two friends kicking each other's asses. He just seemed to like the excitement.

Freja stood at the edge of the throng, her eyes narrowed at us like a disappointed big sister. She realised she'd just missed her window of opportunity to intervene, something she had recently taken on as her personal responsibility. Her head began to throb and she tried to decide whether to scream at us, tear her hair out or start stamping her feet.

Violet tugged on her blazer to try and distract her. She hammed up her shock, curling into Freja's side with a hand clasped over her mouth, the other hand trembling against her cane. These were the only times she hammed up her stiff legs. She knew Freja's attention was better used on her; something I agreed with. Freja hugged her, tutting as if the embrace was all for Violet's benefit. She cupped her head, letting them ground each other.

"Alright, that's enough!"

There was a sharp tug on my arm as the monitor took hold of me. The crowd around us scattered like deer after a gunshot. Noah had to drag Enzo away by his sleeve; Enzo whining like a three-year-old who had been told he couldn't have any more sweets. Freja backed away only by a few metres, watching us disapprovingly.

"Fuck you, Barbarian!" Ocean hissed, kicking out like a toddler. He looked almost manic, his long hair ruffled and stuck up Robert Smith style from the static.

"Right back at you, prissy-headed freak!"

"Enough!" the monitor screamed again, separating us with a firm yank. "To the head's office, both of you!"

The on-lookers who had been chanting encouragement minutes ago now broke out in a mocking, synchronised "ooh!" My cheeks burned as I was swiftly kicked from my pedestal of renowned warrior to bratty child. I dragged my feet, watching Ocean from the corner of my eye. His cupid-bow lips were sporting a full-on pout. I wiped my nose with my already ruined sleeve as more blood trickled down my front.

Light footsteps followed us to the door. I winced at the first 'tut,' feeling Freja's disappointment burning into my back.

Ten minutes later, Ocean and I were sitting on the lumpy sofa outside the headteacher's looming metal office door. I was holding an ice pack to my nose while Ocean clutched his stomach.

"Shithead..." he mumbled.

I scowled at him, ready to come back with something equally devastating, when the creepy door opened slowly. The smell of cigarette smoke wafted out of the office, followed by a pathetic hint of vanilla air freshener. I noticed Ocean's nose twitch before he bit the skin on his thumb.

Tempest looked down at us with his jailer's stare, his bulky arms folded across his faded felt jacket. He blinked slowly, sucking in his teeth to stifle a yawn. "You two again?" He sighed, stepping aside and gesturing for us to follow him. "Alright, let's get this over with."

I noticed the small pinch of satisfaction in his face when he saw us wince. We stood up, his receptionist snatching the ice pack from me. Her nose was turned so far up it looked like she was fascinated by the ceiling.

With my hands free, I shoved Ocean out of the way before he even got a chance to step in front. Ocean shoved me back, tripping me slightly on the way to the plastic chairs opposite the headteacher's desk.

The office was one of the smallest in the school, despite being assigned to the headteacher. It was a narrow, rectangular room with a varnished mahogany wooden desk at one end. The desk was a bit too long. Tempest had to edge himself through the gap between it and the wall every time he wanted to get to his chair, his gut balanced over the surface. His desk was in its usual state of organised clutter, with a stack of papers a foot tall on one end, all stained with ink and pages jutting out. The other end had a heavy outdated desktop monitor that looked more like a plastic paperweight than a computer and a hastily emptied ashtray, coated in a thick layer of grey dust.

Rather than having peeling white paint like the rest of the school, Tempest's walls just had exposed crumbling brickwork, covered in tattered half-filled cork boards and various posters aimed at students. I took in promises of support for drug users, anti-bullying measures and safe spaces for LGBTQ+ students. The gaudy colours of each poster made my eyes sting.

The door swung shut behind me with a bang. Tempest's office could be covered in sunshine, glitter and the softest plush toys; and the heavy, thick metal door could still make me feel like I was entering a prison.

Tempest stood watching us like a stone statue, waiting for us to settle down.

I had always thought there was something very stony about the headteacher. Everything about him was so grey; his eyes, his hair- even his skin had a strange, grey tint to it, even if he didn't look particularly unhealthy otherwise. Despite being pure silver, Tempest's hair was still rather thick. It was combed back away from his eyes, showing a very slightly receding hairline. He was the kind of man I thought could have been very attractive when he was younger, with his chiselled jaw and sharp eyes. These days, however, he looked perpetually exhausted, like he slept every night on a bed made of rusting spikes. Wrinkles pulled at the corners of his eyes and a permanent glare was carved onto his face.

When we were sat down at last, the two chairs placed as far apart as we could manage in the small space, Tempest dragged his heavy wooden desk chair across the floor and sat down himself.

"So, what was it about this time?" Tempest asked, leaning forward.

"He said my hair looked like pubes!" Ocean whined, running his fingers through his wavy hair, still knotted from our fight.

"You started it, you fancy-ass bitch!"

"Enough!" Tempest slammed his fist down on the desk. "What on Earth has gotten into you both lately? Do you want to get suspended again, Hamasaki?"

"No..." I griped. As much as I hated school, I definitely preferred being around Enzo and Freja than the host family

I had been placed with before. I gagged, imagining spending another week babysitting and eating stale biscuits.

"Good. And Jónsson, do you want to lose your place on the Paris trip?"

"No," Ocean sighed, gritting his teeth.

"Good. So, you'll both stop this?" Tempest gave us a stern look as we sulked in our chairs.

We shot death glares at each other before mumbling reluctant agreements under our breath. Tempest decided to take this as a good sign.

"I want you to consider yourselves very, very lucky that I have a meeting to prepare for this afternoon," he said, speaking very slowly, as if one word out of place would activate a hidden bear trap. "You can consider this your absolute final warning on the matter. If I had the time right now, it certainly wouldn't be. As it is, I'll take your word one last time."

He grabbed his pen and wrote out two detention slips.

"You know the drill; I'll give you an hour and a half after school and write to your families... again." He handed us the slips before waving us out. "Now please, get out of my sight and stay out!"

We stormed out of the office, shoving each other again for good measure while snapping, "Pig head" and "Frizzy priss!"

From the corner of my eye, I saw Tempest bite the end of his pen. Just before the door closed behind us, I heard a mutter of: "Those poor boys," followed by a heavy sigh.

~*~

"Sounds like you guys got off easily," Freja said, running her long thumbnail over her fingertips in a peculiarly threatening manner.

Our group had gathered in the dorm common room for the gap between classes and detention. It was a dusty, ragged-looking room with limited, long suffering furniture, some of which seemed to have been in place when the school was first opened. There were a few worn, felt sofas, an Edwardian bookcase with half the glass smashed and swear words in a variety of languages carved into the wood, and a plastic round school table in the centre, circled by four rickety folding chairs. All of which seemed to tilt to the side the moment its user got their focus back. Along the east wall was a pokey kitchenette with seventies-style plastic cabinets, two rusty hobs, and a microwave that looked and smelt like it had never seen soap or a scrubbing brush. Ocean hovered beside it, making a round of tea with the limescale-encrusted kettle.

The dorm was one of the oldest buildings in Averesch International School- an old school of around one to two hundred pupils, placed right out in the ass-end of nowhere. Both the dorm and the main entrance building were stone Gothic-period structures with very few modern upgrades on the outside. The only other original building was a crumbling Lutheran chapel at the end of the field. It held services on Easter and Christmas for any students who couldn't go home and the unfortunate teachers who had been sentenced to watch over them. Occasionally, some quirky couple would commandeer it for their rustic, historic wedding ceremony. So far, all couples seemed to regret their decision, learning only after the service began how much the roof leaked and how marshy the surrounding undergrowth got.

Between the three buildings were various others that looked increasingly more out of place than the next, including a dull grey sports hall, a plastered white science building and a tiny swimming hall jammed in between the church and the forest border. There hadn't even been space for more than four changing cubicles inside, so most sessions ended with a hoard of students, dripping wet and hugging themselves, trudging back to the sports hall wrapped in their towels, with their flip-flops slapping against the grass.

I thought it represented the school very well. It looked fancy from the front, with its arches and old brickwork, and produced good enough exam results to convince parents from all over the world to send their children there; while the inside failed to adhere to the promised standards they were charged for. They were standards that seemed to decline the longer a student attended the school. When I'd first arrived, aged thirteen, I was ordered every day to take my earring out or to wash the gel out of my hair. Nowadays, as a senior, I dyed my hair whatever colour I wanted, wore a nose ring every day and rarely bothered combing my fringe forward to cover my eyebrow bar. I was still nagged for them, only now there was nothing the teachers could threaten me with since it was my final year anyway, and ignoring their lectures led to little or no consequence.

"I was sure you guys were going to get kicked out this time," Freja said loudly, narrowing her eyes at the silence.

"Please," Noah scoffed. He sat on the windowsill, his back and braided hair pressed against the glass. His knees were pulled up towards his chest, his drawing pad resting on his thighs. He was the only one of us who bothered to get changed when classes finished, possibly so he wouldn't get smudges of pastels or paints on his uniform. He was wearing an orange t-shirt and a pair of ripped denim jeans with sharpie stick figure doodles along the seam. "That would mean missing out on the school fees. As bad as it would look for you guys to get kicked out of this pretentious place, it'll hurt the school even more to lose your money and fill two year thirteen places a month into a term."

"It's probably not worth Tempest's time," I said, shrugging, stretching out on the sofa so I could place my shoes casually on the armrest. "Since it wasn't a big fight." Freja's eyes rolled in blatant disagreement. My sore nose throbbed, as if backing her up. "We were just going at each other!"

"As per usual," Freja muttered. Her thick eyebrows crossed above her swamp-green eyes, her lip protruding out as she blew a strand of hair away. During the warmer months, her hair would lighten the tiniest bit each time it was in the sunlight, gradually turning to a fairy-tale strawberry-blonde, which tended to take the edge off her fierce looks. Unfortunately for us, the autumn gloom had brought it back to her usual mousy brown with small streaks of orange. It was currently twisted into two tight buns on either side of her head, with green velvet ribbons that trailed down to her shoulders.

The tension was thick as the others waited for her verdict. Even Cam seemed quiet. She sat on one of the opposite sofa with her copy of *Sandman* in front of her, letting the distorted, undead creatures on the cover face Freja instead of her. Noah quickly copied her, holding his drawing pad up as he scribbled furiously.

Freja scoffed and threw her arms up in exasperation. "Are you idiots trying to get kicked out? You know, you may both be morons, but we do actually like having you around!"

Ocean gripped the counter while he stared at the kettle. Freja pinched his elbow, making him jump. I snorted, so she gave the sofa a kick. It bounced half a centimetre off the ground and I had to scramble to stop myself from falling off. "Are you guys just bored or something? This really isn't funny anymore."

I looked at the ceiling while Ocean picked up the boiling kettle.

For a friend group as close as ours, arguments were inevitable. I knew Freja and the others supposed it was lucky that out of everyone, only Ocean and I clashed. Except Ocean and I had been clashing more and more in recent weeks. What had started as a simple one-upmanship was rapidly turning into a bloodbath.

The rivalry had been comforting at first—something everyone in the group could join in with.

It had started almost at the very beginning, the second week after Enzo had introduced us. Enzo being the 'centre' of our friend group. He had a wide smile and warm brown eyes that just seemed to attract people to him. He was bouncy and energetic, with charm oozing from every pore of his being. Everyone in the school knew who Enzo was and, on some level, I considered myself very lucky to be one of his best friends. He was kind to most people but selective about who became his friend. Friendship with Enzo was like a blood oath; so when he dragged Ocean to his fourteenth birthday party, we just accepted that Ocean was going to be one of us now.

A little while into the party, I had bet Ocean I could eat more jalapeños than him. I don't know why- I had barely said anything to anyone since the party had begun, let alone a new person. There was just something about the way Ocean raised his chin up, his posture and the twitch in his button nose that begged me to challenge him in something.

Ocean had scoffed and accepted the challenge, which immediately had the rest of the party up and cheering. The contest had ended in a draw after I threw up, due completely to some expired eggs I'd eaten for lunch, and Ocean had to wash his face to stop the waterfalls that poured out of his nose and mouth.

Afterward, when we were both cleaned up, we laughed and shook hands.

The following week, we had been playing football on the lawn, with our non-sporty crewmembers watching from the sidelines with bemused smiles. One by one, every member of the group joined them, more interested in seeing Ocean and me tackle each other than playing themselves.

Ocean had won the tournament by four goals to three. I protested for weeks that it was Noah's fault for not paying attention while in goal.

The dynamic had built up over time, various creative jibes being thrown around; mostly settling on our favourites of 'Barbarian' and 'Frizzy'. It hadn't been until the beginning of the current school year that the insults had picked up. The words themselves hadn't even changed. While before Ocean would scoff and bite back with a sparkle in his eye if I made a comment about his pre-treated morning curls or other grooming habits; now his eyes just darkened and his pink lips curled into a snarl.

His words didn't feel the same either. It was harder to let 'barbarian,' 'cave-boy' and 'freak' roll off my back when they were spat at me with pure venom, rather than being sung with an airy laugh. The jibes no longer carried the same sense of good-natured fun, and our tussles were now so intense that some of our friends were starting to suspect we actually wanted to seriously hurt each other.

From the moment I had muttered the off-hand comment about Ocean's hair back on the field, the entire group had backed away.

It was a routine we'd almost perfected at that stage; so much so our last few fights could be played side by side and appear almost in sync. In the beginning, we would circle each other like wild cats fighting over dominance; eyes running up and down the other as we searched for weak spots and breaks in their guard.

Now there was no build-up. We had our rival's movements, strengths and weaknesses embedded in our brains and never let an opportunity slip.

Noah winced when he saw Ocean glare at me, pressing his face further into his drawing pad.

"For God's sake, get your shoes off the armrest!" Ocean snapped, his voice rising out of nowhere.

I deliberately rubbed my shoes against the tattered felt.

"You sound ridiculous," I mumbled.

Ocean spun back around, hair bouncing.

"Open your mouth and speak properly! I'm not going to be lectured by some lazy fat-ass lounging around with his stupid-ass punk hair!"

I just scoffed, ruffling through my short, spiky, dyed red hair.

"At least I don't have to straighten mine..."

Ocean lunged across the room. Enzo and Violet jumped up to grab his shoulders.

"Screw you!" Ocean screeched. "This is all your fault, you unbelievably stupid—"

"Ocean," Violet said in a calming voice. Her puffy hair was pushed back with a uniform headband, showing off her large wooden hoop earrings. She looked at Ocean with a pleading yet firm expression as she rubbed his arm gently. "It's just the communal sofa and you'll be going to detention before you get a chance to sit there, anyway. Your hair is lovely and Ru isn't fat."

Ocean swore under his breath, nudging Enzo and Violet out of the way. Enzo backed off, but Violet clasped Ocean's hand.

Until recently, Violet had only been a causal part of our group. The sort of friend who would tag along to events she happened to be into anyway and would wave at us with a smile in the hallway. Enzo had made it clear she was always welcome, giving her the same bear hugs and toothy grins he gave all of us. Violet returned each one gracefully while still maintaining several connections throughout the school, sitting with a different circle at lunch almost every day.

Her connection with us grew when she'd started dating Freja at the beginning of last year. Now she was as latched on to the friend circle as the rest of us.

I had first thought that Freja's fierce temper had been reigned in simply by her having a girlfriend. However, after getting to know Violet a little more, I saw the particular way they complimented each other.

She was the only person who could stand up to Freja and match her persuasiveness, even if she didn't have the same commanding tone. Her voice was light and somewhat enchanting. Nothing she said ever increased the tension or instigated anger. She just simply stated things as they were and let people reflect on their actions.

"I'm sorry," Ocean whispered, squeezing Violet's hand back and patting Enzo companionably on the shoulder, "give me a minute."

Ocean grabbed his bag and stormed out of the room. Everyone stared at his dramatic exit before their eyes swivelled towards me. I stood up, dragging my feet on the carpet.

"Go easy on him," Violet said calmly.

"What?" I looked at her like her head had just spun all the way around. "You've seen the way he speaks to me!"

"Ocean's just like that sometimes," Enzo said, grinning, kicking his feet as he perched on the table.

"Well, 'most' times these days," Noah mumbled.

"And you guys just put up with that?" I met each pair of eyes. "He comes back all sensitive and prissy and you're taking his side!"

"We're not taking anyone's side," Violet said cautiously. I crinkled my nose, raising my brow at her patronising tone. "Look, I know you and Ocean won't ever get along properly and we won't try to make you. Still, maybe you could... tolerate each other? Like you used to."

I paused at the sincerity in Violet's face.

"Exactly," Freja said in her haughty tone, folding her arms. "We're seniors now. It's time for you both to grow up!"

I ground my teeth. I could still feel Violet looking at me—it was the only thing that stopped me from telling Freja exactly where she could stick her remark. I knew I'd regret it later when I was lying in bed; the perfect put-downs floating around my mind and keeping me awake. In the moment, I thought more clearly than I would in the future. I knew that there was nothing I could say to make Freja truly understand.

Everyone had already decided it was my fault.

I could see why. Ocean was clean, attractive and was usually steady; at least with things that didn't involve me. I was just the big, clumsy rebel. There was nothing I could say that would make them or Ocean think any differently.

Instead, I helped Violet sit down on the sofa, placing her cane carefully beside her, before turning to storm out of the room in a slightly less dramatic fashion than Ocean had.

My shoulders dropped when I entered the dorm room, looking around for any sign of Ocean. I sighed heavily after confirming that it was empty and shut the door behind me with a satisfying 'click'. We had an unspoken truce when it came to the dorm room, but I wasn't sure if I could hold myself back before I'd had some time to breathe. My body felt heavy, even more so when I bitterly realised that I didn't have enough time to have a proper nap before detention.

I looked at Ocean's perfectly made bed. The bottle of hand lotion, hairbrush, glasses case and photograph of him and his foster father were placed precisely on his nightstand as they always were. Noah and Enzo had once started moving them slightly whenever Ocean was out of the room, only to be poked every time he came back and saw what they had done.

Noah and Enzo had just laughed, of course. Ocean had rolled his eyes, waggled his finger at them, and laughed too. My body felt heavier when I thought of Ocean laughing. It was always so sudden it would make me jump; long cheery hiccups as his lips stretched wide. He'd cover his mouth with his hand in an attempt to silence the loud inhaled giggles, but it never made any difference. His laugh sounded so stupid that everyone else would start laughing, too.

It had been so long since Ocean had laughed properly. He had 'laughed', but we knew it wasn't real. It was forced, sharp exhaled laughter, not the inhaled honks we knew were sincere. I wondered if we'd ever hear Ocean's real laugh again. A heavy lead weight sank from my chest to my stomach.

A bolt of lightning struck suddenly in my brain. I stormed towards the end table and knocked every item onto the floor with one sharp, impulsive swing.

"Fancy bitch!" I collapsed onto my bed, trying hard to get Ocean's face out of my mind.

My nose stung when I pressed it against the pillow. I could feel a strange tingling warmth spreading through it. It wasn't a feeling I would describe as painful, just a throbbing reminder of Ocean's head crushing against mine. Something knocked against my bedpost. I peeked out from behind my pillow to see a solid tube of hand lotion beside my bed, rolling side to side on the carpet.

I reached down, scooped it up, and placed it back on the nightstand.

Chapter Two

Ru

I reported to the detention office two minutes before four o'clock. I wasn't surprised to find Ocean standing outside already, his hands stuffed deep in his pockets. His hair was once more neatly combed and scraped back into a ponytail, that familiar small blue vein throbbing on his forehead. He hadn't had time to straighten it again, so I could see the waves and kinks sticking out. He looked up, his nose twitching as he stared daggers at me.

Ocean looked at the ground when the door opened suddenly, focusing hard on the linoleum floor as if it held the secret to some generational mathematical equation.

Neither of us recognised the teacher on duty. He looked both of us up and down before handing us buckets of cleaning supplies and ordering us to the gym to clean the equipment, with a promise to come pick us up at five thirty. I was sorely tempted to drop everything and just head to the gym when time was up. Judging by the teacher's bored face, he likely had no idea what state the gym was currently in anyway. He didn't even walk us there. He just ushered us off with a wave before shutting the office door in our faces.

I have, of course, thought a lot about what would have happened if I had skived off detention that day. It certainly wouldn't have been the first time. If I believed in that kind of thing, I would have imagined some celestial force dragging me and my cleaning bucket along.

I picked up my bucket and followed Ocean as he walked speedily through the side door and across the field towards the sports hall.

Despite being at peace with my punishment, I didn't feel the need to hurry over with the same determined speed as Ocean. I let him rush ahead, losing track of him in a matter of seconds. I kicked at a jagged stone in front of me, staring at it as it bounced across the grass.

I decided that if I could kick seven stones before I reached the sports hall, then I would activate a hidden time machine to take us both back to before the fights. I would enter the gym to see Ocean wagging his pink tongue at me before making some snarky comment about how this was probably the closest I had come to soap in weeks. I would snap something back and splash Ocean with water. Then Ocean would smile at me again; a wide, genuine grin that showed his pearly teeth and made his eyes shine.

My toes ached by the time I reached six. I felt my cheeks heat up as I focused on one last round pebble near the sports hall door. I dug my heel into the ground and reared up for a kick. My foot slipped over the stone, my sole brushing the surface- before I fell backwards. I landed hard on my butt, my cleaning supplies falling out over the pathway.

Ocean was already at work when I caught up, a bucket of soapy, warm water beside him and the gym mats splayed out on the floor, surrounded by net bags of balls and abandoned gym equipment. He scowled at me before dunking his brush so hard in the water it splattered everywhere.

I scowled back. I dropped my bucket, grabbed a bottle of cleaning solution and aimed it at one of the punch bags. I sprayed furiously, immediately assaulting the bag with so many droplets it looked like it had been left out in the rain.

We worked in silence. Ocean kept his back to me, no matter which way he turned. Every time he spotted me from the corner of his eye, he scrubbed a little more furiously. He didn't stop until the brush scraped against his hand, his skin red from the cheap soap.

"Shit, I'm getting blisters on my palms," Ocean whined. "This is all your fault!"

"Whatever," I mumbled as I wiped down the punch bags.

Ocean raised his sore and soapy hands, looking at them like they were about to shatter.

"I need my lotion."

"You're such a girl."

"What did you say?"

Before I could think, Ocean's foot hit the small of my back and I surged forward into the bags.

It didn't hurt that much. My still sore nose got squashed when I fell on my face, but it was more the suddenness of the attack that threw me off balance than the kick. I shook it off before slowly turning around.

"What the hell is your problem?" I screamed. The mild irritation inside me burst into full-blown rage the second my mouth opened.

I shoved him hard. Ocean tried to duck out of the way, but I still got him. He barely recoiled. He sprung straight back with a slap ready. I blocked it. I threw myself against Ocean, causing him to fall onto one of the damp mats.

"I just cleaned that you shit—"

I cut him off with a punch right on his stupidly high cheekbone. His head bounced on the mat. He blinked. With a shriek, Ocean punched me right back. His nails dragged at my cheeks and collar. His usually bright eyes pierced into me. They were dark and almost deranged.

The tension between us rose catastrophically. We went through the usual repetitive motions. So much so, they almost felt rehearsed. Ocean slapped my cheek. I retaliated with a punch to Ocean's arm. Ocean lifted his leg to knee me in the stomach. My breath hissed through my teeth. My ears were primed for the sound of Freja's voice screaming that we were immature morons. My shoulders subconsciously braced, waiting for someone to pull us away from each other or to beg us to stop.

Nothing came.

The sounds of our fight echoed off the walls of the gym. Every slap, smack, and punch rang out like thunder. I tried to force myself to breathe. I tried to remember Tempest's threats that morning or my promise to Violet.

I let go of Ocean suddenly. He landed with a thud on the mat, looking both dazed and furious. I scooted back a few feet. I closed my eyes, trying to count back from a hundred in my head.

Before I reached eighty, long nails scratched over my eye. I saw white beneath my lids. The tight coil in my chest snapped.

"You think you're so fucking perfect!" I roared. Ocean tried his best not to wince as my knee hit his shoulder. "You think you're so smart and oh, so fucking tough! You're not! You're just a dumb, pompous asshole! No one—"

I had no idea what the end of my rant was. Whatever I was about to say got cut off by Ocean punching my throat. I coughed as I struggled to breathe. I was starting to feel dizzy from the adrenaline and lack of air, but I couldn't let Ocean know that.

I immediately pounced on him like a wild tiger. I grabbed at Ocean's wrists, pinning him down to try and give myself a moment to regain my breath.

"Shit!" Ocean hissed.

Ocean's nails clawed at my grip. Clearly, neither of us was ready to give in. I straddled him, sitting upright on his hips in an attempt to pin him down and subdue him with my superior weight.

Ocean stiffened. His face went ghostly pale, his eyes wide as he looked straight up at the ceiling. His back was pressed flat against the mat.

I looked at Ocean, startled by the sudden change, yet still gunning to get one over on him. My breath sounded like a wild boar's snort as I let the rage pump through my body. There was a voice in my mind telling me the same thing over and over. That Ocean deserved this. It didn't give reasons or explanations. It just kept repeating: *Ocean deserved this.*

I pressed my weight more firmly against Ocean's hips. I narrowed my eyes, ready to strike.

"No, stop!" Ocean croaked in a dry whimper, "I... I give up!"

My heart skipped a beat. I blinked rapidly, pulling my mind back into focus. "You what?"

I sat stiffly on top of Ocean as I tried to figure out what could be going on. Our hips shifted at the same time. I finally noticed what was pressed against my thigh. My arms dropped to my sides.

"Get off!" Ocean's eyes were covered by a thick blanket of hair, glued to his face with tears. His ponytail now looked like a limp rat's tail drooping at the back of his head. My heart sank with a strange new form of empathy as I heard my nemesis practically begging. "Please, just get off me."

"Ocean..."

The pause in the fight gave Ocean the opportunity to free one of his legs. He swiftly pulled it out from underneath me, kicking wherever his foot would land. I fell backwards, crashing into the bag of volleyballs beside the mat. I hissed as I sat up, my body aching. Ocean curled into a ball on the mat, burying his face between his knees. I swallowed a lump in my throat.

There was no denying what I had felt. And there was no denying how much it had scared Ocean. I couldn't even try to deny how much the reaction calmed the rage inside me. It was as if the bucket of murky cleaning water had been dramatically thrown out all over it.

The bucket balanced on the edge of the mat, the water rippling as Ocean trembled.

"Hey, Frizzy..."

"I'm not gay!" Ocean snapped, clinging to himself tighter.

"Hey..." I crawled closer. The adrenaline was still pulsing through me, allowing me to momentarily turn my brain off. "It's okay."

"Ru..."

I swore I could see Ocean's heart beating. His body was trembling so hard it looked like he was vibrating. Sweat poured from every inch of his skin, making the white of his school shirt almost see-through.

"Please, don't tell anyone. Especially Cam! Please!"

I recoiled, realising that Ocean was definitely begging at this point.

"Ocean, it's okay." I gripped his shoulders with both hands, deciding to grant my rival a small moment of humanity. "I'm not going to tell anyone. Stop freaking out, okay? It's not a big deal."

Ocean whimpered. He looked like his entire world was crumbling down, all because of the strange turn the fight had taken. The fight, which had started out like every other, had changed things. For both of us. There was no going back to the old routine now.

My stomach clenched at the sight of Ocean looking so vulnerable, so afraid. A strange weightless feeling passed over me; my heart trembling at the thought that followed.

After everything Ocean and I had done to each other, after how we had ended up in the gym together to begin with, the last thing that would make sense would be to react in the way I was thanking out. Right then, I wasn't capable of logic. None of my thoughts were coherent. I couldn't even remember Ocean getting on my nerves to the extent I felt the need to get into a fistfight just five hours earlier. I couldn't even remember the reason why we had started fighting five minutes ago!

Looking into Ocean's eyes, I could only think about how they were the colour of the sea – blue with a hint of green. His face was smooth, without a trace of stubble on his chin or upper lip. I looked at his tiny, slightly upturned button nose, his high, sharp cheekbones and thin, pink cupid-bow lips. They were impossibly soft-looking, even as they wobbled.

I don't know how long I stared at Ocean's face. I wasn't as stupid as people thought I was. There were feelings inside me that I knew about, feelings that I couldn't have ignored even if I bothered to try. I didn't even hate Ocean for giving me those annoying feelings. If anything, I hated myself for being dumb enough to have them. I was sure the feelings were partly responsible for why Ocean got on my nerves so much, although I'd never even dared to hope that Ocean's antagonism towards me was caused by the same thing.

At least until now.

The scent of disinfectant stung my eyes and nose, but I didn't pay it any mind. A meteorite crashing through the roof of the sports hall wouldn't have taken my focus away from Ocean. A gigantic dinosaur could have been smashing through the school, surrounded by screams declaring that I alone could stop the terrorising monster and I still wouldn't have been able to move until I acted on the stupid instinct pulling at every string in my mind.

I scratched at the mat with my blunt fingernail, pulling a trail of soap residue with it. It wasn't like the stupid instinct would change anything more at this point; other than possibly snapping Ocean out of his panic. I had nothing to lose.

So I went for it.

I gently cupped Ocean's cheek before leaning in and pressing my lips against his.

I felt more than heard Ocean's small gasp, our lips vibrating together. Ocean froze, letting the kiss continue for a short, wonderful moment, before pushing back. The shove was weaker than before, but just as frantic. "Don't," Ocean mumbled. He gripped my blazer. "Stop, please. Don't make fun of me."

Ocean's tone confused me even more. He sounded so defeated it was almost off-putting. I wanted the sass Ocean had used when he snapped at me in the common room! It spurred me on, hitting me with a sudden need to bring him back.

Deciding that I had already gone this far, I took Ocean's hand and squeezed it tight. I grabbed a handful of Ocean's soft hair and crushed our lips together, laying Ocean against the workout mat. I loosened my grip on Ocean's hand so I could lace our fingers together. I made sure to leave a little give in my hold, wanting Ocean to know he could push me off at any time. With every second that passed, I hoped a little more that he wouldn't.

"Ru," Ocean whispered. He pulled one of his hands free so he could run his fingers over my shoulder. The touch sent a pleasant buzzing sensation down my spine. "This... This isn't too awful."

I smirked. "That's probably the nicest thing you've ever said to me."

Ocean rolled his eyes and cupped the back of my neck.

"And this..." Ocean took a deep breath. "You want to do this?"

"You know I do," I said bluntly. I placed my hand on Ocean's hips. Ocean's eyes widened before he finally let them close, a long breath of relief escaping from his lips.

I knew the moment he opened them again he was going to panic. Instead, he kept himself in the moment and let himself enjoy my hands on his body. Ocean sighed audibly, as if surprised that I was such a good kisser. My tongue moved steadily against his, while I stroked his hair with a gentle touch I didn't think myself capable of. We both let ourselves get swept away in the kiss, embracing the moment for what it was.

I pushed closer against Ocean with every flick of his tongue. For a brief moment, I felt like I was going to die. As if Ocean was holding me above a high cliff and if he let go of me for one second, I would fall. I didn't want it to stop. It would soon. The pressure was so high it was ringing in my ears. The feeling was so electric, almost heavenly; yet also bitter sweet.

Because the moment it was over, I would have to let go of Ocean.

Without a chance to prepare, the pressure burst, exploding inside my head and in my stomach. I pressed into the skinnier body beneath me, harder than I intended. Ocean didn't seem to mind. He trembled, gasping into my mouth as he rode through the moment himself.

I rolled off of him, lying next to him on the red workout mat, breathing heavily. We both stared into space.

I slapped my hand against the mat until I found Ocean's. He wrapped our fingers together.

~*~

Enzo sat up on his bed when I opened the door. A lollipop stick hung out of his mouth and a comic book lay open on his stomach. Noah was sitting by the window again, playing something on his tablet with a pile of textbooks and homework next to him.

"Ru, Ocean!" Enzo said with a grin. "How was detention?"

"How do you think it was?" Noah asked sarkily, not looking up from his tablet.

I looked at Ocean. My rival was staring back at me. His end table was once more perfectly arranged, as if it hadn't been disturbed at all.

"It was fine," he mumbled. "I'm going to take a shower."

I leaned against the door as Ocean pushed past me into the bathroom, my eyes following him.

Chapter Three

Ru

"Mr Hamasaki!"

I sensed others jump at the sharp tone in the teacher's voice, but I didn't bother looking up. I let the scolding fly over me, continuing to tap my pencil against the desk. A hand decorated with beige nail polish slammed against my textbook.

"Mr Hamasaki!" Mrs Tempest sniffed sharply.

"Yes?" I said irritably. I hated the way Mrs Tempest said my name. She always hissed it, her voice dropping as if she were swearing.

She placed her hands haughtily on her hips. "That's 'Yes, Mrs Tempest', surely?" she said huffing, "could you please be so kind as to stay in the real world with us?"

I didn't react.

I hated that condescending tone some teachers used – as if I was wasting Mrs Tempest's time just by existing in the same universe as her. The insistence that the right way to behave was to just take whatever crap she gave me and that would somehow prepare me for real life.

Unlike her husband, I didn't think Mrs Tempest could look like anything other than the thin pencil of a woman that stared at me now. Her face was plastered with far too much make-up, so much that her crinkly lips made wet noises when she smacked them in rage.

I knew how to end this situation: apologise and let Mrs Tempest give me that disapproving glare before she continued her lecture. Unfortunately for her, today I really couldn't. I opened my backpack, sweeping my books off from the table so they fell inside.

"Excuse me!" Mrs Tempest said, her tone going up a few octaves. "Where do you think you're going?"

I didn't reply. I threw my backpack over my shoulder and walked straight out of the classroom. I didn't even slam the door behind me. It just swooped back, leaving Mrs Tempest standing in the centre of her classroom and the rest of her students in a state of either amusement or shock.

"Stupid freaking..." I shook my head.

Mrs Tempest really wasn't worth my anger. As annoying as she was, with her squeaky, huffy voice that made her sound like a stupid little girl while she acted as if she were the most important person to ever grace the face of the earth, hers wasn't the irritating face that kept flashing in my mind like a strobe light.

For the first time since I'd started her economics class, I wished I could have focused on her. It would've at least kept the image of my dumb roommate out of my head.

Since the incident with Ocean in the gym, we'd been avoiding each other as much as possible for two people that shared a dorm room and a friend group. Luckily, the only class we shared was Ms Khil's history lesson twice a week. This allowed me to be buried in my thoughts during the rest of my classes rather than staring across the room at Ocean.

I was convinced that Ocean thought what happened between us was nothing more than a terrible, confusing nightmare. He obviously hadn't mentioned it, but I hadn't been expecting him to avoid me as if I stank like the plague mixed with sulphur. If our eyes did happen to meet, he'd go so pale he was almost see-through. When it happened in the dorm he'd cough loudly before stretching, acting as if he had drifted off for a moment. This, of course, made me want to scream my lungs out! Watching him make such a big dramatic show out of this had me wanting to throttle him.

Then there were the times outside of the dorm. Ocean would hold a long blink before pretending to look straight past me. Even when there hadn't been anything there other than the dark, wild forest. That made me want to punch myself as hard as possible and bury myself away somewhere where I'd never get in his way again.

I didn't think I'd ever been this confused in my entire life.

I'd never fussed about crushes before or spiralled into doubts about things like 'attraction.' I'd realised I liked guys maybe four or five years ago, even if I hadn't yet acted on it or announced it to my friends. It wasn't that I was embarrassed or ashamed of being gay, I just didn't see why it was anyone else's business and hadn't been in a situation where it seemed relevant to bring up. The only person I'd told so far was Freja, simply because she'd been the only person who'd thought to ask. I never understood why other people's romantic affairs were supposed to be interesting to those not involved.

I didn't mind being perpetually single. I wasn't even sure what romance consisted of. When I was a child, people would call my friend Mio my 'girlfriend' because we were always together. I knew I liked her a lot. She was fast – faster than me – and always full of energy. I was impressed by everything she did, leading to a companionable relationship of challenge and competition. Every time we came across a hill, one of us would bet the other that we could run up it faster. It never mattered who'd won since we'd both roll to the bottom cackling. If we went swimming, it would be 'who can hold their breath the longest,' when it snowed it was 'who can build the best snowman,' or win the snowball war that broke out every single time.

I guess I had been too naïve at the time to know if my feelings were romantic. Still, that had never stopped the adults around us, including my dad, calling her my 'girlfriend'.

We never cared, we just carried on with our games. I remembered running outside with Mio the moment the rain stopped to see whose toy car could roll down the mud hill the quickest. Mio always won that. She had much better cars than I did. Mine were all secondhand and most had busted wheels. Mio's were mostly new and brightly coloured. I didn't matter since she always let me play with hers.

If that was what having a girlfriend was, I thought I could handle it. It wasn't until middle school that my innocent fantasies of play fights and car races had been crushed.

I'd been forced into a group of lame boys who I never really considered friends. I hung out with them, purely out of boredom and lack of a better option. When my dad packed me off to Averesch a year later, I didn't miss a single one of them and struggled to remember their faces after a few months. Of course, by then I was Enzo's friend.

I remembered the lame boys going on about some model, fawning over pictures of her and saying how hot she was. I knew he couldn't care less. I'd be damned if I can remember her name, but then again, I'm pretty sure none of those jerks knew it to begin with.

I was more impressed with the men in my health magazines and boxing manuals. Even if I wasn't completely smitten with them, as my friends had seemed with the model, I knew I was certainly more interested in them. Then again, my admiration hadn't been exclusive to the male champions.

There had also been a cute female bodybuilder, with short blonde hair. I loved watching her compete. There was something rather dainty in the small jump step she'd take back as she dropped her weights to the ground after a victory. She was just as strong as some of the men in my magazines and a lot more persistent.

For a while, I had been certain that I was just attracted to strong people. Strong women and strong men – whatever the 'sexual' term was for that. Because I'd put up posters of the female bodybuilder and watched her on TV over and over, this seemed to qualify her as my first crush.

It wasn't until last year that I finally decided I found the male fighters just that little bit more appealing. Those thoughts might have been prompted for the first time when I tripped up my *actual* first crush during a game of field hockey, sending him face-first into the mud. He'd pushed himself up, spluttering and almost shrieking. His blue eyes narrowed at me as he flicked his now grimy ponytail over his shoulder- before slamming his hockey stick into my ankles. I flipped over, almost landing right on my head with my legs in the air. Laughter surrounded me, the loudest being a sharp, inhaled giggle.

I clutched my backpack strap tighter at the memory, speeding through the school. I burst through the doors of the gym, happy to see that it was mostly empty, with only a few other seniors using their free period to work out. My stomach tightened when I saw the unused mats stacked neatly in the corner; instantly reminding me of rolling over them with Ocean in my arms. I tried not to run past them. Instead, I walked swiftly into the locker room.

I threw my backpack on the floor, furiously popping open the buttons of my school shirt. I winced when I saw myself in the mirror, catching the swells of fat around my hips and stomach. I hadn't thought it was possible for them to get bigger overnight, but now I wasn't so sure. I pulled my t-shirt on so quickly my head almost got stuck in the armhole. I wrapped my hands before making a beeline for the punching bag. I didn't always train this way; usually I focused on weights outside of club practice. Today, however, the bag seemed to be calling me, dragging me over by the flames of my anger.

I took quick breaths, keeping my stance as I had been taught, throwing fast punches at the bag. The world around me seemed to stand still as the bag swayed, bouncing backwards as I threw my weight into it. The chain holding the bag to the ceiling creaked. I didn't bother to worry about whether it would break. Again.

I shut my eyes. I wanted to picture Ocean's face in front of me instead of the blue leather punching bag. I'd been in this position many times after a trivial argument; imagining I was punching him right in his prissy face, bloodying that stuck-up nose.

This time, when I swung my fist at him, those shiny eyes filled with terrified tears. My fist stopped, stuck in place as it hovered stiffly a half-inch from the ethereal Ocean.

I collapsed onto the crash mat beneath me, ignoring the strange looks from the others. Luckily, they all decided I didn't need any attention and left me to my misery. My irritation grew as warmth pooled in my stomach, remembering being in this position less than a week before.

I couldn't blame myself for my interest in Ocean. Ocean had those long legs, a cute smile and beautiful, bouncy hair. He was strong but slim, with skin so smooth it was like glass. If I were watching a Hallmark movie and Ocean walked in,

I would know immediately that the protagonist would end up with him, no matter how long they had known any other potential love interest or how stupidly rushed the relationship got.

As objectively attractive as Ocean was, I hadn't thought there was anything between us other than reluctant friendship. While I had been honest with myself about the not-so-random 'feelings' I would experience during our conflicts, I'd never put too much into it. It had to be one-third attraction to Ocean, one-third rush from the fights, and a final third of virgin frustration.

Now, I'd seen a side of Ocean I hadn't seen before – a vulnerability and softness to the usually snippy tool.

I growled in frustration, again forgetting the others in the gym. Most of who were now staring a little too stiffly at their own targets.

I needed to clear my head. Now.

~*~

Something in my brain really hadn't been wired right that day since instead of just texting Freja and asking her to meet me like any normal person would, I decided to go down the old-fashioned route of just heading back to the common room to see if she was around. It wasn't a completely stupid thought. If Freja didn't have class or swim practice, she'd likely be there. Then if no one from our circle was there, I'd just grab a snack before going to lie down.

I didn't stop to think my plan through until I was taking wide steps down the upper corridor, my shoulders hunched. I hadn't showered after my stint at the gym, so the straps of my backpack were practically sticking to my shoulders. I clutched the left strap, my knuckles white as I squeezed. The door to the common room was open, with two voices trickling out. I strained my ears for Freja's.

My ears burned. I felt the back of my neck grow hot at a familiar soft voice. I froze in the corridor, my palm sweating around the strap of my backpack. I pressed against the wall, peeking through the gap in the door hinge. Ocean was there. Most of his face was so pale he looked like he was about to keel over, but the tip of his nose was bright pink, as if he had a cold. He was sitting at the table next to Cam, several textbooks open in front of them. Cam looked about ready to tear up the exercise book in front of her. Ocean just sat up straight as if he were dining with royalty, serene and calm.

"Oh, God!" Cam fell back in her chair, her short hair sticking up at odd angles. "This is so stupid!"

"I know." Ocean placed a comforting hand on her upper back.

He looked at the scrawled mess that was his friend's French homework. Even from where I was spying, I could see there was more ink blotched in the margins than on the actual page.

"How do you remember all these rules?" Cam rubbed her eyes. "Just makes me feel like a right spanner!"

"I know," Ocean said again. He took out a pencil, turning to a new page of Cam's notebook. "How about you tell me what you want to write? Then we can discuss it together."

"No, I can't have you write my homework for me again," Cam said, pouting. "Last time you did that, Mr Maes noticed after the first sentence. He was really narked about it!"

Ocean nodded, looking at his own work. I imagined Ocean's neat, swirly cursive handwriting. It in no way compared to Cam's scrawling.

"How about I write it out first and then you can copy it, okay?" Ocean flipped to a fresh page in his workbook, placing

Cam's homework sheet beside it. "Alright, so an activity you enjoyed at the weekend."

"We had netball practice on Saturday?" Cam said, shrugging.

"Okay so: *Le Samedi, nous avons eu pratique de netball.*" Ocean wrote out the sentence carefully. "Can you read that?"

Cam cleared her throat.

"Okay: *La samedi—*"

"*Le*," Ocean corrected gently, "because it's a masculine word."

Cam just groaned again, scrunching her face before screaming at the ceiling. "It's so dumb! This is dumb! They're words."

"Yes," Ocean said, sighing. "But those are the rules." He put his pencil down, staring at the sentence he'd written out for his friend.

"Hey!" Cam scooted closer. "You okay? Are you sick of explaining this to me again?"

Ocean smiled, his cheeks trembling.

"I'm completely fine, Cam. I mean, I'm with you after all!" He took her hand off his shoulder and patted it gently before setting it next to her homework.

"Stop being so flowery, Ocean. It's creepy," Cam said sharply. "I wouldn't mind some tea, though."

"Of course!" Ocean took his glasses off and hurried to the communal kettle. He rummaged through the cupboards for teabags, gritting his teeth when he saw they'd been shoved right to the back behind a stack of ramen packets and a dusty jar of pickles that I was sure had been there longer than I had.

I twitched, torn between guilt and pride, remembering that I had moved them there this morning just to piss him off.

Ocean tapped his hands on the counter, staring at the kettle as it boiled. He looked over when Cam scoffed, catching her pulling an exaggerated, goofy face at her homework. She flipped her paper off, rubbing her eraser furiously over the page, turning it into a fuzzy mess.

"You behave," she said playfully, giving her book a light smack.

I looked back at Ocean. He watched her endearingly, leaning against the counter with his arms folded across his waist. I dug my nails into the wallpaper.

Cam stared at her paper with her hazel eyes, her brow furrowed in concentration, the pink tip of her tongue stuck out of the corner of her mouth. She admittedly did look cute. Cam was funny and always tried at school, even if she got distracted in every single lesson. It wasn't really her fault. It just seemed to be her funny way. Sometimes you'd be talking to her, and she'd get this glazed over look in her eye. After a while, she'd shake and grimace when she realised she'd missed most of what was being said.

No matter how frustrating Cam seemed to find French, not having a head for languages, she would keep at it, letting Ocean guide her as he tried to explain the rules.

A sickening feeling spread through my stomach and up towards my throat as I watched Ocean stare at Cam. I may have understood why he felt the way he did about Cam, but that didn't mean I wanted to be anywhere near it. My gut squeezed in on itself as I saw Ocean open his mouth, silently rehearsing what he wanted to say. I considered what to do; stand here and endure it, or speed off at the risk of Ocean hearing and noticing I was there. He could be speedy and might possibly get to the door before I made it to the stairwell. Out of that worry or maybe just twisted curiosity, I stayed, digging my fingers so deeply into the wall I could feel the plaster pushing under my nails.

"Hey, Cam," Ocean said quietly.

He lifted the boiled kettle the moment it clicked, filling the teapot. The dread inside me loosened a little at the familiar movement. Ocean lived by the philosophy that everything, even awkward or embarrassing conversations with a crush, were better with a cup of tea. I couldn't say he was wrong.

"Yeah?" Cam's confused face immediately turned into a bright, sunny smile. She cheered as the teapot was brought over, as if it were a grand prize rather than a simple hot drink. "Thanks, Ocean!"

"You're welcome." He poured them both large mugs of black tea, adding milk and three sugars to Cam's. "Can I ask you something?"

"Sure!" Cam picked up her mug. Her face remained a picture of joy.

Ocean straightened his back in the chair, lifting his chin and squaring his shoulders. His hands curled around the mug as he brought it closer to his body.

"I like you," Ocean admitted. My hand scratched down the wall, leaving a trail of claw marks. "A lot. And we've been doing this for a while."

Cam whined in dismay. "I know! I'm sorry, Ocean. I'm not trying to be a dumbass about this, I promise!"

"No, you're not," Ocean said quickly. "That's not what I meant. I just meant we've been friends for a long time. We've spent a lot of time together and I was wondering... do you like me?"

"Shut up, Ocean!" Cam batted his cheek like a kitten. "You think I care enough about French to sit here struggling beside someone I didn't like? You're the best!"

Ocean's lip wobbled while his jaw stayed perfectly still. I swallowed, my mouth suddenly dry.

"So... would you go out with me?" Ocean blurted. "Be my girlfriend?"

Cam's face fell. I watched Ocean's heart drop into his shoes.

"Oh, Ocean..." Cam let go of his cheek. "I don't think that'd work. I like you, but you're my friend, you know? I don't think I could see you 'that' way."

"I see." Ocean turned to the teapot. He kept his stiff, snooty posture despite the shake in his voice. "I would be a good boyfriend. I promise. I'd do anything you'd ask of me."

Cam didn't quite cover her mouth in time to stop her laugh. She cringed, quickly straightening her face, the corners of her mouth still quivering. She picked her mug up, blowing before taking a sip of her tea. "Well, you already do everything I ask," she said, winking. "Besides, that's not the relationship I want. I can't think of any girl who would want that kind of relationship."

"What do you mean?" Ocean looked at her, confused.

"I don't want someone who will just do anything for me at the drop of a hat," Cam explained. "Like, literally, if a hat drops! Remember when Janie's hat flew off in the wind and you went running halfway across the field after it?"

"She said she needed it to keep the sun out of her eyes," Ocean protested. "Besides, it looked nice on her."

"That was sweet of you," Cam admitted, "but honestly, girls don't need to be pampered in the way you seem to think we do. I want a boyfriend who acts like an actual person. Not just a robot who goes along with everything that makes me happy."

"Seeing you happy makes me happy!" Ocean looked at her pleadingly.

"Exactly," Cam said frankly. "You think shit like that is charming, but it's creepy as all hell. I know you think you like me, but it seems like you just want someone to take care of. You need someone you like for more than that. Do you understand?"

Ocean didn't look like he understood one little bit. He clutched his stomach; his lips straightened as if he were about the throw up. There was a sharp snap. Ocean clutched one half of a pencil while the other rolled away across the floor and underneath the bookshelf. He bit down so hard on his thumb I could see a bead of blood swelling up underneath his tooth. He was shaking so hard Cam slipped her cardigan off and draped it over his shoulders.

"Do you want to stop?" Cam said delicately, closing her French book.

"No." Ocean quickly stopped her, picking up the remains of his pencil to write out the answers for Cam to copy. "I said we'd finish this, so we will. It's no trouble."

Cam didn't look sure at all and I couldn't blame her, given how Ocean looked like a kicked baby goat. Still, she picked her own pencil back up, seemingly deciding not to deny him a distraction if he needed one. Although she also probably couldn't have afforded to miss another French assignment.

"Thank you, Ocean. You're a good friend."

"Thank you." Ocean dusted the eraser shavings off the page. "Come on, I have a piano lesson in an hour."

Before I could decide what to do next, someone pushed past me to get to the door. I jumped before shoving my hands into my pockets, turning my head as I leaned against the wall. I was trying to make it look like I was waiting for someone, but they didn't seem to care. They just gave me a quick, curious glance before stepping inside and giving the door a weak shove. It bounced off the rusted lock before swinging back with a creak.

I took this as my opportunity to run. I turned back down the corridor, throwing my sleeve over my eyes while I typed out a text to Freja.

~*~

Around an hour later, I was lounging on the grass, staring at the slightly grey clouds with my hands folded behind my head. I checked my phone, wondering what was taking Freja so long.

I grit my teeth in frustration. I'd been considered 'very big for my age' for as long as I could remember and was often denied 'under 18' prices. Yet when it came to buying hard alcohol, I was always asked for ID. Freja, on the other hand, didn't even need to change out of her uniform. She just took off her blazer and tie, snapped open a couple of shirt buttons, and every liquor store employee was just all too happy to help her.

I reminded myself that next month I would be eighteen and permanently free from Freja's ridiculously inflated commissions.

"Ru!" Freja called triumphantly, making her way up the path towards me. Her hips swayed exaggeratedly as she held up her yellow, ink-splattered tote bag with pride.

"Aren't you cold?" I asked spitefully, staring at her bare legs and open shirt. I sat up, sitting cross-legged as a chilly breeze hit both of us.

Freja just grinned and stood next to me with her hand outstretched. I reluctantly reached into my bag for my wallet. Freja waited patiently as I counted out every euro. She snatched up the money, giving me a smug grin as she tucked it into her bra. She reached into her bag, pulled out a twelve-ounce bottle of store-brand rum, and tossed it at me. I caught it, immediately twisting the screw cap with my teeth.

"Thanks," I mumbled, before drinking a small mouthful.

"What's up with you today?" Freja sat opposite me, mirroring my position before pulling out a litre carton of rosé wine. She unscrewed the plastic cap before shoving a blue crazy-straw into the opening and taking a long pull.

"What do you mean?" I said. My voice was muffled around the bottle.

"You – you're all tense and confused looking," Freja teased, nudging me with her foot. "You only look like that when you're trying to think." Freja's grin grew wider than it had when she'd taken my money. "Is it about a boy?"

I clicked my tongue at the excitement in Freja's voice, tapping my finger against my bottle.

I knew that the lack of fights between Ocean and me and the blatant ignoring of each other had been chalked up to Tempest's threats. So far, no one had commented on it, assuming we were just trying to resist the urge to beat the shit out of each other. My chest tightened as I looked at Freja's hopeful and ever so slightly concerned expression. She'd been dying to talk about this ever since I told her I thought I was gay and I badly needed to talk about what had happened. My attempt to throw out my frustrations at the gym had just left me sweaty and hyped up. I was just as confused as I had been since it happened, as well as being out right frustrated! I'd disappeared into the bathroom a few times during the night after hearing Ocean moaning lightly in his sleep. In the morning, Noah had asked if I was sick!

I knew I shouldn't think too much about any of it. Ocean's reaction during our fight could have been completely random, and he'd gone along with things purely out of horniness or embarrassment.

Even so, I couldn't shake how terrified Ocean had looked when I'd felt him against me. He'd looked adorable- and like his entire world was about to collapse. Ocean had never seemed scared before, especially not with me. I needed to know what that meant. I couldn't help agonising over whether

Ocean liked me or was, at the very least, attracted to me. Maybe his overtly chivalrous behaviour with the girls was exaggerated, so no one found out he liked guys too, or instead. He'd never indicated that he liked me before that afternoon, but then why hadn't he punched my lights out instead of kissing me back?

I'd promised Ocean I wouldn't tell anyone, and I intended to honour that, but I figured that if I didn't give Freja any damning details, it would probably be okay. It was highly unlikely that she would figure out I was talking about Ocean – she still thought I hated him, and more importantly, that Ocean hated me. A month of fistfights seemed like a pretty good scapegoat.

"Yes," I admitted, preparing myself for Freja's reaction. "It's about a boy."

Freja squealed, clapping as best she could while clutching her carton. She shuffled closer to me. "Who is it? What happened?"

"It's no one you know," I said quickly. "And even if it was, he was pretty insistent that he 'wasn't gay'. I think he's going through some shit, so I wouldn't feel right telling you his name."

"That's fair," Freja agreed. "So, what happened?"

I took a deep breath. "It's complicated. I've kind of liked this guy for a while," I admitted. "A long time, actually. Then again, I also kind of... don't like him? He's just really... I find him really hot!" I shook my head, certain that my feelings wouldn't make sense to anyone. Not when I couldn't navigate them myself. "Anyway, I never thought he liked me at all. Then, the other day, out of nowhere, we kind of..." I trailed off.

"Tell me more," Freja pressed, sipping enthusiastically on her wine.

"We were alone," I continued. "We were arguing about... something, I don't even remember what. Then we started fighting. The whole thing escalated so quickly. Then all of a sudden, I feel—" I stopped, thinking I was getting too graphic. "We started kissing."

"Your first kiss with a guy!" Freja cooed, leaning in closer. "How was it?"

I certainly wasn't going to lie.

"So, fucking good!" I practically groaned. Even if I couldn't figure out how I felt about Ocean overall, I was willing to admit that the kiss had been overwhelmingly brilliant. "His lips were so goddamn soft. His mouth was so hot! It was pretty perfect."

"Aw!" Freja pulled her straw out to screw the cap back on her wine. She laid down on the grass next to me and rolled over onto my side. "So, what's the problem?"

Now she'd asked the difficult question. I wrapped my arm around her, letting her cuddle me.

"No problem as such," I said, trying to sound casual. "We haven't spoken. Not properly. I'm not sure what to do next."

"Well, have you tried asking him out?" Freja said.

I craned my neck to stare at her as if she'd asked if I'd tried shoving a live snake down my shirt. "What do you mean? Just like... asking him on a date?"

"Yeah." Freja sat up again. "Just tell him you liked what you did and that you'd like to spend more time with him. The worst he'll say is no."

I tipped my rum bottle up and down, listening to the liquid gloop. As obvious as it sounded now that Freja had brought it up, I hadn't considered outright asking Ocean for a date. Presumably, Ocean wasn't ready for that kind of thing with another guy, even if he did like me back. He'd likely just tell me he wasn't gay again, and we'd go back to fighting. The thought gave me a heavy feeling in my gut; like I'd thrown up a little bit into my mouth and was now worried I'd start projectile vomiting over everything. Even so, Ocean blatantly rejecting me didn't seem like the worst thing to ever happen to someone. At least then I would get some closure. The way things were now, not knowing why what had happened, had happened, and not knowing how Ocean felt about it, was driving me more insane by the minute.

"You're right," I said. "I'll talk to him, get this over and done with."

"Maybe you'll end up with your first boyfriend!" Freja teased.

"I doubt it," I mumbled, "but thanks for your help anyhow. I'll, um, let you know how it goes."

"Please do." Freja shifted, kneeling beside me so she could resume sipping on her wine. "So, was it just a kiss?"

"Nope," I said proudly. "We did some hand stuff!"

"Oh, my!" Freja put on a daft southern belle voice, fanning herself with her hand in an exaggerated manner. "You make it sound so romantic."

"Well, as romantic as a sweaty tumble in the gym after school could get."

"Gym?"

I choked on my rum. "Um, yeah," I said quickly. "He's on the boxing team. It was after hours, we stayed late to do some extra shit. Things just heated up."

"Huh..."

I lifted my rum bottle. "Could you get me another one of these?" I asked. "You know, for after I get rejected?"

"Sure," Freja said, standing up. She smiled deviously. "I can go to the store on Limbretch Street, but it'll cost you a thirty percent commission!"

"Whatever." I took another sip.

Next month couldn't come soon enough.

~*~

I wasn't sure how, but I could sense Ocean was around the moment I approached the dorm. I knew Enzo, Freja and Violet had gone swimming, Cam was at board game club and Noah was at the library with his girlfriend Janie. Perhaps part of my brain had decided that since I didn't know where Ocean was, he must be in the dorm room. I could almost smell his powdery, flowery scent as I pushed open the door.

Sure enough, Ocean was standing next to his bed. Perhaps he had sensed me too, given that he didn't even flinch. He just carried on as if nothing had changed, not even looking at the door. He unplugged his hair straightener, leaving it to cool down on his bedside table with the plug across his pillow. Next, he looked at himself in his hand mirror, making sure his bangs were perfectly straight, parting them so the layers came down on the right side of his forehead. He ran his fingers down his cheeks, inspecting his skin carefully as he turned his face from side to side.

I stared at him, my palm sweating around the door handle.

Ocean had taken off his uniform and was now wearing some impossibly tight, grey skinny jeans with decorative rips at the knees and thighs, revealing another black layer of denim underneath. He'd paired them with a tight, cosy looking black sweater that came down to his thighs, with its own small decorative tear on the lower right side. On his left wrist were five rubber bangles hanging loosely over his slim arm. His hair looked so silky, smooth and perfect, nothing at all like the frizzy mess it was when he woke up or the tight, stiff ponytail he wore to class.

"Ru?"

The coldness in Ocean's voice snapped me out of my trance. I looked at the bathroom, confirming to myself that the light was off and that we were definitely, one hundred percent alone. I didn't know when we would be alone again.

I had planned on waiting a while; taking the time to think about what I should say. Now that I was face to face with Ocean, I realised it would be better to get it over and done with. I was ninety percent sure this would end with a foot in my stomach or a slap across my face, but those odds would be the same if I planned this for ten seconds or ten months.

"You look scruffy, Blondie," I teased in a weak attempt to break the ice. "What's the occasion?"

Truthfully, despite his strangely casual attire, Ocean looked just as sophisticated and classy as ever. He stood up, back straight, his shoulders squared as he huffed.

"If you must know, I'm going to the library in the city," Ocean said, reaching for his black messenger bag.

"You know there is a library on campus, right?" I questioned, as if it were obvious.

"Yes, but you see, not every library contains every book in the world," Ocean said, speaking very slowly and rolling the words around his lips. "The library on campus doesn't have the book I want, so I reserved it in the library in Antwerp centre. Now, if this interview is over...!"

He slipped his feet into two sleek black boots. He looked even more elegant with the inch and a half heel and the leather shine going halfway up his calf.

I pressed my legs together, hoping Ocean wouldn't notice.

"God's sake, Barbarian!" Ocean jutted his left hip out, hand resting over the bone, right foot pointed out in front.

While Ocean probably thought his pose made him look dangerous, it made me want to wrap my arms around him and squeeze. I leaned against the closed door—more to stop the others from coming in than to keep Ocean from leaving.

"I wanted to talk to you," I said bluntly, "about what happened."

Ocean's attitude shifted completely. He tapped his fingers against his lips before he started to bite his nails.

"Ru..." Ocean cringed. He tried his best to sound confident, but his voice came out in a small tremble. "What happened was..."

I looked at the impossibly beautiful boy. My heart warmed, the same as it had in the gym when Ocean curled into a ball. Ocean looked vulnerable, scared, and impossibly cute!

"Listen, Friz—" I stopped myself, rubbing the back of my head. "Ocean. If you want, we can just pretend it never happened." I crossed the room, sitting down on Ocean's bed and gesturing beside me.

He shuffled for a minute before reluctantly sitting down, putting as much space between us as he could.

"I won't tell anyone, and I won't mention it ever again." I clenched and unclenched my fists. While the idea of pretending Ocean and I had never kissed broke me a little, I knew I could do it if that was what Ocean wanted. I'd always give him that much respect.

"I can tell you have issues," I continued. "Hell, we all have shitty issues. Stuff we'd rather not deal with. These are the shittiest years of our lives after all!" Ocean couldn't stop himself from laughing a little bit. He looked up from his lap to finally meet my eyes. "I can't deny... I'm totally into you." I felt the heat spread to my face. I hoped Ocean couldn't tell. "So, if you're into it, I'd really like to go out together."

"G...Go out?" Ocean stammered. "Like... boyfriends?"

"Well, yeah." I tugged on my hair. "Don't worry, though. If you're not ready for that, or if you just don't like me, I totally understand. Just, maybe resist the urge to be a tool about this! If you tell everyone I like you, I'll kick your ass so hard you'll taste it!"

I slouched on the bed, leaning on my elbows in a pitiful attempt to seem like I couldn't care less what he'd say next. I expected Ocean to quip back that I 'couldn't kick his ass in my wildest dreams,' or perhaps burst out laughing at the whole thing. My stomach muscles were braced just in case there was a punch. Instead, the only noise was the scraping sound of Ocean rubbing the edge of his now-stubby nail against his wool sleeve.

"Ru," Ocean paused to breathe, "while we're being honest, I... I do like you." I twisted his duvet in my fists. "I'm sorry, this just isn't easy. I mean, I'm not gay!" He flinched again. "I mean, I like girls!"

"I know," I said, trying to keep a matter-of-fact edge to my tone, "but it doesn't have to be that black and white, you know?"

"I'm starting to come to terms with that," Ocean admitted. "Or at least I'm trying to."

My heart was beating a thousand miles a minute as Ocean looked me up and down. I tugged at my shirt, realising that my first three buttons were open. I smoothed my rolled-up sleeves back down, hoping to hide my chubby arms. Ocean crossed his legs, trying to sit up straight with dignity.

He smirked.

"You know, you look a lot less gross up close," Ocean said, his voice teasing but soft. "I can actually see your eyes properly."

"Huh?"

Ocean gave one hiccupped laugh. "I can see your iris. Your eyes aren't just black, soulless pits." He tilted his head. "And your dimples are deeper than I thought. I guess they're not completely swallowed up by your chubby cheeks!"

I bit my tongue. I could tell Ocean was waiting for me to respond, but I was too scared of saying the wrong thing and ruining everything.

Ocean hesitated, pushing his finger through the decorative rip in his jumper.

"Look, Ru. I don't have a girlfriend. I also don't appear to be anywhere near getting one." He grimaced. I could tell he was thinking about getting rejected by Cam earlier. "I don't think I like guys. At least no guys other than..." Ocean's mouth continued to move, even if he didn't finish his thought. He looked like a cartoon character that had been muted.

Ocean edged his hand across the stiff school sheets. He linked his fingers with mine, not even flinching at how sweaty my hand was.

"I'm not ready for anyone else to know yet," Ocean explained carefully. "If you're okay with that, then I'd really like to explore this."

I blinked. I stared bewildered at Ocean- before a dumb grin broke over my face. "I understand that," I said, nodding. "Don't worry, we can keep it a secret."

"Good."

We sat on the edge of the bed for a while, smiling warmly at each other.

"So," Ocean said, eventually, "this date?"

"Well, I could come with you into the city," I suggested. "I'm sure we won't run into anyone." I could tell from his expression that Ocean wasn't sure about that in the slightest. "If we run into anyone, we can always tell them Tempest ordered us to hang out after school until we learn to get along."

Ocean snorted. "Do you think anyone would believe that?"

"Violet and Freja might not," I admitted, "but Enzo and Noah definitely would!"

Ocean tutted, but he still smiled at me. My grin grew wider until it felt like my cheeks were stretched right across my face.

Ocean's smile turned into a grimace when he noticed the grass stains on my rumpled shirt and the mud streaks on my trousers.

"You'll have to get changed first. I'm not going out in public with you when you look this wild, Barbarian!"

I scoffed, but stood up to go through my drawers.

"Whatever, Frizz Head. Just don't let your blonde brain lead us into oblivion."

Chapter Four

Ru

Ocean shoved his hands deep into his pockets the moment we stepped out of the coffee shop. I kept my distance between us now that we were outside rather than hidden away in our cosy corner of the cafe, but it was as if he could sense my presence behind him.

"That was fun," Ocean said, his voice only slightly timid. "We should um..." He smacked his lips before hunting in his black denim jacket for his cigarettes.

"It was," I agreed. I pressed the tip of my shoe hard against the step in front of the coffee shop. "So, you needed to go to the library, right?"

Ocean nodded frantically, exhaling a long line of smoke in my face. My eyes watered, but I didn't get the chance to protest or even rub them on my sleeve.

"Right," Ocean said, stepping backwards. "I'll see you in the dorm!"

He turned on his heels, his boots clicking against the cobbled pavement. I watched the almost twisted figure as it got further and further away before turning left at the end of the street.

~*~

I rammed my shoulder into Enzo as he ran towards me, slapping the basketball with so much force that small stones bounced off the tarmacked ground and ricocheted off my ankles. Enzo winced a little, but he had been braced for the tackle. He turned around, ducking in front of me to steal the ball and run towards the hoop. I tried to catch up with him but didn't get there in time to stop Enzo from leaping up and scoring the winning basket. Enzo whooped in victory, catching the ball as it bounced just so he could throw it back at me.

"Best out of five, then?" I said, catching the ball with both hands.

"Yeah, if you like." Enzo grinned wickedly despite his heavy breathing, showing off all his large, chunky teeth like a friendly shark. He lifted the bottom of his shirt up to wipe his face. His thick black curls were tied into a top-knot right in the centre of his head, small ringlets spilling out and sticking to his sweaty forehead.

Despite the autumn weather, we were more than willing to play on the outdoor court. It was nearly always free during the colder months and it gave us the motivation to push ourselves a little bit harder. I bounced on my toes to warm myself back up before throwing the ball at Enzo.

"Hey! Take it easy!" Enzo gasped, the air knocked out of his lungs from the hit. The ball dropped and rolled away. Enzo brushed the hit off and ran after the ball. He tossed it up in the air and caught it, only to lose it again when he tried to spin it on his finger. "You taking your frustrations out on me?"

"Huh?" I came at him to try and grab the ball. Enzo just dodged out of the way, cackling.

"You know," Enzo teased. "Trying not to invoke Temp's wrath!"

He ran backwards, dribbling the ball in front of him. I lunged for it, but Enzo shot the ball over my head. This time, it bounced straight off the hoop and rolled to hit the chain-link fence surrounding the court. We both ran after it, but this time I managed to successfully ram Enzo out of the way and grab hold of the coveted ball. I tossed the basketball into the air a few times, Enzo jumping up to bat at it like a kitten. I slid to the side and threw it straight into the net. I spun around, flipping Enzo off with both hands.

"Won't you look at that?" I taunted, ignoring Enzo's previous victories.

Enzo just returned the gesture before grabbing the ball and tossing it from one hand to the other.

"Okay, seriously, is everything alright?" Enzo asked bluntly. I screwed my face up before making another grab at the ball.

"Everything's fine," I said, running around him in a circle. We heard Violet chuckle from where she sat at the edge of the court, a book in her lap. "Stop trying to distract me. You that scared you'll lose?"

"Okay, first of all—," Enzo dodged past me and effortlessly threw the ball through the hoop, "I don't need to distract you to win." He smiled smugly as he stepped to the side and scooped up the ball. "You seem super eager to beat me today. Presumably, because you're too scared to challenge Ocean to anything in case Temp makes good on his word."

My cheeks flushed at the sound of Ocean's name. I tried to snatch the ball from Enzo's grip in a play to distract him. Enzo just took a step forward with a straight face. He dropped the ball, letting it roll away as he pressed the tip of his nose against mine, standing stiffly and breathing right over me.

I batted him away.

"I'm not scared of Temp," I mumbled. I turned, walking away to grab my water bottle. It was just for something to do other than look straight at Enzo. I hated how well he could read me sometimes.

Enzo wasn't exactly book smart. He was the student who was constantly told he could be top of the class if he applied himself, but who didn't have the time to study when he could be doing everything he actually wanted to do. With the exception of Ms Khil, teachers seemed to have it out for him, giving him D grades in his mock exams after weeks of him not handing in the study material. Then when it came to the actual exams, he'd come out with mostly Bs and be perfectly content with that.

I was incredibly jealous that he seemed to get away with putting in the minimal effort. Not enough to make me actually work harder or complete assignments on time, but enough to make my teeth grind when I came out of the same exam with a C+ after Enzo had spent exactly the same amount of time as me playing video games and one-on-one basketball when the rest of our group had been studying.

"Okay fine, so you're not scared of Temp," Enzo said, shrugging. "Noah's right, he's got better things to worry about than one-on-one battles between you shitheads. Still, it raises the question..." He picked the ball back up, deciding to occupy himself by bouncing it repeatedly against the rattling metal fence next to my head. He grinned when he saw my eye twitch in irritation. "Why did you suddenly make it your life's goal to kick Ocean's ass this year?"

Goosebumps prickled up my arms, and I quickly began rubbing at my skin as if I were cold.

"Because he's annoying." I took a swig of water. It went down the wrong way, making me cough violently. My eyes stung, water trickling from my nose. I turned around, clutching my chest, dragging it out for longer than necessary as I tried to put my thoughts together into an answer.

Things had seemed mostly fine during our impulsive first date. Ocean appeared to be having a good time and conversation had flowed between us better than I could ever remember it doing. I'd even made Ocean laugh! I could remember clearly his head jerking back as he covered his mouth with his hand, wheezing as his body trembled and his eyes looked ready to bulge out. I couldn't remember what I had said that had made him laugh so much. All I could see in my mind was his full-bodied, carefree laughter, followed by a sigh and a smirk. He'd sunk back in the cushy sofa, clutching a tall, glass coffee mug with both hands. His eyes stayed on me, filled with softness and joy, rather than anger and desperation. I wasn't sure why, but that look made my hand move under the table until it rested on top of Ocean's thigh.

He was so warm I thought for a split second that I'd burn myself. My tongue pushed at the roof of my mouth as I carefully moved my hand a few centimetres up his thigh, then back down as fluidly as I could.

Ocean sipped his latte, his eyes flicking down. He didn't return the favour or hold my hand, but he didn't slap me away either.

As far as I could tell, Ocean had enjoyed himself. It was just the aftermath that had been a little confusing. I wasn't a dating connoisseur, but was pretty sure dates weren't supposed to end as awkwardly as my coffee date with Ocean had.

"Dude?"

I turned to see Enzo grinning at me, gesturing crazily to the basketball. I threw my water bottle down and ran over, only for Enzo to jump past me and dribble away.

"So, you're for real done with being an angry asshole?" Enzo asked, keeping himself and the ball moving.

"Yeah, it's fine. Sorry for scaring you guys," I said between grabs for the ball, my arms flapping around like an angry goose. "It's not going to happen again."

"Did you and Ocean agree on that?"

"Why do you care?"

I snatched the ball from Enzo and threw it towards the hoop. The illegal and overly ambitious attempt fell predictably flat. The ball dropped and bounced along the ground before it even came close to its target.

Any taunt that Enzo wanted to throw at me was cut off by the sound of slow, sarcastic clapping. Enzo and I turned to look at Violet. She was clutching her book. All three of us looked at the metal doorway of the court. A girl was smirking at us, her school tie loosened halfway down her shirt and her skirt hitched up midway down her thigh.

"Bravo, Ru," she said in a flat, dull voice. She turned to Enzo. Her sour face morphed into a shy smile. "Hi, Enzo!" She tossed her hair a little too obviously, her eyelids batting as she pressed the tip of her tongue against her top teeth.

"Hey, Marie," Enzo called, holding his hand up stiffly. "What can I do for you?"

I patted him on the shoulder before running after the ball. I tossed it casually from one hand to the other while walking over to Violet, who hummed with her eyes fixed on her book. The humming got gradually louder with every second. Her eyes focused so hard on her page she looked like she was trying to turn it with the power of her mind. I started to bounce the basketball repeatedly, letting the thudding noise cover whatever words were being exchanged at the other end of the court.

"Okay!" Enzo called. He ran back to us, looking more out of breath than he had when we'd had been playing. "Let's start over."

"What was that about?" I asked, holding the ball under my arm. Enzo shrugged, not even trying to make a grab for it.

"Nothing," Enzo said simply, "she just wanted to ask about something."

"'Something,'" Violet mocked back in a squeaky voice. Enzo just shrugged again.

"Yes, literally something," Enzo insisted.

"Everything is 'literally something!'" Violet stuck her tongue out, grabbing her cane to jab it at Enzo's ankles.

Enzo just made a game of it, jumping up with both feet whenever the cane got close.

"There's a party at Martine's family's cottage this weekend," Enzo said between jumps. "She wanted to know if I was going."

"Isn't that awkward?" I asked. "I'm pretty sure finding out if the person who dumped you is going to be at an out-of-school party is more than *something*." I looked at Marie, who was now sauntering away with her hips swaying. Two other girls intercepted her, squealing as they ran over. I cringed, wondering if dogs could hear them.

Enzo took advantage of my distraction and knocked the ball out from under my arm. He turned around, throwing and bouncing the ball off the side of my head. I grimaced and lunged at him. Enzo threw the ball over his shoulder, jumping out of the way of my attack. He wrapped around me, hanging off my back like a gibbon.

"What would you know about it, huh?" Enzo teased, tightening his grip around my shoulders.

"Right." I pushed him off. "How would I know?"

"Aw, don't be like that!" Enzo looped his arms around my waist, pulling me so close his sweaty shirt stuck to mine. "I'm just messing with you."

"Get off!" I demanded, my arms hanging limply at my sides.

Enzo just squeezed tighter, calling for Violet to come join him. She shook her head without looking up from her book.

"Come on!" Enzo shouted centimetres away from my ear. "Super platonic bro-love time!"

I stood there stiffly as Enzo pressed slobbery kisses into my cheek. I could see Marie out of the corner of my eye. She was sandwiched between her friends, all of them glaring while her ex-boyfriend refused to let up.

"Stop it!" I gave Enzo another shove, wriggling away. "You're all slimy and gross!"

Enzo pouted, but finally relented. He pulled his arms away to grab the now stationary basketball. He ran backwards, raising it up above his head triumphantly, as if getting hold of it had been his plan all along.

"I should probably go," I said quickly, grabbing my bag from underneath Enzo's. I threw the strap over my shoulder, wincing at the squelching sound it made when it hit my sweaty skin. "I have to take care of some things."

Enzo shrugged, his cheery grin still painted on his face. He threw the ball at the hoop, fully prepared to turn the two-player game into a solo expedition.

"Hey," Violet said suddenly. She put her book into her bag and grabbed hold of the fence, pulling herself up before we could offer to help. "Do you want me to come with you?"

"No," I said, wincing when I heard my own curtness. "I mean... I'm going to shower, then nap. Just a little drained."

Violet didn't look convinced, but she didn't pry. She nodded, slipping back down the fence to stretch her legs out in front of her.

"You'll be okay getting back?" I asked automatically.

"Shut up," Violet shot back, her soft voice not carrying any real poison. She picked her book up, licking her finger and flicking back to her page. "Bye now!"

I didn't say anything more. I turned, leaving Violet to her book and Enzo to his ball as I walked broodily back to the dorms.

~*~

I went straight to the shower the moment I returned to my room. I let my sweaty tank top and shorts drop to the floor before picking them up with my feet, balling them up and tossing them into the laundry basket by the bathroom door. I tried to focus on the tiled walls as I scrubbed my hair. Ocean's bottle of blueberry scented shampoo seemed to be mocking me from the shelf. It always made the bathroom smell unbearably sweet after he used it, but when I'd smelt it up close in Ocean's hair, it had seemed much subtler. Comfy even.

My mouth moved silently as I talked myself through various speeches in my head. My brain was mostly sure that *something* had to be said, but as Enzo had rightly pointed out, I had no way of knowing what that something was.

I wasn't any closer to a conclusion when I got dressed in a pair of faded black jeans and a t-shirt I'd picked up at a local concert last year. The words *Acid Mouth* were scrawled across the front in faded red lettering above a Pegasus horse bleeding from the mouth. The band had been a fairly fun night away from school, but I doubted I'd see them again, at least not with the same name. Still, the shirt was loose fitting, even over my flabby stomach, and comfy enough.

I collapsed on my bed, swearing under my breath as I rifled through my bag for my earbuds. I turned the volume on my phone up high, closing my eyes to let my heavy metal playlist soothe me and calm the chaos of my thoughts. I knew it wasn't the most conventional music choice for calming down, but I found if someone was shouting in my ear, sometimes in a language I didn't understand, it could drown out pretty much anything I was worried about. It compensated for all the screaming I wished I could be doing myself.

I frowned, opening my eyes reluctantly when my playlist was interrupted by a notification. I slapped against my side table, feeling around blindly for my phone. I craned my neck to read the text. I sat up when I got to the end, my eyebrow raised.

~*~

"I didn't think you'd come so quickly," Ocean teased. "I thought you might be in bed given that it's already past five." He looked up from the floor of the storage cupboard. He smiled playfully as he hugged his knees. "Are you going to be my little lapdog now that you're my boyfriend? Coming anytime I whistle for you?"

"Shut up!" I hissed. I slammed the cupboard door behind me, the sudden darkness making me blink.

Ocean tutted. He pulled out his phone, turned the flashlight on and placed it on the shelving.

"Thank you for coming," he said, his tone now a lot more sincere. "I wanted to see you."

"Yeah, I got that much," I muttered as I sat down on the floor opposite Ocean, crossing my legs. "So, what do you want?"

Ocean reached into his bag and pulled out a biscuit tin, a large can of craft beer, and two small water glasses. He cracked open the can and poured equal helpings into both glasses, before pulling the lid off the tin.

"Here," Ocean offered it to me, "Violet made me madeleines as a thank you for making snacks for the swim team last week. I thought we could share them."

I snatched one up. The small cake crumbled instantly in my tight grip. I held my breath, my hand hovering. Ocean just laughed good-naturedly, scooting closer. He set the tin down in his lap, balancing it between his knees while he carefully placed a glass in my crumb-coated fingers.

"I'm sorry for yesterday," Ocean said, his voice quiet but honest. He leaned against my shoulder, his soft cheek rubbing against the worn fabric of my band t-shirt. "I just didn't know what to say. Or what to do."

I stiffened. He felt so warm! I looked straight ahead, wrapping my arm around his shoulders. My fist tapped lightly on his back before I stretched and cupped his upper arm.

"You seemed fine in the coffee place," I couldn't help but point out, "why did you suddenly freak out when we left?"

"You know why!" Ocean said brattily. "And it was justified! I'm pretty sure Tempest walked past us at one point."

I scoffed, tightening around Ocean and resting my chin on his head. It might have been my imagination, but I did conjure the image of Temp glancing through the coffee shop's large window as he strolled past laden with shopping bags.

"You think Temp is going to think we're suddenly all romantic just because we had coffee together?"

"Shut up, Barbarian!"

My grip on him loosened. I grinned, kissing the top of Ocean's head.

"Alright, so Temp might have seen us having coffee together," I said carefully. "So, you invited me to have our second date in a supply cupboard?"

"Technically, yes," Ocean mumbled against my shoulder. He kissed my neck lightly. "I thought it would help me loosen up a bit. I can talk freely to you here; I don't have to worry about other people seeing or hearing anything."

My head started to throb again. I put my beer on the floor before picking up a piece of the broken cake. I chewed it thoughtfully, Ocean plucking crumbs from the faded logo on my shirt. I took a second piece and nudged the sponge against Ocean's lips. My boyfriend opened his mouth easily, letting me feed him.

"I don't mind this," I admitted. "I mean, maybe not every time you want to talk to me, but I don't mind it." I felt a stab of pain underneath me as one of my legs fell asleep. I dragged it out, stretching both legs in front of me to lean against the wall. "And I know shit about how any of this stuff is supposed to work. So, I'm happy for you to take the lead here. We'll do what you want, alright?"

Ocean lifted his head to flash his perfect teeth at me.

"Interesting. I was expecting you to tell me you could 'relationship' a thousand times better than me. This is surprisingly refreshing." Ocean nudged my ribs playfully. "Aren't you scared I'll coerce you into something?"

"You really think you can make me do anything I don't want to do?" I shrugged against the wall. "You're not that tough, Blondie."

Predictably, he jabbed me hard in the chest.

"Are you forgetting already what went down last week?" Ocean swung his leg over and stamped on my shin, gasping in mock offence when I didn't flinch. "I can remind you."

"I remember quite clearly kicking your stupid, fancy-ass!" I turned, biting Ocean's hair.

Ocean twitched, a usual sign that I was starting to get on his nerves. I couldn't stop my grin of pride, but quickly tightened my arm around him when he tried to sit up.

"It was a draw," I said quickly. "They interrupted us before we got to the good part."

"So, you admit I *could* have kicked your ass if I'd been given the chance!"

"Do you really want to do this now?" I sighed, quickly grabbing one of the cakes and shoving it into my mouth before it could break apart.

Ocean hummed thoughtfully, leaning back as he gripped my t-shirt. He shrugged, springing back up to kiss my cheek.

"No, I guess I don't." He sipped his beer. "I suppose we must be growing up."

"Sure," I mumbled through cake. "Why not?"

Chapter Five

Ru

I'm sure most of us would have said my birthday party had gone perfectly. Ms Khil had taken dorm duty that Friday night and had agreed with us beforehand that we could have the party on the condition that we weren't too loud, turned the music off by ten so we didn't draw attention from other rooms, and at least pretended to hide our beers when she came to do her rounds. She even agreed to join us at eleven-thirty, before "escorting" the girls back to their dorm at midnight.

It had all gone to plan. We blasted out Ramstein, Children of Bodom and all the other bands I liked that the others normally could stand, throwing in the occasional Queen song everyone could sing along to. Keeping it all at a reasonable volume, of course. We ate masses of pizza and played the stupidest, rudest drinking games we could think of. Everyone seemed to be having a good time. Even Ocean didn't seem all that tense. He sat on the floor beside his bed with a half-smile, only getting up to refill Violet's water bottle for her. That was until, during a game of 'Reveal', Cam had asked a fairly innocent question.

"Ru," she said with a cheeky smile, "which girl at school are you most into?"

Everyone, bar three, stared intensely at me, waiting for the answer. Enzo clearly wasn't interested, focusing on shoving pizza in his face. Freja smirked, her eyes sparkling with my secret. Ocean looked awkwardly at the carpet.

"Well," I said, then took a large swig of beer, "I don't really like any of them."

"Really?" Noah scoffed, leaning back on the beanbag. "I don't get you, Ru. You're eighteen and you've never had a girlfriend!"

"Says the guy who only got a girlfriend this year," Freja jibed.

"Yeah, well, I got one!" Noah countered.

"It's not that weird," Enzo said between bites of pizza. "Ru doesn't like girls!"

I looked at Enzo. He didn't seem to have noticed or cared what he had implied. He just swayed on the floor as he peeled stuck cheese off the roof of one of the boxes. I shook my nearly empty beer can, feeling surprisingly casual about the whole situation. There was no point in hiding things. Or at least I couldn't think of a reason why I should.

"Yeah," I admitted before swallowing the rest of the beer. "I'm pretty sure I'm gay."

Everyone was quiet.

"Oh," Noah said, clearly a little shocked by the sudden declaration. "That's cool."

Cam's eyes went wide. "Really?"

"Yeah," I said. My brain told me I should say something more, but it wasn't giving me anything. It wasn't like I had prepared for the big reveal. "Is that..."

"It's fine!" Freja reassured me. Her eyes darted about to give everyone equal amounts of attention, daring them to say something. She had come out herself two years ago and while our friends had been okay with that, she knew enough of the world to be aware of double standards; particularly from men.

Her eyes locked on my boyfriend.

Ocean sat stiffly on the scratchy carpet, biting down on the edge of his cup so hard he was leaving grooves in the paper.

"It is fine," I said suddenly.

"Yeah!" Violet crawled over and threw her arms around me. "Congratulations, Ru!"

Freja pursed her lips, keeping one eye on Ocean, but after Violet beckoned her over, she softened and joined her. Cam giggled in delight, springing up to turn it into a full-on group hug. I stretched my arms to hold all my friends as best I could.

"Thanks, guys."

Cam wrapped her arms around my middle, squeezing tight. "I withdraw my question," she said through laughter. "Happy birthday!"

"Happy birthday!" Enzo cried, his mouth still filled with hot, cheesy pizza. He fell against Noah, spraying crumbs over him as he tried to lead everyone in singing: *'Happy birthday to you!'*

I sighed in relief as subtly as I could. Cam took Enzo's hands, spinning him around in a crazy dance. Noah and Janie clinked their beer cans together so enthusiastically their drinks fizzed over as they mouthed the words to the birthday song- ignoring Korpiklaani's *A Man With a Plan* blaring in the background. I pushed Freja and Violet together, encouraging them to dance. It seemed to distract Freja away from Ocean, a grin forming on her face as she jumped about with Violet.

I collapsed on my bed with a satisfied smile, grabbing a fresh beer on my way down. I looked at my boyfriend. Ocean's eyes were focused on the wall, five inches away from his face. Beer trickled down his wrist from the grooves in the cup.

He didn't move until a few hours later, after Ms Khil had left with Freja, Violet and Cam. He grabbed his blazer, mumbling something about wanting to sneak outside for a cigarette. I lay still for a while, trying to figure out what to do. I checked on my roommates and saw Enzo lying bloated on the floor while Noah cleared up around him. I downed the last can of beer, frustrated that I wasn't even feeling a little bit of a buzz, before grabbing my leather jacket and heading out the door.

I knew where I'd find Ocean. My boyfriend had a very good system for sneaking cigarettes at school. He knew exactly when the groundskeepers would be on their rounds and how often they would cross the sports pitch. He even knew where the blind spots were in case the teachers on duty happen to look out of their windows.

Sure enough, Ocean was standing behind one of the old equipment cabins on the east side of the sports pitch, inhaling deeply on a cigarette. The bright orange glow of the tip guided me to him like a beacon in the almost pitch-black night. It hadn't snowed yet, but the air was crisp and cold, biting at any exposed skin. Ocean was hunched up. His neck pulled in and his shoulders pushed up to his ears. His hands were hidden inside his blazer sleeves, the two fingers holding the cigarette poking out. He stared straight ahead, as if focused on something invisible in front of him.

He heard me approaching; my boots were squelching pretty heavily in the mud after all. I was relieved to see him relax a little when he saw it was me. He smiled before turning away to take the final drag of his cigarette.

"Hey," Ocean mumbled, stubbing the cigarette out in his metal portable ashtray.

It was almost mechanical the way he slipped the ashtray into his left blazer pocket with one hand as the other reached into his right trouser pocket for his pack. He pulled out his cigarettes, tapped out a fresh stick and placed it between his lips. Each movement was precise and fluid. It was a quirk I was strangely proud to recognise in my boyfriend. I still wasn't entirely sure what it meant, but I knew to tread a little more carefully.

"Hey." I leant against the wall of the wooden cabin. My head jolted suddenly as the multiple cans of beer finally settled into my system. "I'm really sorry, by the way."

"Don't be." Ocean lit his latest cigarette. I heard him suck the smoke in sharply before he blew it away from me. "You're allowed to come out whenever you feel the time is right. I just…" He cringed and looked at the ground. "I'm really not ready."

"That's okay!" I took his hands, careful of his cigarette. "I was ready, but you're not and that's okay." I pecked Ocean's soft lips. "You're worth the wait."

Ocean snorted. "Don't be sappy, Barbarian!" He snapped back, shaking his head. "I really can't believe this."

"Hm?" I creased my brow, thinking he was talking about my coming out. "What's so unbelievable about it?"

"That you're saying these comforting things with your stupid barbarian brain," Ocean teased, "when a few weeks ago your English vocabulary seemed to consist mainly of four-letter words."

I scoffed, lightly ruffling Ocean's hair. I shivered as the silky strands glided through my fingers. The ends were returning to their slightly frizzy state after the long day. They smoothed out as I stroked, before pinging back into place, settling just below Ocean's ears.

"Whatever," I mumbled, "dumb blonde."

"Oh yeah." Ocean smirked triumphantly. "That sounds more like you!"

Ocean exhaled slowly, watching the shapes of his smoke against the black sky. He leaned against me.

"It's more than just... figuring out what I like," he mumbled. "I'm figuring out some stuff about myself, too. Stuff I'm really not ready to address yet. I can't..." He pressed his lips against the butt of the cigarette. "I can't talk about it now. When I can, you'll be the first to know, okay?"

I nodded. While I couldn't figure out what Ocean meant, I knew better than to pry. I pulled him closer, stroking his hair again. He pressed his cheek against my jacket, his face turned awkwardly to the side as he finished his cigarette.

An eerie silence surrounded us, the trees barely rustling.

Finally, he pulled back, kissing me lightly on his lips. I hummed at the contact, pleased to have this rare moment alone with my boyfriend.

We'd tried to casually sneak away a few times for longer dates after telling the others that we were just going off into the city to run a few errands. Separately of course. It never worked. Someone else would always chime in, saying they wanted to tag along or had things they needed to take care of themselves. I could never think of an excuse to get rid of them and Ocean would melt at any request from the girls. They would go off together and I'd have to mull around like a loner until the next train, wandering through shops I never bought anything from.

It had been a month since we'd started seeing each other and I could only count four dates in total. On our last, Ocean had admitted he'd gone on twelve with his last girlfriend by that point. He'd marked each of them off in his calendar and even planned a candlelit picnic for the official 'one month' mark, with fresh strawberries and sparkling wine. While I didn't expect or want anything that frilly, a movie together or even just a walk alone would have been nice.

"Hey," Ocean said softly, poking my forehead. "What are you thinking about, huh?"

"Just..." I shrugged, "how we don't really get that 'get to know each other time?' Like you're supposed to do when dating, you know?"

"Do we need to?" Ocean paused to think, taking out his ashtray to get rid of his latest cigarette. "I mean, we already know each other well enough.

"I know your favourite colour is blood red. Your favourite food is pulled pork. Your favourite book is *Jam* by Yahtzee Croshaw, for reasons you've never successfully been able to justify, and that you hate ice cream because it's too cold. You love the taste of dark ale and can't stand sugar or milk in your coffee to the point where you can't drink it if the same spoon has been used."

I didn't know what to say to that. I closed my mouth with a clunk when I realised I was gawking. Both of Ocean's arms looped around me, squeezing me tighter.

"The important thing is that we can spend time together; either in a group or in these unexpected moments. These are what help me figure out my feelings. Towards you and... Myself."

"I would like more time with you," I admitted. "Where I can just..."

I shut myself up before I accidentally said something too sappy!

I definitely preferred these spontaneous moments over sneaked dates – times when Ocean would just let himself be held without twitching or whispering. It was strange how much between us had changed since our detention in the gym. Like a switch in my brain had been flicked and suddenly all the things I hated about Ocean were now things he loved about him. Like the way he ironed his clothes, straightened his hair and kept order in the dorm room.

I kissed Ocean's hair, running my hand down his back, feeling him through his blazer.

Ocean slipped his ashtray back into his pocket. He looked at me, his eyes shining, looking at peace for the first time in a long while.

"Come on, Barbarian," he said with a sly grin. "I have another present for you."

My hand grew sweaty again as Ocean pulled me back towards the dorm. It wasn't until we were climbing the stairs that I realised Ocean was still holding his hand. The thought made me grin dumbly, even if the halls were empty by now.

Ocean peeked into our dorm room to make sure the light was off and Noah and Enzo were in bed.

"Wait here." He snuck into the bedroom. There was some light rustling before he stepped outside with a small purple shopping bag held closed with Velcro.

Ocean took my hand again, pulling me to the empty common room and pushing me inside without a word. He locked the door, the key presumably slipped to him by Ms Khil, and closed all the curtains, shutting out the outside world. Despite the secrecy, I kind of liked it. At that moment, it was just Ocean and me. Nothing else mattered.

Ocean opened the bag, pulling out a soft, embroidered comforter. He pushed the scruffy sofa back with his foot and spread the comforter out over the floor. Next, he took out several tealight candles in glass holders, lighting them in a circle around us. I continued to watch as Ocean pulled his shoes and socks off, leaving them next to the sofa. He laid his blue blazer over the back before lying down on the blanket, reclining on his elbows. He brought his right hand up to his chest, slowly popping his shirt buttons open to reveal his smooth skin.

I shuddered, shuffling next to the door. Ocean seemed to notice my awkwardness. He smirked and held out his hand. "Come on, Barbarian."

The three words snapped me back to the moment. I kicked my shoes away, pulling off my leather jacket to throw it over the table. I knelt and crawled over to the comforter, leaning in to press my lips to Ocean's. He wrapped a leg around my waist, pulling me closer. I stared into his eyes, noticing the way Ocean's ridiculous, frizzy hair framed his face.

Only I wasn't going to lie to myself anymore – I loved that beautiful, sexy, frizzy hair!

I leaned in for a bruising kiss, my lips opening against Ocean's. Our eyes closed as I rolled us onto our sides, our tongues moving together enthusiastically. Ocean relaxed, letting himself be kissed for a few moments before pushing my shoulder. I pulled back immediately, separating us by a few centimetres.

"Hey, Ru," Ocean mumbled, "I want to give you your present."

I felt a delightful tingling feeling in my stomach and forced myself to take a few deep breaths. I was painfully aware of how easily I could become overwhelmed during moments like this.

Ocean pushed me back further until we were both kneeling in front of each other. He reached up, tucking his hair behind his ears. "Let me take my time," Ocean said gently, "but I want to do this. I promise."

I nodded, still not sure where Ocean was going with this. But I was hopeful.

"Alright then." Ocean reached into the bag again. My heart sped up when he pulled out a bottle of strawberry-scented lube.

"I don't want to… you know," Ocean said nervously, "'Go All the Way'. I'm not quite ready. But sometimes… I like to use my fingers on myself." His cheeks went pink. My heart trembled at how impossibly cute he was. "I thought maybe you could try using fingers on me."

My mouth went dry. I had no idea how he did this to me every single time. It was another advantage of knowing each other so well already. Whenever the door was locked and we found ourselves alone, there was no need to waste time talking. I could just cup Ocean's face and kiss him hard.

I pounced on Ocean, his bottle falling to the floor. I kissed him again, straddling him on the comforter- until I felt my belly press against Ocean's flat stomach.

"Wait!" I jumped back. I saw the startled expression on my boyfriend's face. "Sorry. I was worried that I might, well, crush you."

Ocean snorted surprisingly delicately, slapping my shoulder playfully.

"I'm not made of twigs, shithead!"

I pinched his skinny arm. "You sure about that?"

"Shut it!" Ocean wrapped his arm around my neck, pulling me back down.

I sucked in my gut, trying to hold it back as best I could. Until I saw the trust in Ocean's eyes. He strained upwards to brush his mouth against mine. It was like an off switch. I relaxed, exhaling against his lips.

"Get comfortable," I whispered. "I'll go slowly, okay? And, you know… let me know if you need to stop."

"I will," Ocean promised. He reached down, taking hold of my wrist. "Also, I want you to know that after we do this, I'm open to doing other things. Not 'the thing', but if there's something you've been thinking about that you might like me to do to you, I'd like to hear it, okay?"

I grunted sharply, almost like a pig, before sitting on my heels. I looked at the ceiling, my face screwing up tight, trying my best to think where the line was. It felt as if I was caught in a life-altering dilemma.

"You don't need to break yourself," Ocean said reassuringly. "I just thought since this is a 'me thing' and it's your birthday..."

"Yeah, but I don't want you to feel obligated to do something to me just because it's my birthday," I said. "I don't want you to feel pressured."

Ocean sat up, hugging his knees with his ankles crossed over each other. I couldn't help but notice how differently Ocean carried the same position in here with me than he did back in the dorm room with the others. In here his lips curled in a smirk, his eyes sparkling with mischief.

"Look, the 'fingers' thing-," Ocean let go of his knees to give air quotes, "-that's not what I was intending for your present. I just thought it might relax me before I do what I was actually considering for your present."

I looked Ocean up and down. He puckered his lips slightly.

"Oh..."

"Yeah!" Ocean reached underneath my untucked shirt, pulling my leather belt. He stared at my flushed face. I felt both embarrassed and unbelievably elated.

Our hands pulled at each other's clothes. I knew I was being a little awkward since I was still unwilling to put all my weight on Ocean. Ocean was tougher than he looked. My nose still twitched sometimes when I thought about our last battle in the field. But when we were holding each other like this I became all the more aware of how bony he was.

Ocean didn't seem bothered. He took my hands, guiding them along his body. Every time I tensed or felt my fat brush against him, Ocean made a soothing noise and ran his hand up my arm.

I popped open the cap of the lube. When I spread it over my hand, I found it wasn't as sticky as I had feared. It was thick and gooey but felt quite nice as it glided smoothly over my palm. I turned to Ocean, unsure of what to do next. He took my hand and guided it between his legs.

Ocean whispered in my ear the entire time, coaching me on speed and pressure, guiding me to do it the way he liked it. The tension in my gut finally melted away completely. I kissed him again, letting our lips linger together.

I had seen several of Ocean's girlfriends come and go over the years. I'd scoffed every time a new one was introduced, wondering how they could possibly put up with him being so prissy and high-strung for any amount of time. Now, I understood completely. Ocean's hands definitely felt good, but there was something else there, something that made me feel safe. I didn't feel self-conscious when Ocean touched the chubby flesh on my hips or embarrassed when it didn't last as long as I would have liked. Ocean kept me in the moment and kept my thoughts on him. I knew I didn't have anything to compare it to, but I knew what a positive experience felt like.

I knew I would appreciate this moment for a very long time.

"Ru." Ocean sat up, kissing me tenderly, his thumb tracing the shell of my ear. "Happy birthday."

I laughed giddily, reaching to stroke Ocean's cheek. I stopped myself last minute, remembering where my fingers had been.

"Thank you," I said, brushing our noses together. "Should we go? Head to bed before anyone comes looking for us?"

"Soon."

Ocean reached for his bag, pulling out a packet of wet wipes. He gently ran one over us both, passing me one for my hands. When we were both clean, Ocean leaned into my side, sighing contentedly.

"Hey, Barbarian?" Ocean said, eventually.

"Yeah?"

Ocean rested against my chest. It felt like our bodies were as close as they could possibly be. "I... I really like you," he admitted.

I chuckled, turning to kiss Ocean's temple. "I really like you too, Frizzy," I whispered soothingly.

Ocean smiled against my collarbone, his long limbs wrapping around my waist, trapping me. Not that I minded in the slightest.

Chapter Six

Ocean

My eyes felt heavy as I looked up at the orange sky. I chewed on my bottom lip as I tapped my last cigarette against the metal lid of my ashtray. I knew I shouldn't, if not for the obvious health risks, but because I only had enough money left for one more packet before my allowance arrived. As I shifted on the cold, damp grass, I found myself placing the stick between my lips against my will.

I smoked it slowly, pulling Ru's leather jacket over my shoulders. It swamped me, the zipper opening reaching my sides as I held it closed.

Ru was back in the dorm room. I'd hefted him there soon after we had recovered, insisting that he needed to lie down. Ru didn't protest. He could barely stand at that point. The alcohol had hit him hard when he came down, making him behave rather giddily. I smiled to myself, thinking about bundling my boyfriend into his bed, watching as he slept spread out like a giant starfish, his mouth hanging open.

I took another drag of my cigarette, running my free hand through my hair. I recalled feeling so good just a few moments ago in the common room with Ru. It had been something

I'd been planning for over a week and had been completely certain I was ready. Only now, I felt a twisting feeling in my stomach, with no idea how to settle it.

After I finished the cigarette, I finally concluded that smoking wasn't helping. I stubbed the butt out in my ashtray, jamming the lid closed when it threatened to overflow. I didn't think I felt drunk. I'd only had one and a half beers, yet somehow I couldn't keep a straight path as I staggered back to the door. I winced when I rubbed my hand over my lightly stubbled chin.

"I take it you had fun at the party, Jónsson?"

I jumped at the steady, calm, familiar voice, quickly shoving my ashtray back into my blazer pocket.

Ms Khil looked me up and down, twisting her lips into a small, knowing smile. Her slick, black hair was pulled into a doughnut bun with two silken straight locks framing her face, a large rock of turquoise hanging around her neck on a silver chain.

I shuddered at a sudden pang of pain at the front of my skull.

"Sorry, Ms Khil," I mumbled. "It's Ocean. Remember?"

"Ah, yes. Sorry!" Ms Khil frowned with what I took to be honest remorse, stepping away from her place in the doorway. "Come on, Ocean, let's get you some tea. And just so you know, dear," she lifted herself onto her toes so she could whisper in my ear, "you do a good job at hiding the sight from us, but you need to come up with a new system for the smell."

I nodded, deciding to save being embarrassed for later, letting Ms Khil pull my arm over her shoulders so she could lead me inside.

Five minutes later, I was back in the common room with a cup of hot tea in my hands. I rubbed my thumbs along a chip in the mug's ceramic rim, my brow creased in thought.

"Ms Khil?"

"Yes, Ocean." Ms Khil looked up, her fingernails trying to slip her key back on its chain.

I felt my facial muscles tense as I took a long sip of tea. "Is it normal to agree to date someone even though you're not sure how you really feel about them?

Ms Khil didn't stop her sigh, letting the keys fall onto the table.

"I'd like to say: 'for your age, yes'," she said. "I suppose a more accurate answer would just be a straight 'yes'."

I collapsed to the side, my neck resting on the arm of the sofa.

"It's not that I don't like—." I stopped myself with another sip of tea.

"You don't need to overthink things," Ms Khil said quickly. "The great thing about relationships is what they teach us about ourselves. It might not always seem like it, but it's completely fine to just take things day by day and see what comes. It's so easy to fall into a pattern of over analysing your feelings." She twirled her finger around one of her loose wisps of hair. "Again, I'd say that it's normal for someone your age to overthink or over-analyse relationships, yet I'm afraid I know people who took a long time to grow out of it. Myself included. Anyway, my point is, if you like who you're with now and enjoy their company for the time being, you don't need to fret about the past or the future."

"I get that," I said. I brought my legs up, folding them underneath me as I sat on the edge of the sofa. "Thanks."

"Anytime. And you know, Ocean," Ms Khil bowed her head, forcing her eyes into my line of sight. "If you ever need to talk about something, anything at all, you can come to me. Alright? Even if you just want someone to listen."

"I know, Ms Khil."

"Good." She stood up, placing her keys back in her pocket where they belonged. "Now, I know it's Saturday, but you need to get at least some sleep. Alright, Mr Jónsson?"

I winced, resting my forehead on my mug.

"Sorry! Ocean," Ms Khil corrected quickly.

"Thank you." I smiled, my tired eyes crinkling. "I'll go to bed in a minute."

I sighed heavily as the door clicked shut, reaching underneath the sofa to pull out my hidden purple shopping bag. I ripped the Velcro open, digging around until I pulled out a small black and gold book, my fountain pen strapped to the side. I flicked it open in my lap, my hand trembling as it marked inky blotches across the page. The scribbles didn't match my usual careful handwriting by a long shot, but it didn't matter. No one else but me would ever read it; or if they did, this meant they wouldn't associate it with me.

I turned to stare out of the large, murky window. I curled up on the sofa, content to sit there quietly for a while.

~*~

"Ocean!"

I recoiled as I stepped inside the dorm room, Noah's face suddenly uncomfortably close to my own.

"Um... Hello there?" I said cautiously.

"Help me?" Noah whined.

I blinked. "With what?"

Noah snatched my phone out of my hands and thrust his crumpled school shirt at me. I looked at it. Then back up at Noah. "This answers no questions."

"Can you help me iron it?"

I raised my brow at him, thoroughly unimpressed.

"By 'help you iron it', I assume you mean you want me to do it for you?" I said exasperatedly. "You're all going to have to learn basic life skills at some point."

"I'm sorry, I just don't have time. I'll ruin it if I try to do it," Noah said with a pleading expression, "and I'm supposed to meet Janie soon."

I looked at the shirt again, becoming less impressed by the second. "You're wearing your school shirt?"

"Janie wants us to wear smart clothes tonight. She said it'd be fun."

"And you're wearing your school shirt?" I threw the shirt onto his bed as if it were a slug I'd found on the bottom of my shoe before heading to my drawers. "With your face, you can't afford to be so half-arsed! You think you'll ever pull another girl like Janie?" I looked over my shoulder at Noah. "I'll lend you a shirt and iron this for tomorrow."

Noah sighed in relief, peeling off the yellow t-shirt he was wearing.

"Thank you, Ocean! I really owe you one."

"You owe me several," I muttered. I produced a blue flowered shirt with black buttons and black lining on the inside. "Put that back on! I don't want you getting your germs and body odour on my things. It's cold outside, anyway."

Noah obeyed immediately and pulled the t-shirt back over his head. He slipped the black and blue shirt on, wincing as he tried to push his arms through the sleeves.

"It's a little tight," he noted, "and long."

"That's fine. Just roll the sleeves to your elbows." I carefully folded the cuffs and slipped the sleeves up Noah's arms. "It'll look 'smart casual', which will be more fun. So long as you can button it up, you'll be fine."

Noah nodded, quickly buttoning the shirt up as instructed. I stopped his hands at the top button before snatching my phone back from Noah's pocket.

"There. A presentable looser!" I gave him a faux-regal wave, reclined on my bed and resumed scrolling through nothingness.

"Thank you," Noah said again. He went to grab his school shirt, but I shooed him away.

"It's fine. I want to iron some jeans tonight, anyway."

Noah tilted his head to the side, his fingers still fiddling with the top button of his shirt.

"Iron your jeans?"

I didn't rise to the bait. I threw my phone down and returned to my drawer, pulling out my pair of stark black skinny jeans. I could feel Noah's eyes on me. I turned around, furrowing my brow when I saw the wide grin on my friend's face, rather than the mocking smirk I'd been expecting.

"What?"

"You have a girlfriend!" Noah said, cackling.

My throat tightened; my cheeks prickled with embarrassment and dread.

"I don't," I said quickly, with a tremor in my voice.

"You do!" Noah scoffed, pointing at the pair of jeans in my hands. "You only iron your jeans if you have a date. And those are your 'date jeans'."

"I do not have 'date jeans'," I insisted. "I have various pairs of jeans I wear at varying times." I opened the shared cupboard to pull out the ironing board, placing my folded jeans at one end. "And today, I just happen to want to wear these jeans. Now give me your damn shirt!"

"You're not going to tell me who it is, dude?" Noah threw his school shirt at my face, smirking at my grimace. "Come on. I'm not going to tell anyone."

"Only because you'll tell everyone, you arsehole!" I stormed into the bathroom to fill up the iron. I kept my eyes ahead of me, catching a glimpse of myself in the mirror. My cheeks were so pink they looked like they'd been scrubbed with sandpaper! I squirmed, feeling uncomfortably warm despite the window being wide open.

On the edge of my reflection, I saw Noah's face poking through the door.

"Is it who I think it is?"

"Yes!" I said without thinking. I slammed the iron down on the counter before shoving Noah out of the way. "Now get out of here. If you're late, Janie will start to remember how much better she can do!"

I kicked the door shut, immediately locking it and turning the shower on.

"Shit," I mumbled to myself, shaking my head furiously. "What the hell just happened?"

I grabbed my towel from the rack, deciding to take a shower anyway now that I was here. I unbuttoned my school shirt whilst peeling my long grey socks off with my toes. My uniform fell to the floor casually. I clicked my neck as I picked up each piece of clothing and placed them folded on the closed toilet lid. From the corner of my eye, I saw my reflection again in the slowly misting mirror. I couldn't stop myself from looking up and down my pale, naked body. My heart continued to pump dread through my veins. It was as if I were standing above a freezing cold lake, knowing at any moment I would be plunged into its depth.

I picked my towel back up and draped it over the mirror.

~*~

It had been raining hard through most of the Sunday, leaving the air in the common room thick and warm. Now it had calmed to a light drizzle, but the bored, silent atmosphere still hung above us, the raindrops steadily tapping against the window, paired with the tick of the wall clock. Ru was more focused on the clock than his history textbook. I smirked at his endearing huff.

He was spread out across the wide sofa while Enzo sat on the floor in front of him with his own history homework. Freja, Violet, and I were sitting at the round table opposite them, each with our own textbooks. Ru shifted on the sofa, rubbing his lower back against the cushions. I could tell he honestly was trying to study, but I knew rainy afternoons turned his brain to mush. He had been staring at his book for almost two hours now, with only short breaks to scroll through his phone.

He yawned loudly before his eyes met mine. I wrinkled my nose to force my glasses up a little bit. I rarely wore my glasses around the others. There were a few occasions during the day where I had to squint, but I only really needed them for reading. Ru had mentioned during our last 'cupboard date' that he wished I'd wear them a little more often. He'd claimed they looked 'adorable on me', talking about how my nose twitched and my eyes opened a little more than usual.

My eyes stayed on Ru's and I blessed him with a silent smile. Ru let the history book slip down to rest on his abdomen, smiling back.

A loud bang made everyone jump, our eyes immediately turning to the door. Cam stood there with an open palm pressed against the door, her eyes zoned in on me. She shoved the door again, the wood banging so hard against the wall it left a mark in the worn paint.

"Cam?" I stood up sharply, frowning in concern.

Cam didn't answer. She stormed over and in half a second had grabbed the collar of my black t-shirt.

"What's wrong—?"

I was cut off abruptly, the last few letters muffled, as Cam suddenly pressed her lips against mine.

"What the hell?" Freja fake-whispered to Violet, her face half amused and half bewildered. "What... What?"

Cam pulled back, her nails digging in through my t-shirt. "Oh, didn't you hear?" She said, her voice scarily light and overly sugary. "Ocean and I are dating. Didn't he tell you? Apparently, that's what he's telling people?"

I stared at her, bewildered.

The realisation crashed over me like a tidal wave, the blood draining from my face. My Friday night conversation with Noah passed through my mind.

My mouth dropped open, producing only a long, throaty groan.

"Oh, so *now* you don't have anything to say?" Cam shrieked. She finally let go of me, letting me stumble backwards into the table. Guilt pulled my organs into a tight knot as I took in how genuinely hurt she looked. "I tried, Ocean. I knew you had a crush on me, but I honestly thought you were mature enough to just let us be mates."

I grabbed at my hair, tugging it until my scalp burned. I shook my head, my groan turning into a desperate whimper as I tried to put everything together.

The sound of heavy footsteps echoing down the corridor turned my stomach acid to lead.

I took in a deep breath, my chest clenching so tight I began to wonder what a heart attack felt like. I went to squeeze Cam's shoulder but quickly pulled my hand back at the last minute, shaking it in the air as if I'd accidentally grabbed something hot.

"Well!" Cam snapped.

I swallowed, my breath puffing through my nose.

"I'm sorry," I said finally, my voice quiet and strained. "It was a misunderstanding." I tried to squeeze past her, but Cam just grabbed me from the back.

"Don't you dare walk away!" She yelled. "Why did you tell Noah we were dating?"

Freja snorted in laughter, while Violet and Enzo leaned in closer, eager to hear everything.

"I didn't!" I slipped my hand into my pocket to stroke my cigarette packet. I flipped the box open, running my thumb over the filters to count them in my head. I stood still, forcing myself to take one breath for every stick I touched.

Cam stood opposite me waiting, her hands on her hips as she pouted like a housewife in an old sitcom.

When I reached eleven, I cleared my throat.

"Noah asked if I had a girlfriend and I guess he assumed it was you."

"You have a girlfriend?" Violet asked, tilting her head in confusion.

"No!" I threw my hands in the air with a furious scream. Even Cam recoiled, watching bewildered.

My nails scratched over my cheeks, leaving angry red lines down my face. The room began to spin around me as I tried desperately not to start crying.

"Ocean?" Enzo said, propelling himself up off the floor. "Are you alright?"

"I'm fine!" I snapped. "I just..." I balled my hands into fists. I closed my eyes tight as I tried to regulate my breathing.

"Ocean." Enzo wrapped an arm around my shoulder. "Come on, man. Five things you see, right?"

I shook my head. I fumbled in my pocket, pulling out one of my cigarettes. I placed it between my lips, taking a few imaginary drags. Enzo rubbed my shoulders, his thumbs moving in deep circles. I counted my breaths slowly; until a prickling feeling of relief spread down my cheeks and chest.

"Alright," I said, my voice still shaking. "Cam. I'm sorry. I didn't mean to make Noah think we were dating. I asked you out, and you said no. I'm alright with that."

Cam clicked her tongue, raising her eyebrow. I felt her cynicism hard, but I couldn't really blame her.

"I mean it." I tried to keep my voice firm, despite the rising humiliation of having three of my friends watching. "I'm not interested in you anymore, Cam. I swear."

Cam didn't look away. She kept her mouth in a straight, pursed line across her face, tapping her foot sharply. Violet, Enzo, and even Freja all held their breath as our staring contest continued.

Finally, Cam threw up her arms.

"Alright, fine! But I better not hear any shit like that again!" She jabbed her finger into my chest. "If I do, I'll knock your teeth in!"

She pushed past me, ramming her shoulder into mine. I let her do it, counting backwards from ten as she stormed away. The moment I reached one, I shoved my now steamed-up glasses in my pocket and ran out of the room.

~*~

I pushed the large gym door open slowly, the creak of the rusty hinges echoing almost ominously. I peered inside, already hearing the rattling chains of the punching bag. The gym was almost completely dark, only moonlight trickling in from the clerestory windows.

"Hello there." My hand hovered above the light switch, but I decided I wasn't that cruel. "Are you going to tell me why you stormed off like a child?"

Ru ignored me, continuing to focus on slamming his fists into the bag. I leaned against the frighteningly sticky wall, my arms folded across my chest. Ru seethed through his nose, sweat trickling down his cheeks. He threw one last full swing at the bag, his deep voice crying out in exasperation as he turned to glare at me.

"Fuck you, you dumb blonde!"

"Is that all?" I looked into the rage-filled eyes of the young man opposite me. "Although perhaps it would have been too much to expect something more eloquent."

"Fuck you!" Ru pointed his finger at me. "Don't you dare sit there-!"

"I'm standing."

"Fuck you!" Ru slapped the bag so hard it spun on its chains, swaying heavily to and fro. "Don't you dare try and act superior when you're the one who—"

"You really are the stupidest piece of shit in the entire world, aren't you?"

Ru snapped.

Our bodies slammed together with a hard smack, the crash shaking the entire sports hall. I tried to keep my feet, but ended up falling backwards. My arms looped around Ru, bringing him with me as I tumbled to the ground. Ru didn't waste time. He raised his fist. I caught it easily. I cupped it, slamming my knee into his side. Quite predictably, Ru winced.

He braced himself, expecting a slap. Only to grunt in pain when I slipped the nail from my pinkie finger through his nose ring.

"What the—!"

I yanked lightly on the piercing. Not enough for it to snap, but enough for Ru to cringe and sit up on the workout mat.

"Are you just trying to get me to screw around with you in here again?" I said, tutting.

"That's not what—"

"I know." I let go of Ru's nose, tickling him lightly under his chin. "And I'm sorry." I shifted on the floor, crawling forward until my nose pressed against Ru's.

"Ocean..." He looked at me with a combination of horror and disbelief as the reality of what he had done began to catch up to him. I continued to stare back, keeping my face as still as I could.

"Come on." I pecked his cheek peacefully. I stood up, dusting my knees off before holding my hand out. "Let's take a walk."

"Where to?"

"How about the lake?"

Ru recoiled, as if the offered hand was crawling with live ants.

"You want to go to the lake?" he said. "With me?"

"Yes." I wriggled my fingers. "What's the matter? Are you embarrassed to be seen with me?"

Ru scoffed exaggeratedly. "No more than anyone normally would." He rubbed his hand on his thigh before slapping it against mine, gripping tight.

~*~

Ru wasn't surprised when I dropped his hand the second we stepped outside the gym. Luckily, the cold wind hit us in full force. Since Ru hadn't remembered to grab any gloves or winter wear when he'd stormed out of the common room, he seemed content on this occasion to keep his hands inside his pockets.

His shivering appeared to increase when I told him the full story.

"I'm, um, sorry," Ru mumbled. He cringed, no doubt playing his storm out over in his mind.

"Oh, come on." I hip-checked him, smirking at his bashful expression. "Yes, you were an idiot, but..." I poked him in the side of his head, "*I'd* probably have ended up being an idiot if it had been you."

I took out my cigarettes, wincing when I saw the one I'd pulled out earlier was bent and torn, shreds of tobacco now lining my pocket.

"Yeah, well, thinking about it, I guess I would have known if you were dating Cam." Ru tried his best to keep his tone light, but I could see his lips trembling. "You've had a crush on her forever. If she'd agreed to date you, I would have been dumped in a nanosecond."

I nudged him good-naturedly, slowing down to look over the lake.

During the warmer months, the lake was incredibly popular amongst students. The sandy bank would be covered with towels and people peacefully sunbathing, or groups sitting around chatting together in the warm rays. The grass behind it would be equally packed with students running around or playing a variety of outdoor games; like a mini-Olympics. The lake would be filled with paddle-boarders, dinghies, or just swimmers screaming and shoving each other in the water.

When it got colder, it was obviously quieter, although most days the grass and sand still had a few people curled up reading or finishing their homework in peace and quiet while the waves lapped on the shore. That evening, it was completely empty. As it had been snowing most of the week and raining most of the day, the sand was coated in a thick layer of mushy, slippery ice and the lake was almost completely frozen, the remaining snowflakes dancing off the flat surface in the harsh wind. The white snow was vibrant in the moonlight and showed every inch of the empty, murky lakeside.

I tested the ground with my foot, grimacing at how soft and wet it felt. I sat down on the bank anyway, squishing against the ground. At least my trousers were protected a little bit by my winter coat. I slipped it off and spread it out beneath us so we could both sit on it.

"It's alright," Ru said quickly, "you don't have to do that."

"Shut up." I grabbed Ru's wrist, tugging him sharply until he sat down next to me. I leaned into Ru's side, tugging the sleeves of my blazer as far down as they would go. Ru took the opportunity to sneak his arm around my waist, holding me closer for warmth. If anyone approached, we'd hear their footsteps crunching on the ice and snow long before they got close enough to spot us. There was no reason not to hold each other.

"I don't think I ever really had a crush on Cam."

"Hum?" Ru pressed our foreheads together.

"I think it was just easy to convince myself I had a crush on her," I admitted. "She's easy to be around, she's funny and even you have to admit she's pretty."

Ru shrugged. He cupped the back of my neck, his fingertips gently dancing over the faded smattering of freckles I had left over from the summer. I wriggled away, shielding myself from the wind, to finally light my cigarette. Ru raised his hand to help, cupping it around the stick.

We could hear ominous rumbling sounds echoing around us from the ice shifting on the lake. The strange noise was both eerie and comforting. I exhaled a long line of smoke, watching as the grey shapes merged with Ru's icy breaths.

"It's good that she turned me down," I said, only a touch wistfully. "I think if we'd ever actually dated, I would have realised pretty quickly we were better off as friends. I just like having a girlfriend."

"Oh yeah?" Ru leaned back, ignoring the freezing ground and balancing himself on his free hand. He was trying to sound casual, but I could see his nostrils flaring. "How do you like having a boyfriend?"

I hummed thoughtfully as I pressed my cheek against Ru's shoulder. A moment later, Ru lowered his head, resting it on top of mine.

"It's growing on me," I said cheekily.

We sat in silence after that, leaning against each other for as long as we could bear the cold, listening to the rumbling of the shifting ice.

Chapter Seven

Ru

Ocean glided forward, keeping his hand clasped firmly around mine while I shuffled awkwardly beside him on the tips of my blades. His arm jerked when I slipped. He turned around just in time to watch me landing firmly on my butt like the clumsy dork I was.

He laughed so loudly other skaters turned their heads, looking confused as he wheezed. Ocean adjusted his blue bobble hat before hauling me to my feet. He tugged playfully on the thick, grey wool scarf I had borrowed from Freja before pulling me in to steal a quick kiss.

"This is so perfect," Ocean whispered against my lips.

"Yeah," I whispered back.

It was perfect.

It was exactly what we needed after months of tiptoeing around our friends. By now, we had perfected the art of sneaking around. We would hang out with the group, remembering to criticise something dumb or call each other a 'barbarian' or a 'priss,' before sneaking off to give each other affection – and hand jobs.

It was something we'd become a lot more confident in since my birthday. Recognising when the group's social battery had run dry seemed so obvious now that we both felt a little stupid for not recognising it before. Like the night after we had all gone to the hog roast festival together and our roommates had collapsed into bed the moment we got back to the dorm. Ocean looked at me from across the room while Noah and Enzo snored like barn-animals stuck in porridge.

He had slipped out of his bed and over to mine, tiptoeing carefully, even if he wouldn't have woken the others if he'd stomped across the floor in iron boots. We'd shifted around under the covers, trying to find a comfortable cuddling position. We finally settled on Ocean lying flat on the mattress with me half on top of him, my head against his chest. Ocean stroked my hair, craning his neck every now and then to kiss me.

I didn't think I'd ever slept as well as I had that night. When I woke up in the morning my boyfriend was half asleep in his own bed, his eyes fluttering open and closed. Despite hating how empty my bed seemed after he'd left, my insides felt warm and full for the whole day.

There was just something about being close to each other, something about being together even for short, stolen moments, that made the simple everyday things easier.

Only now the Christmas break was looming and our group was preparing to head back home for two whole weeks off school. My chest literally ached at the thought of not being able to see Ocean for such a long time. Especially since straight after the holidays, Ocean would be heading off on the Paris trip for an extra two weeks!

I squeezed Ocean's hand tight- before turning away, cringing. I wondered when I'd become such a sap!

"Aw!" Ocean pinched my chin. "Barbarian is getting all pouty!" He winked at me, skating away to show off with a quick jump and twirl. "Don't worry, we can stop now."

I shrugged, my skates scraping against the ice as I shuffled after him.

Ocean had been the one to suggest that we sneak off on Friday evening to a winter festival in Brussels. Everyone had been exhausted after hearing about all the homework they were expected to do over Christmas and from rushed end-of-year summary exams. Even Violet had gone straight to her room without a word. Ocean and I had just left the building without any explanation and met up at the train station. Being so far away, with all our friends back at school, there would be nothing to hide. We could act like a couple for a little while before separating for the holidays.

I could also tell that this was a little bit of a test run for Ocean. Presenting as queer in public and learning that the real world didn't care all that much. That while internet comment sections were more toxic than Dzerzhinsk and while certain jerks at school would make stupid jokes about 'butt sex,' the real world could be a different place; far from the anger of repressed students or resentful teachers.

I watched my boyfriend as he pulled his skates off. He had that look in his eyes again. That thoughtful, glassy look as he stared off into the distance. The one he'd had when I'd found him behind the cabin on my birthday. I felt more uneasy every time I saw it and wished I knew what on earth Ocean was thinking about.

It was something I'd started to pick up on after my birthday party. I'd thought a lot about Ocean nervously telling me that he had some things he 'wasn't ready to address yet', but I still wasn't any closer to figuring out what he'd actually been talking about. Whatever was troubling Ocean was *really* troubling him; that much was clear. More and more frequently, I woke up in the middle of the night to see Ocean sitting on the windowsill chewing on his sleeves, tears brimming in his eyes.

"Hey."

Ocean flinched in surprise. A few thick curls slipped out of the tight rim of his bobble hat. I took his hand, running my fingertip over the remains of the black nail polish he had painted on before we left. I lifted the hand to my lips and kissed Ocean's knuckles.

"You okay?"

Ocean didn't hesitate to lean in and pinch my cheek.

"I'm fine, Ru," Ocean insisted. He pulled the zippers up on his boots and stood up. "How about you go get us some mulled wine? I'll wait next to the market."

My stomach twisted. As often as Ocean was getting that faraway look in his eye, more often, he'd paste that smile on his face. The corners of his mouth turned up, while his brow crinkled with what looked like fear.

I sighed but didn't call him out on it. I knew it would be better to let Ocean speak when he was ready. It was a trust I wanted to earn.

"Sure." I squeezed his hand again, giving him a reassuring nod. Ocean cupped the back of my neck before giving me one last smile and walking away to return our skates.

I stared after him.

I decided a little detour on the way to the bar was in order.

~*~

"What the hell, Ru!"

I almost dropped the steaming cups of mulled wine when Ocean ran towards me. The snow was still quite thick, Ocean having to pick his feet up with every step to lift his boots out of each sink-hole they created. It didn't stop the fury twisted in his face, or the little huffing sounds he started to make when he got close enough for me to hear.

"I've been waiting here for an hour!" He said dramatically. "What happened? Did you get lost or something?" He stared in confusion at the mugs, noticing the steam still coming off the top.

"Of course not," I muttered, walking past Ocean to an empty table. He sat opposite me, snatching his mug to cradle it with both hands.

"Well then, what took you so long?"

I grinned.

"I got you something." I pulled a black box out of my pocket, pushing it forward on the table. The edges easily ploughed the light dusting of snow out of the way.

Ocean looked at it suspiciously.

"I thought we were doing presents at the Christmas party on Sunday?"

"Yeah, but I thought I'd like to give you this one in private." I leaned back in the chair, smiling smugly and feeling very proud of myself.

Ocean continued to look at me, crinkling his nose. He flipped open the lid of the box and instantly clapped a hand over his mouth.

I grinned. I took the box and pulled out the long sterling silver chain. On the end was a small globe with seashells, tiny pieces of seaweed and grains of sand embedded in the glass. It shimmered when it caught the light. The glass inside was misty, with tiny bubbles of air framing the decorations. It almost looked like a miniature rock pool compressed inside a ball.

I looped the chain around Ocean's neck; the tiny glass orb bounced on his black coat. He admired how the colours swirled when he turned it around in his hands.

"So you'll think of me," I leaned in to kiss my boyfriend's ear, "when you're away."

Ocean threw his arms around me and squeezed me tight.

"If you wanted to remind me of you, shouldn't you have got a barbaric symbol of strength or something punk-like?" He teased, although his voice was soft. "It's beautiful. Thank you."

Ocean pulled back, pressing his lips against mine. I kept my eyes open. It was the first time he'd kissed me outside without looking over his shoulder first.

"I didn't think you were capable of something like this," Ocean jibed. "Are you sure you're the same barbarian that didn't have anything better to do than give me shit about my hair?"

"Well, your hair is stupid," I huffed back. My hand pounced, snatching Ocean's hat and ruffling his curls until he slapped me away. "Are you sure you're the same dumbass who couldn't think of better insults than fat jokes?"

To my surprise, Ocean cringed.

"I'm sorry, I shouldn't have said those things," he said. "You're not fat."

I scoffed. "I'm not *that* fat." I clapped my hand over his mouth before he could protest. "Look, it's okay, I get it. I deserved it."

Ocean poked my gut lightly. "You think you deserved it? No one deserves to be made fun of because of something dumb, like their weight."

"Yeah, well, no one deserves to be punched just because someone made fun of something as dumb as weight." I sat up. "You remember the last fight we had?"

"In the gym?" Ocean ran his fingers up my chest.

I shook my head.

"No, before that in the field," I said, my voice low. "We got really pissed off at each other about some things we said and got sent to Temp's office."

"Oh." Ocean's face fell into a neutral expression. "What about it?"

I picked up my mug, needing the hot drink. The wind was so sharp my teeth hurt!

"It was my fault," I said quickly. "I know I said it was your fault, but it wasn't. It was my fault." I could practically feel the words tumbling off my tongue. I let them fall, knowing I had to get everything out before I changed my mind. "Around this time last year, I started to have feelings for you. I don't know why, they just crept up on me. I didn't want to like you because I thought you were straight and couldn't stand me. So, I just kept building you up as this demon inside my mind. Then when I saw you again after school started, I just snapped! Every time I looked at you, I told myself you were the worst because there was just part of me that really wanted to be close to you. I just let everything descend into that screwed up madness."

I risked looking at Ocean. My boyfriend just blinked, continuing to stare with the same blank face.

"I hated that you were kind to everyone but me," I continued, "and when I realised it was because I started things, I hated you even more. When we were fighting, it was the only time I didn't have to think about it. It's shitty and horrible, but all I can do is apologise."

I drank my wine so quickly I burned my tongue. Ocean's face was so still it was almost chilling! He cupped my cheek, forcing me to maintain eye contact.

"No, it wasn't," he said soothingly. "*I* started the fight in the field, remember?"

My frown deepened. "No, you-."

"You said my hair looked like pubes, which it doesn't, but that's not the point, so I kicked you," Ocean said in a blunt, matter-of-fact way. "The time before that was when you shoved me because I called you fat. The time before that I don't remember, but it could have been either one of us." He ran his thumb over my brow, as if he were trying to smooth out the creases. "Even if we count all the way back to the start, we would both still be guilty. There were so many times when I could have walked away. I was never forced to hit you back or call you hurtful things. I chose to." He pecked my cheek. "You shouldn't feel ashamed about our fights when I did nothing to stop them. And if it weren't for our fights, we wouldn't be here right now."

I couldn't stop myself from laughing, as sweet and sincere as Ocean's speech was.

"You telling me some 'fate' shit brought us together?" I teased, brushing my nose against Ocean's hat.

"Ew, no." Ocean chuckled. "I just want to put everything that happened before behind us. I've liked these past few months and I like how I am when it's just the two of us."

"Yeah?" I prompted.

"Yeah." Ocean placed our hands together. "It's pretty cool."

"Cool." I ran my thumb tip lightly over the side of Ocean's hand, unsure if the shiver that followed was due to excitement or the cold. "And just so you know, I'm not going to hurt you ever again. Even if you kiss Cam or call me fat! I'm not going to let anyone hurt you again."

Ocean pinched my side.

"You can't promise something like that, dumbass." Ocean smiled shyly. He picked up our mugs, handing me mine. "Come on. It's time to head off."

"Oh yeah?" I fumbled in my pocket for my phone to check the time. "When does the last train go?"

Ocean shook his head, flashing his pearly white teeth.

"We're not going back to school. I got us a hotel."

~*~

The streets weren't overly crowded, especially considering the time of year. There were just a few people hurrying around, completing their Christmas shopping, some pulling along screaming children. Ocean walked beside me, his arm linked through mine. His cheeks were pink, although I didn't think it could just be the cold.

"Hey, babe?" I said eventually.

Ocean's cheeks flushed deeper. "Yeah?"

I pulled him into a doorway beside a bright department store window. Creepy elf figures with shining faces and fixed smiles swayed back and forth, waving candy canes taller than they were.

"Look, if you're not ready for anything, we don't have to do anything, alright?" I tried to reassure him, rubbing a comforting hand over his shoulder. "Just because we have a hotel room doesn't mean—"

"It's not that!" Ocean said quickly. He looked at his heeled boots, kicking snow behind him. He pulled out his cigarettes, hesitating for a moment, before remembering he was far away from school. "I was just thinking... shouldn't we get some condoms?"

I blinked. It was my turn to shuffle awkwardly, rubbing the back of my vibrant head; now dyed a bright shade of turquoise. Mrs Tempest had given me a stern glare during her class this morning when she saw the new dye-job, but even she seemed to have accepted that there was no point in chastising me. Especially since I was no longer being dragged into the head's office every other day.

"I hadn't thought of that," I admitted. "I guess we don't, um... have to? I mean, I'm totally, completely virgin over here. Nothing to pass on."

"With me, there's been... a couple of girls," Ocean admitted. "I'm clean, I swear," he kicked the ground again, taking nervous puffs on his cigarette, "but I think I'd feel better if we used them."

"Okay." I nodded. "Then we'll get some."

Ocean exhaled, his face relaxing. He nodded back, continuing our walk down the high street.

We stopped at a small convenience store on the way to the hotel, Ocean bashfully leading the way to the pharmaceutical section. He looked over the selection before picking up a small package.

"I don't want to assume anything," Ocean said, again growing embarrassed. "I know that um... with guys, either of us could..." He trailed off, clearly unable to say what he was thinking inside the store.

It was mostly empty, but a little old woman with a wheeled shopping bag was browsing juice cartons just a few metres away. I tried my best not to laugh as Ocean's eyes darted around, looking anywhere but at the stranger.

"It's okay. We can decide all that when we get to the hotel."

I turned to go pay, but Ocean grabbed me. "Ru... have you ever measured yourself?"

I gave him a weird look. "What do you—" It dawned on me. I looked at the display of condoms, then back to the box in Ocean's hands. "I see."

My eyes flicked over the selection on the shelf. Truthfully, I had measured myself. Freja had asked about it when I had been staying with her family and we'd used her sauna together.

When she found out I hadn't, she had accused me of: 'Suffering from a dangerous lack of curiosity.'

To me, size wasn't a big deal- despite me being a little self-conscious about my puppy fat.

The word 'big' had been thrown around a lot when I was growing up. I'd been the tallest person on my street back in Kawaguchi since I'd surpassed my uncle's height at fifteen. At school I wasn't considered 'tall', being roughly the same height as Noah, a little shorter than Enzo, and only a bit taller than Ocean. Although I supposed my body was still 'thicker' than average. I was so used to having my overall size pointed out to me; I just couldn't be bothered to think about *that* size. While I was secure enough to know it didn't mean anything to *me*, I'd heard others talk about it like it was the only thing that ever mattered.

Finally, my eyes landed on a packet of condoms that seemed appropriate. I reached for them, but Ocean quickly pressed a kiss to my lips so he could snatch the box before I could. I let him do it, kissing him back.

"Did you bring lube?" I asked, trying to keep my voice down as the woman moved a little closer.

"I have a little," Ocean patted his bag, "but I suppose more doesn't hurt."

"One would hope not." I grinned at the light kick to my shin, taking a bottle of lube from the shelf.

"It's okay," Ocean said, plucking the bottle from my hands. "This is my treat."

"Hey!" I frowned, forgetting to be subtle as I chased after my boyfriend. "Come on, you paid for ice skating and a hotel. I can get these."

"Oh, really?" Ocean raised his brow.

He straightened up as the elderly woman passed us, covering the condom boxes with his hand and smiling at her sweetly.

"Tell me," he said in a snide voice, "would it damage your pride more to let me pay for these now or bashfully confess that you need train fare tomorrow?"

I paused, mentally calculating how much cash I had left. Ocean laughed, linking his arm through mine as he positioned us behind the stranger in the line for the register. "Don't worry yourself, you paid for the wine, and besides," Ocean gestured to the globe around his neck, "you've already gained boyfriend points this evening."

I still didn't stop my pouting when Ocean approached the cashier, my brain trying to form a decent comeback.

When Ocean slipped his purchases into his messenger bag, nodding his thanks to the cashier, I caught the way he fiddled with the ocean globe.

It was enough to make me let things go.

~*~

The hotel was much nicer than I had been expecting. It wasn't very big, just a double bed, a chest of drawers opposite and a small en-suite with a shower, but it was clean and white with a crisp, comforting smell.

Ocean ushered me into the room, leaving the key-card in the holder by the door as he shut it firmly behind us. I stood there awkwardly for a minute while my boyfriend carefully unzipped his boots and slipped them off.

"Hey," I said.

I wrapped my arms around Ocean as he straightened up, burying my hand in his hair and pulling him in for a slow, sweet kiss. I melted against my boyfriend, Ocean's hands gripping tightly at my shoulders.

"Ru," Ocean whispered excitedly against my lips. "Please. Come on!"

I kicked my shoes away and yanked my socks off, throwing them aside. I paused when my fingertips brushed along the hem of my t-shirt, feeling the rolls of fat underneath.

"Hey." Ocean took hold of the t-shirt, carefully tugging it over my head. My arms went up automatically, as if I were a toy for him to manipulate. "You're beautiful."

Ocean ran his fingers over my torso. It was so strange the way he stared at me. I had expected to feel uncomfortable, being exposed with his hands moving up and down my sides. What I really felt was amazement, mostly. Ocean was looking at my body as if it were a fascinating work of art. He bowed his head, kissing my collarbone as he splayed his hands over my chest.

"Frizzy!" I shut my eyes tight.

I wanted Ocean to take his time, so we could explore each other properly, but I was pretty sure my dick wouldn't be able to handle the wait! Instead, I pushed Ocean onto the bed, capturing his lips in another kiss.

"Wait," Ocean whispered. I immediately climbed off him.

"What's up?"

"Which one of us..." Ocean paused to breathe again, "goes first?"

Based on the slightly scared look in Ocean's eyes, I could figure out what he meant.

"Whichever," I said, shrugging, "we've got all night."

Ocean hummed in agreement, drumming his fingers on the duvet. "In that case... could I take you first?"

I couldn't help feeling a little taken aback. Not that Ocean wanted to go first, but that he looked convinced I would tell him no. I edged closer, kissing him tenderly. "Sure."

Ocean's shoulders dropped. He reached for his bag, searching for the condoms and lube. "You can go next, I promise."

"It's alright, babe." I laid on top of the pillows, pulling my belt and jeans open. "This is good."

Ocean nodded. He stood up, eyes fixed on me as he slowly popped the buttons open on his shirt. My heart sped up when I saw the small globe pendant resting against Ocean's skin. He folded his shirt neatly and placed it on the drawers. My mouth dropped open as Ocean's black trousers fell to his ankles. We'd been dating for three months now, had done *things* together, and had lived in the same dorm room for around two years. Yet somehow, this was the first time I'd seen Ocean fully naked. The first time I was able to take in the length and majesty of those long legs, his slim, angular upper body and the bouncy hair that fell over those piercing blue eyes.

"Come here." I held out my hand, encouraging my boyfriend back to the bed. I pulled Ocean against me, holding him as close as I could.

~*~

I didn't know how long I'd been asleep; probably only a few hours. All I knew was that the bed was far too empty when I woke up. I sat up, slapping the empty space beside me.

I spotted my boyfriend sitting on the windowsill.

Ocean was curled up, his coat pulled over his otherwise naked body, holding a lit cigarette out of the window. It could only open a few inches, but Ocean had managed to wriggle his skinny wrist through, his head bowing down each time he sucked on the filter. He was shaking slightly as he stared at something on his lap. When Ocean took a long drag from the cigarette, I saw through the smoke that his eyes were wet.

I didn't like seeing my boyfriend cry, especially when I didn't know why, but over the past few months of our relationship, I'd started to become honestly impressed. I could barely remember the last time I cried.

"Frizzy?"

Ocean turned, almost dropping his cigarette. "Shit, Ru! I'm sorry. I—"

"What's going on?"

The simple question seemed to send Ocean into a panic. I noticed a medium-sized diary being snapped closed in his lap. Ocean crossed his legs over each other, squeezing tight. He stared at the book. It was mostly black, the cover decorated with an intricate pattern of golden honeycombs. It had gold trim on the edges of the pages and an elastic strap to keep it shut.

I slipped out of bed and walked naked towards the window. My boyfriend clutched the diary protectively.

"Babe," I said, "whatever you're going through, I mean..." I pinched the bridge of my nose, not sure what the right thing to say was. "I'm here if you want to talk about it. Okay?"

Ocean sighed heavily. He took a final drag of the cigarette before throwing it out the window and digging his nails into the book. "I know," he whispered. He turned, rubbing his face against me. "I'm... I'm going to miss you so much."

I sat down on the windowsill next to Ocean, pulling him into my lap. "It'll just be a little while. Less than a month."

"I know."

I rocked Ocean gently, the diary crushed between us.

Chapter Eight

Ocean

I slipped hurriedly inside the front door, kicking my shoes off and heading straight for the stairs.

"Seahorse."

My footsteps paused.

"Yes?"

"Can I talk to you?"

I peered through the gap in the bannisters. I could see Theo through the open doorway to the living room, sitting stiffly in his chair. "What did I do?"

Theo sighed, rubbing his wrinkled eyes. "Just get in here before I drag you!"

I mumbled out a string of curses, reluctantly walking back down the stairs.

Theo tapped his foot against the floor, his thick sock making a repetitive 'pap-pap' noise against the carpet. It almost drowned out the loud, threatening tick of the old grandfather clock that stood proudly next to the cast iron fireplace.

Theo hadn't changed the decor of the living room for almost forty years, not wanting to mess with what he considered fine, no matter how much I insisted that it was old-fashioned and stuffy. The room certainly was old-fashioned, with a dark hardwood coffee table, a nineteenth-century armchair with polished leather and a stuffed bookshelf filled with old hardbacks, giving the room its earthy scent. I knew the familiar feel of the room brought Theo a lot of comfort, especially after a long day. It was a place he could sit down with a cognac, a book, and, most importantly, no one bothering him.

Which was why it was disturbing to not only be invited in, but ordered without any explanation.

"What do you want, you old—"

Theo watched the blood drain from my face as my eyes locked onto my black and gold diary. Rather than being tucked away safely in my bag upstairs, it was sitting on the coffee table right in front of Theo. Tears trickled from my eyes, rolling down my pale cheeks.

I watched as any small hope that this might have been a misunderstanding or a joke faded from Theo's mind.

"Sit down." Theo leaned back in his armchair, trying to collect himself. I didn't move. "Seahorse, sit down now!"

I quickly scurried to sit opposite him on the table, my lip trembling. My fingernail dragged against the hardwood as I gripped the edge.

Theo rubbed his brow again, realising that he would have to do the talking. "I found this in your room." He pointed at my diary.

"What the hell were you doing in my room?" I hissed, my voice filled with justified anger. "Why are you going through my stuff?"

"I thought it might be your notes for Paris," Theo explained. He leaned back in his chair, the leather creaking. "I shouldn't have read it. You're right. But, Seahorse... Seahorse, look at me."

My watery eyes turned to face Theo.

"Is this true?" Theo tapped the diary. "What you wrote in here? Is this how you feel?"

The clock was interrupted by a dry sob. My head slowly nodded.

"I see..." Theo leaned forward, linking his thumbs and resting his forehead on top of them.

I was gripping the coffee table so hard my diary trembled with me. I felt like I had been dropped into a pool of freezing cold water. The cold jabbed into me from every angle and when I looked up, all I could see was a thick sheet of ice, trapping me underneath.

"I'm so sorry," I sobbed, my voice shaking. I hugged my knees, curling as deep into myself as I could, melting into a weeping, coughing mess.

Theo winced in sympathy.

"For God's sake, don't cry about it," he grumbled. He strained himself, reaching out and dragging me into his arms. He placed me upright on his knee, as if I was once again his tiny little Seahorse. He rocked me carefully, swaying back and forth. I balanced on his knee, my legs bent over the armrest. Theo cupped my head, letting my tears fall onto his scratchy jumper.

He pulled his handkerchief out of his pocket and dabbed at my tears. He held it against my nose, waiting until I blew loudly into it.

"Come on now," Theo soothed. "We're going to figure this out, okay? I mean it! I don't know how exactly... But we're going to figure this out. I promise."

I nodded against his shoulder.

~*~

Ru

I stared at the cracks on the ceiling of the dorm, counting the lines. I looked at every stain and every mark, knowing them all by heart. My eyes, wide in the dark, flicked to each corner before following the tracks of black mould that were too high up for anyone to ever bother about.

I couldn't sleep. I didn't think I'd ever sleep again.

I rolled over, staring at Ocean's empty bed. The bed had been empty for far too long. I was used to seeing it undisturbed during the day. Ocean would pinch Enzo and Noah hard enough to bleed if they ever dared to leave anything within two feet of it. Every morning after crawling out, eyes heavy and frizzy hair sticking up, Ocean would smooth out the covers straight away. There were hardly any creases anyway, Ocean being the only freak on the planet I knew of who ironed their pillowcases.

I'd watch Ocean as if I were watching a nature documentary. He would tuck the sheets back into place, plumping the pillows and folding down the thin duvet at the top. When Ocean finally walked away, the bed would be as pristine as it had been the previous morning, as if it had never been slept in.

Seeing the pin-neat, empty bed during the day was freaky, but at night it was spine-chilling.

As far as I knew, the Paris trip had ended two weeks ago. I had seen students from the trip walking through the corridors, looking fine for the most part. Not that I knew them especially well- or cared.

Except that Ocean still hadn't returned to school.

I pressed my pyjama sleeve over my mouth, biting my wrist hard. I didn't know what to do.

Halfway through the winter break, Ocean had stopped contacting us. The day before, Ocean had been texting how much he missed me and how much he couldn't wait to see me again. He'd shown up to every one of our scheduled group video calls, acting his usual stuck-up, pain in the ass self. Straightened hair looking bouncy, beautiful, and soft. Then, out of nowhere, Ocean had disappeared. He stopped texting, stopped showing up for calls- all contact had just stopped. I'd heard nothing. There were no explanations. Ocean just wasn't around anymore.

When I cornered other students from the Paris trip, they just shrugged, saying that they'd seen Ocean twice the entire time. Once on the first day during orientation before Ocean left to stay with relatives instead of at the hostel, then again on the next-to-last day when they needed to hand in their work experience forms. Ocean hadn't even been on the coach there or back.

No one knew anything more. Freja hadn't heard anything. Enzo hadn't heard anything. Literally everybody had been trying to call, but Ocean just wasn't answering.

Violet even tried calling Theo's restaurant. She'd calmly asked the maître d' if she could speak to him, but she'd just been told rather curtly that Theo was on family leave. She'd tried to push further, asking when Theo would be back or if Ocean was working, since he sometimes did kitchen prep work or food running during the holidays. The employee just repeated that they didn't have any information about Ocean or Theo. Finally, they told her that if she didn't want a reservation, they would have to end the call.

I stood by with clenched fists. We could all hear the employee's dismissive attitude through the phone, acting as if our friend wasn't missing! I'd come close to snatching the phone from Violet a few times to demand to talk to Ocean, but she'd calmly held up a single finger while Freja held me back.

I turned over in my bed and grabbed my phone to check if there were any messages. There was still nothing. Not that I expected anything.

The damn frizzy-freak had never been one for social media, so it wasn't like there was an Instagram or Facebook page I could stalk. Even so, I had Googled him a few times – just in case… Well, just in case.

I didn't know what to say or do. Part of me wanted to curl up with Freja during our drinking sessions on the grass and sob about how much I wanted my boyfriend back. Only Freja didn't know I had been dating Ocean. No one did, as far as I knew. I couldn't betray Ocean by mentioning it. Even if Ocean had disappeared from the face of the planet.

I could have joined in with the rest of our friends in their mourning over Ocean's disappearance.

Enzo had full-on cried about how he missed their Friday pizza nights where Ocean would make individual pizzas for all of us in the big home economics kitchen. Jalapenos and olives for Noah, barbeque chicken for Janie, mushrooms and vegan bacon for Cam, tuna and pineapple for Freja, bell peppers and pepperoni for Violet, plain cheese for Enzo, and a pizza with shrimps for me. I noticed that after we'd started dating, my pizza had subtly grown.

Ocean wasn't even that into pizza, saying it was too greasy. He never made one for himself, plating up everyone's favourites and only eating one or two slices of whatever was left over. It didn't stop him going through the same routine every week, taking the same orders and making any requested changes without complaining.

Cam was upset because Ocean would always dye her roots for her. She'd tried to do it herself, only to turn up in the common room, looking both surprised and terrified with brown streaks down the side of her face and hands that looked like they'd been dipped in mud.

I supposed I could have come up with my own reason like that for missing Ocean – a mundane favour that Ocean would do for me that I missed, but I wasn't very good at improvising. Besides, as far as the friend group knew, Ocean and I were still rivals. Two people who clashed at every opportunity, only pretending to be civil for the sake of their friends and to not piss off the headteacher. I almost wished that was still the case. If Ocean had gone missing six months back, I would have been concerned, but I wouldn't have been broken.

I didn't know what could have happened. I thought things had been going well with us, especially after our secret date to the winter festival. And the hotel room afterwards.

The memory hit me as I looked at the empty bed. My stomach clenched. I couldn't stop wondering how much of Ocean's happiness had been faked. It was clear, to me at least, that he had been hurting, with his strained smiles and faraway stares.

I couldn't stop myself from wondering if Ocean was still alive.

A noise like an angry goose left my throat before I could stop it. I threw back my covers, running to the bathroom and locking the door behind me. I leant against the white door as I forced myself to take deep, steadying breaths.

I sank to the floor.

"Please... you shitty blonde shithead!" I whispered. "Please, just let me know if you're okay."

~*~

Ocean

"You didn't have to drive me the whole way," I huffed, leaning against the window.

"Yes, I did!" Theo snapped.

I rolled my eyes. Theo had been acting as if a six-hour round trip car journey was little more than a mild inconvenience to his day. He'd had the same tone when I was eleven and accidentally tipped Pepsi all over the backseat. He'd arrived late to work because he insisted we had to go home to clean it up straight away.

Theo turned down the winding road; the large school was now visible in the distance. The old-fashioned brickwork beckoned us, looming at me like a final boss fight. Theo glanced over at me, my fingers tapping against the window.

"For God's sake, just light a cigarette. You're seventeen!"

I glared at Theo, but reached for the cigarette packet on the dashboard.

Theo stopped at a red light, taking the opportunity to rest his eyes for a moment. "Maybe we should just go home," he said quietly. "You can start school again after your birthday."

"No. We're almost there now," I said with determination, taking another drag. "The only thing worse than facing this would be running away."

Theo nodded. He looked oddly proud.

"Alright, if you're sure, Seahorse. Remember, I'm just a phone call away. You call me day or night and I'll come to pick you up no matter what. Got that?"

"Yes, you stupid, shitty old man!" I seethed out a long line of smoke, feeling very much like an angry dragon.

Theo looked at me from the corner of his eye as the light changed, just in time to see my fingers fondling that bizarre glass ball.

"You look really pretty, by the way."

"Thank you."

~*~

"You ready, sweetheart?" Ms Khil asked.

I fidgeted on the spot, feeling like a spider in the corner of a bath, looking up at an incoming rolled up newspaper. I nodded.

Ms Khil squeezed my shoulder before knocking on the door. She patted her neat hair bun.

"Come in!" Freja called, casually. She probably thought it was one of the guys.

Ms Khil opened the door.

I peered through the crack. Freja was sitting up on her bed. Violet was lying contently on her lap reading her book. Cam was singing to herself, painting her toenails with a green highlighter pen as she sat on the floor.

"Hello, ladies." Ms Khil held the door open slightly, stepping between it as if she were blocking the entrance. She looked at the girls with a still, enigmatic smile. "I trust you're all well."

"Fine thanks, Ms Khil!" Cam sang. She stretched her legs out, leaning back to look at the ceiling, kicking her feet above her.

"Good." Ms Khil looked at each girl one by one. "Now, as you know, there is an empty space in your dorm." She gestured to the spare bed by the window. "So, I'm here to let you know that as of this afternoon, you'll be getting a new roommate."

"A new roommate?" Freja furrowed her brow. Violet sat up next to her, looking equally confused.

The bed had been there since the start of the school year, all other pupils having their own friend groups already. It was almost unheard of for a student to join our remote school so far into the school year, especially a senior.

"There's a new girl?" Violet asked curiously. "Why now?"

"There have been some special circumstances," Ms Khil explained. "And she isn't new."

"What do you mean, Ms Khil?" Freja asked.

The teacher shrugged and looked over her shoulder. "All yours, darling."

Ms Khil stepped aside. All three girls stared at the doorway.

A tall, blonde girl stepped inside. She'd taken her shoes off and was wearing long, black socks that stopped about ten centimetres above her ankles. Her bare, pale legs were freshly shaven underneath her pleated school skirt. Her long hair fell over her face, bouncing off the collar of her blouse. Blue fingernails tugged at the sleeves of her grey jumper as she shuffled awkwardly. The girl still clung to her large military style duffle bag as if she didn't know if she could put it down.

"Shit—" Freja shifted forward on the bed, face twisted in confusion. She stared at the girl. "Shit... Ocean?"

I flicked my hair out of my eyes, swallowing audibly. I looked up at my friends.

"Hey, Freja."

Chapter Nine

Ru

"Guys!"

Enzo and I looked up, spotting Noah running across the field like he was being chased by a hell demon. I looked at him for a second- before lying back down. I closed my eyes, already deciding that whatever Noah was trying to pull this time definitely would not gain my interest. Enzo looked at him, confused.

"Guys!" Noah said again, a little louder this time. He nearly skidded across the grass, narrowly stopping himself from collapsing into a group of unknown girls.

Noah's mistake of running so hard caught up to him the moment he reached us. When he took his first breath in, the air came out in a long wheeze. He braced himself on his knees, bending forward.

"Noah!" Enzo pulled Noah down so he could rub his back. He reached into the small, familiar pocket of Noah's bag to grab his inhaler. "Here." Enzo shook the inhaler furiously, uncapping it and holding it to Noah's mouth.

He nodded as a way of saying 'thank you', breathing in with another wheeze as he pushed the button. I didn't move throughout the whole performance, continuing to relax on the grass.

"What's wrong, Noah?" Enzo asked, scooting forward on his butt, rubbing grass stains into his school trousers.

Noah spluttered some more, his legs shaking and knees knocking together comically. "It's..." He shuddered again. "It's... Ocean!"

I sat up. "What? What about him?" I blurted. Before I quickly laced my fingers together, placing them behind my head to resume my casual position. "Is he back?"

Noah shook his head. Then nodded. Then shook his head again. "It's..." He made a choking sound in the back of his throat.

"Noah, what's going on?" Enzo asked. "What happened to Ocean?"

Noah shook his head again. He pointed across the field.

I immediately spotted Freja walking down the main path, arms linked with another girl. She was taller than Freja was, with a longer skirt. A black messenger bag bounced against her thighs. Freja seemed to be guiding her, although her companion didn't appear to be taking any of it in. Her head bobbed in understanding without turning to look at anything Freja pointed out. Her hair shielded so much of her face I didn't think she could see anything, anyway.

"Who's that?" Enzo asked. "That girl with Freja? She new?"

"Yes. Well, no. But kind of, yes?" Noah grabbed his hair, shaking his head wildly.

"Oh, come on, fuck-wit!" I scoffed. "What the hell is—?"

I cut myself off. The girl with Freja looked so familiar – a little *too* familiar. I swallowed. I'd never forget those long legs, those ocean blue eyes filled with simple kindness, peeking out through a stupid, sexy mop of blonde hair that would frizz out first thing in the morning before it was straightened. It had grown a little longer now, curls bouncing on her shoulders.

"Ocean." I couldn't stop the name slipping past my lips. I gaped helplessly, staring at her in awe.

"Ocean!" Enzo's scream almost deafened me. He leapt up off the grass, running across the field towards his friend.

I dug my fist into the dirt, tugging up a clump of grass.

~*~

Ocean

"So, will you be joining any of the girls' sports teams?" Freja asked with a grin. "We could use you on the swim team."

"No sorry," I said. "They haven't told me if I can do sports yet. At least competitively."

"What?" Freja shook her head in disgust. "Fucking shitheads."

I squeezed her arm, grateful for the sympathy.

"It's not the school's fault... They have to wait to hear back from the governors or something." I shrugged. "It doesn't matter, honestly. Taekwondo is co-ed, so I'm pretty sure I can continue with that."

"Cool." Freja pulled me in tighter, pointing towards the art building. "Don't use the bathroom on the second floor, okay?"

"Why not?"

"That's where this stupid gang who thinks they're tough shit go to smoke dope. They're not dangerous, but if you get caught in there with the smell, teachers will assume it's you."

I nodded. "Okay. Thank you for the warning." I couldn't help but cringe uncomfortably. It already amazed me how differently girls were treated. If there was a gang who regularly went to one of the boys' toilets to smoke dope, they'd have been expelled long ago. Yet Freja had already told me about some girls who got a week of detention and a letter sent home after having a belching contest – something I was pretty certain a group of boys had done on multiple occasions and turned into a tournament. There had even been a chart on the notice board in the boy's corridor at one point. It was like the school wasn't even trying to hide the double standards.

"Ocean!"

I felt a prickle of fear spread down my spine, recognising Enzo's voice immediately. He let out a loud cry of excitement that would always bounce off every building within ten miles of him.

Sure enough, when I turned around, I saw the long-limbed boy flailing about wildly as he sprinted across the grass. I braced myself internally, waiting for his reaction- only for him to crash against me. I took a few steadying steps back as I was pulled into a familiar hug.

"Um, hey, Zo. I—"

"Ocean!" Enzo interrupted, wriggling with his arms around me. He lifted me a few centimetres off the ground to shake me from side to side. "I missed you, I missed you, I missed you!" The ball of energy pulled back, giving me that thousand-watt smile. "Where did you go? Where have you been? When did you get back? You're back for good, right?"

I gaped at him, feeling bewildered, but on some level not overly surprised that he apparently hadn't noticed there was anything different about me. He just stood there, waiting for an answer.

"Alright." Freja grabbed him by his collar, pulling him off me. "Let's not overwhelm her, okay?"

Enzo blinked in confusion. His eyes went wide. "Ocean! You have boobs!"

I folded my arms across my chest, placing my forearms over my padded bra. I tried to wave off the subconscious feeling the simple statement gave me.

"Yes," I mumbled.

"Cool!" Enzo pulled me back into his arms. "They're comfy!"

"What did I just say, Enzo?" Freja yanked him off again.

I rolled my eyes but couldn't help feeling incredibly touched by Enzo's casual attitude; as immature as it was.

"So, why do you have boobs now?"

I took a deep breath. "Well, Enzo," I said, hugging myself tighter.

Freja stepped beside me, an arm coming around my shoulders. I appreciated the gesture. My roommate grounded me and gave me the courage to make the confession for what felt like the thousandth time in the last couple of months.

"I'm transgender."

"What's transgender mean?" Enzo asked, hugging me from behind. Effectively knocking Freja aside. "Is it a good thing? Can we have a party? We have to have a party 'cos Ocean's back!"

"It's a good thing." Freja stepped in again, noticing how flustered I was getting. It couldn't have been hard to see; my face was flushing so deeply I felt like a flamingo! "Want me to explain?"

I nodded, giving Freja a grateful look. She nodded back before once more grabbing Enzo by his collar, turning him to face her.

"Ocean's a girl," Freja said simply. "We thought she was a boy, but we were wrong. She's a girl. Okay?"

Enzo blinked twice. "Okay!" He turned back to me. "So, we're going to have a party, right? Will you make me those fancy cheese and ham things?"

My head started spinning. As well as this was going, it was a little overwhelming.

"I need to finish showing her around," Freja said, linking her arm back through mine. "Let's meet up in the common room at six tonight, alright? We'll celebrate then."

Enzo whooped and jumped up into the air three times before running around the field in an almost perfect circle of excitement.

"There, that went well," Freja said with a reassuring grin. "Now come on, Ms Khil wanted me to give you the code for the girl's locker room."

She pulled me forward, leading me towards the sports hall.

I looked across crossed the field, past Enzo, who was now wrestling with Noah; the two boys tumbling around on the grass and screaming. My heart skipped a beat when I saw a tall, familiar figure staring at me with dark eyes.

I looked away.

~*~

Ru

The party in the common room had felt creepily routine. Ocean seemed to integrate back into our group quite fluidly. She was cooking in the small kitchenette, making sweet and savoury muffins, including a unique cheese and ham special just for Enzo.

I could see a picture I'd seen a thousand times. Enzo was sat on the sofa having his nails painted by Janie while Cam sat beside them with her homework. Noah was trying to play poker with Freja and Violet, but, of course, was getting everything wrong and losing his allowance at an alarming rate. I was lying on the floor in front of the sofa trying to nap- only for Cam's toes to poke me repetitively in the neck as she reclined back, doodling in her maths book.

It was a picture that could have been taken now or last year, or even the year before if I took Janie out.

Enzo didn't seem to be at all bothered by his best friend revealing that she was a girl. Noah still looked terrified of her, but after getting a death glare from Freja, didn't say anything. Ocean's other new roommates didn't seem to care either; they were just very excited to have Ocean back.

"Hey, Ocean!" Cam jumped off the sofa, almost kicking me in the face. "Look at this one!" She ran over with her phone in hand, linking arms with Violet and dragging her with her. "Could you put this one in my hair? It says it'll go lighter in the sun. Doesn't that sound cool?"

My stomach clenched when I saw Cam and Violet hovering around Ocean. Cam grinned as they chattered about hair dyes and summer colours. I was happy for Ocean. Of course I was. She was back and safe – safe and happy. It was all I'd asked for over the past few weeks.

As happy, relieved and weightless I was just seeing Ocean back, I couldn't deny the twisted feeling inside me. I was terrified of going back to our room later; trying to sleep and seeing Ocean's abandoned bed. I shuddered when I imagined another boy moving into our room, as unlikely as that was. Rolling over at night, expecting to see her peaceful, comforting face, only to see some stranger. Not that I would mention that to Ocean. There was no possible way of saying something like that without sounding creepy as hell.

My chest tightened. I tried to pull myself up while keeping a straight face, mumbling something about going to the bathroom. I was pleased to see that no one else was paying enough attention to acknowledge this. Why would they? Ocean was back.

I walked across the field, my hands in my pockets. I wondered if I should've turned up to the party at all. Ocean had been avoiding me all day. No matter how many times I'd tried to corner her, she'd found some way to disappear. Not that it was hard with everyone else wanting her attention today.

Everyone had been, much to my surprise, tactfully avoiding questions regarding her change or why she'd been away. Instead, asking her how Paris had been and what she'd done for the remainder of the winter break. She had answered honestly enough, showing pictures of a man she'd seen in Paris covered in pigeons and a fairground statue of a tree with a wide grin that looked like the stuff of children's nightmares, before talking about going shopping for clothes with her foster father.

I rubbed my brow, making a beeline for the well-known gap in the hedge so I could sneak off to grab something from the local liquor store. I crawled back twenty minutes later with my usual bottle of rum tucked under my arm. I looked pretty messed up, with twigs and leaves stuck to my uniform. My hair was dishevelled at best and I was pretty sure I could smell the alcohol on my own breath.

I started hoping that no one had heard me say that I was going to the bathroom. If they had, I'd return looking like something had gone horribly wrong.

The field was so much quieter and more peaceful than it had been earlier. It was empty; no groups chatting or running around. No one walking arm in arm down the path. I spotted a tiny orange light behind the equipment cabin. My hand clenched around the glass bottle, my mouth going almost painfully dry. I took another swig of rum, wiping my mouth with the back of my sleeve and ignoring the burning sensation on the shells of my ears.

I staggered as I made my way across the grass. My heavy footsteps alerted Ocean before I was even halfway there. She tensed, her fingers tightening around her cigarette, but she didn't run away.

"Hey." I halted in front of her, shoving my rum bottle back under my arm. I watched Ocean smoke. Her eyes shone in the darkness. The smoke swirling around her face made her look very mystical. For a moment, I wondered if this was all a dream and that would open my eyes to see the dark, mouldy ceiling.

"Hey." Ocean leant against the cabin, shivering. There was a heavy tension in the air that neither of us knew how to handle, even if it was rather predictable.

I shuffled on my large feet, looking at my boyfriend—my girlfriend?

I sighed. I needed to know where I stood. Even if I had a feeling the answer might hurt.

"So where have you been?" I asked eventually. "You were supposed to come back weeks ago."

"Theo thought it would be better if I stayed at home for a little while longer," Ocean explained. She tapped her cigarette out. Forgetting not to leave evidence, she dropped the butt and stubbed it out under her boot. "...while he got things sorted out with school."

"Yeah, that makes sense." I scratched my head. "It's been kind of lonely without you. I mean, without you to keep them in line, Enzo and Noah keep leaving their shit everywhere."

I added the last part quickly.

"I'm sorry," Ocean said. "I know this is awkward."

"No, it's okay." I moved closer, my feet catching in the mud. I quickly grabbed Ocean's hand. My heart sped up. I'd almost forgotten how soft Ocean's hands were. Almost.

I tried to focus on the fact that the person I'd been agonising about for over a month was okay, but I couldn't stop the bitterness that spread through me.

"Why didn't you answer your phone?" I clenched my teeth. "I called you. I called you so many fucking times!"

Ocean looked at the crushed cigarette butt, her bottom lip between her teeth. She looked thoroughly ashamed of herself, which brought me a little bit of comfort.

"I'm so sorry, Ru," she sighed, her voice trembling but sincere, "I wanted to text you. I must have drafted a thousand texts, but I just didn't know what to say."

"I don't know, how about 'I'm alive!'" I stared at her so hard I could imagine her bursting into flames. "How could you do this? After we... you know?"

"I'm sorry, I shouldn't have done that." Ocean looked into my eyes. "Especially after what we shared. I didn't mean to make you think that us having sex didn't mean anything. Because it did, Ru! It meant more to me than I thought it would."

I relaxed a little bit. I was still angry, but the overwhelming relief that Ocean was okay caught up with me again at her confession.

"Frizzy..." I stepped closer, our faces just a few inches from each other. "I know it did. I wouldn't accuse you of faking. I know you too well."

"I know you do."

There was another silence. I folded my arms, my rum bottle lodged in my armpit as I tried to choose the right words. "So, this is your secret, then? What you've... been dealing with?"

Ocean fiddled with the hem of her jumper. She reached into her pocket for another cigarette. I stood quietly beside her.

"Yes," she said plainly. "I've been dealing with these feelings for... well, forever. Although it's only been in the past year, I really figured out what was going on." I started to feel sick, remembering what she had said to me on my birthday. In this very spot. "I know I said I'd talk to you about it when I was ready. I mean to, honestly! You were supposed to be the first person. Theo found my diary. I was sort of thrown into the deep end. He ended up being really supportive about everything, though. He just... wanted me to be happy."

"I see." I tugged on my hair. "Are you happy?"

Ocean smiled. A true, content smile. "Yes, I'm very happy."

"Good," I said quickly. I braced myself to ask what I really needed to. "So... does this mean you're my girlfriend?"

"Ru..."

"Because I'm okay with that! You look really pretty. You've always been really pretty."

"Ru." Ocean held my hand. "I can't be your girlfriend."

I clenched my free hand into a fist. "I mean... I just assumed since you're a girl..." I said slowly, "it's okay. You can call yourself whatever you want. It doesn't matter to me."

Ocean cringed.

My eyes twitched. My bottom lip shook as I tried not to scream. I knew very well what Ocean meant.

"Ru," Ocean said again with a sigh, "I can't date you anymore."

I felt my heart sink into my kneecaps. "Frizzy..." I swallowed. "Don't."

"You can be a really sweet guy. I'm just not in a position to date anyone right now. I have a lot of stuff I need to figure out." Ocean powered through her speech, forcing herself to look at me. "I'm sorry, Barbarian. I've loved the time we've spent together. It meant so much to me. Every single moment with you... it made everything easier."

"Then don't stop it." I tilted my head, taking her other hand. The embers from Ocean's new cigarette tapped against me. I winced, but didn't pull away. "I get this is a big time for you... but I want to understand. I'll listen. Anything you want to talk about, I'm here. We can move back a few steps. We'll take things slowly."

Ocean smiled at me again. This time it was a half-smile. A damning smile. "I'm sorry, Ru," she whispered. She leaned in to press a single, soft kiss against my parted lips. "But..."

I could tell she felt bad. It was obvious in the way she hunched her shoulders and held herself. Part of me knew what she was about to say.

"You're the only openly gay guy in our entire school. It's going to be hard enough establishing myself as a girl. I can't even list the number of disturbed looks I got today alone. If it gets out that I'm dating you... I really couldn't handle it."

I closed my mouth. I didn't like this. I hated everything about this. But I hated even more that I understood Ocean's reasoning. I'd been thinking about coming out as gay for the past year. I'd had been certain for a while that I liked guys. At least I thought I did. Truthfully, I still wasn't that obsessed with random attraction. I'd sat around listening countless times while Noah or Freja had been prattling on about some hot girl, and I'd just nodded with disinterest, as I had done in middle school.

Ocean on the other hand; she made my blood boil. She made me feel happy and safe, in a way only one other person ever had.

"This is why you didn't tell me before, right?" I asked bluntly. "Because you knew you'd break up with me when you did."

"I didn't put off transitioning especially for you." Her tone started off harsh, but she managed to reign herself in. She stroked her thumb over the burn on my hand. "I'm sorry, Barbarian."

"No." I shook my head, letting go of her. "Don't be sorry. That's how you feel."

"Thank you." She reached around her neck for the clasp of her ocean globe necklace. I grabbed her wrist carefully.

"No. It was a present. You can keep it."

She nodded, taking a final drag of her half-smoked cigarette before crushing it on the ground next to her first.

"Alright. Thank you, Ru."

She took pity on me, turning to walk back to the dorms without another word. I listened carefully, waiting until the squish of her boots echoed far into the distance.

I fell to my knees in the dirt, staring at the broken, crushed cigarette butts in the soil. My rum bottle finally fell and rolled beside her cigarettes, my fingers digging into the ground between them.

Chapter Ten

Five months earlier

Ocean

"That asshole," I seethed to myself. "That dumb, hideous asshole!"

I stormed down the corridor with no destination in mind, my boots stomping on the polished floors. I pushed through the doors at the end of the long corridor before running down the staircase, wanting to be as far away from Ru as I could get. The moment my foot hit the bottom step, my mouth fell open in a long scream. I collapsed onto my knees, crawling under the staircase to hide. My fingers ran through my hair and pulled, thin strands coming out in my palms.

"Stop," I whispered to myself, "stop, please."

I didn't know who I was talking to. Ru, Freja, Violet, Enzo. It was all just too much. I turned over, leaning against the wall as I looked up at the dusty old staircase. I shut my eyes for a moment, forcing myself to take five steadying breaths.

"Okay," I mumbled, feeling the heat spreading from my cheeks to the rest of my face. My fists finally unclenched. "You're okay."

I rummaged in my messenger bag, finding my familiar black and gold diary. I shivered as I opened it to my last entry.

Violet asked me to make snacks for the swim team this afternoon! It's still rather annoying that everything thinks I can make shit just because Theo owns a restaurant.

I don't really mind doing it for her though.

I licked my thumb, rubbing at a smudge of ink in the corner before I flipped back another two pages.

I had the dream again. I was in Freja's body this time – it was so vivid, I swore I could feel her perfect boobs bouncing when I ran!

The others are still asleep. At least it's lucky these little shits never wake up for anything. The barbarian looks so gormless. I'm sure spiders must have crawled into his open mouth at some point. That's probably why I haven't seen any in the dorm lately!

I continued to flick through the pages while mumbling more insults towards Ru. I took my fountain pen from its strap, forcing my hands to turn to a new page and stay there. I pressed the nib against the paper, printing splotches on the page in deep blue ink.

Ru made another stupid attack on my hair again today. I just can't stand him constantly making jabs about my appearance when he looks like that with his dumb cheap-looking hair and always managing to have stains all over his clothes. He looks like a fucking vagabond and it makes me want to scream!

I scratched the pen against the margin. I looked around the dark corridor to make sure I was alone.

I think this would be easier if I looked like him or maybe just acted like him. If I was just a normal boy. Not that it would make it any easier to pretend to be a boy, but maybe I would be able to tell everyone the truth then. Right now, I imagine telling everyone that I'm a girl and them telling me how things 'made sense' or that I 'acted like a girl anyway'.

I don't know how a girl is supposed to act. Not that I know how a boy is supposed to act. I don't know how to act to make me seem more like a boy. Or how to act to make people believe I'm a girl. I don't think I want to.

I don't know. I just don't want to feel like I'm proving shitheads like Ru right. He's such a bastard! He hangs around Freja like they're best buddies, then calls me a 'girl' like it's some kind of insult. I don't understand how she puts up with him. As much as it hurts being called a boy, it hurts worse being called a girl by people like him. Being told I shouldn't behave this way and having that shithead mocking me for straightening my hair.

I paused, biting down on the lid of my fountain pen. The rough splotches I'd started with had descended into meaningless scribbles much quicker than I'd been prepared for. My eyes filled with tears.

I just want to be normal.

I shut the diary and wiped my eyes. I could do this. I'd been pretending for seventeen years. I could continue pretending for as long as I needed to. No one ever needed to know.

~*~

The walk back to the dorm from the gym was one of the longest walks of my life. I couldn't bring myself to look at Ru. I tried my best to ignore the boy walking beside me, even if I flinched every time I heard his heavy footsteps shuffling against the floor. His arm brushed against mine every now and then, making me jump. I could still feel his hands on my body; as if I were still pressed into the workout mat.

Ru kissing me, touching me – and me not hating it.

I had no idea what the protocol should be for this kind of situation. In sex education, they'd taught us what sex was and the changes that would happen to our bodies. I remembered the peppy councillor with the big, annoying grin who had come in to tell us that masturbation, premature ejaculation, or losing an erection was 'normal' and 'happened to everyone.' He had laughed along with the boys and put up with the immature banter, while I sank into my chair, begging for it all to be over. I'd crossed my legs so tightly I could swear my crotch was bruised afterwards.

For all the gritty, brutal honesty of the session, the counsellor had never touched on how to actually navigate relationships. No one had ever taught me how to feel or even how to express feelings. The closest anyone had ever come was the 'Auntie' at the big care home I'd lived in before Theo, who had told me very sharply that: 'boys don't cry.'

I wanted to cry. I'd wanted to cry then, when a large boy had ripped the head off my stuffed rabbit and threw it down the stairs. Now, it seemed like I *needed* to cry, otherwise I would explode! It felt like I was filled with a thousand black snakes, all of them slithering around inside me and tying themselves into heavy knots.

"Ru, Ocean!" Enzo cried out. "How was detention?"

I winced at his innocent question. I couldn't tell anyone to know how detention was when *I* didn't know how detention was.

"How do you think it was?"

I could feel my body trembling as I looked up, my eyes latching onto Ru's like two magnets pulling together.

His face was blank. There was nothing there; no pain or regret. He'd said he liked me in the gym, but I didn't know whether to believe him or not. He was the last person in the entire world I would have expected or indeed *wanted* a confession from. For all I knew, he was having me on and tomorrow the whole school would be laughing behind my back.

My goal moving forward would be to keep the laughter behind my back. So long as I never had to hear about this evening again, I could drag myself through to graduation.

"It was fine," I mumbled. "I'm going to take a shower."

I turned the shower on, stepping into the warm spray and hugging my naked body. I could hear my roommates arguing behind the door, and something crashing as it was thrown against the wall. Ru seemed to have fallen back into his routine with Noah and Enzo. Everything was business as usual.

I washed my body slowly. My head was spinning, unable to comprehend what Ru and I had done – in the gym, of all places! That was supposed to be our neutral ground, where we could fight as wildly as we could within the rules. I'd never be able to wrestle with Ru again, especially not on those mats. I didn't know how I felt about that either.

Bile rose in my throat. I didn't hold back. Instead, I opened my mouth, letting everything trickle out and wash down the drain. The only feeling I was sure I felt was confusion. There was so much confusion I didn't even know where to begin!

"I'm straight," I whispered to myself. "I'm a straight man."

My heart clenched. As if I knew deep inside that I wasn't either of those things. I'd called myself a lesbian in my diary a few times, experimenting with the label, but this evening had thrown me for an awful loop!

"Why did you do that, you barbarian?" I hissed to myself, reaching for my blueberry shampoo. I focused my energy on my hair, scrubbing it vigorously. "Do you fancy me or something?"

It was a redundant question. Ru had confessed that he had always got aroused when we fought. He'd kissed me and given me that wild look with his dark eyes that was now burned into my mind.

"I fucking hate you." I scrubbed harder, shaking my head wildly under the shower spray. "I hate you so much, you shithead!"

A loud knock on the door made me jump.

"Hurry up, Ocean!" Enzo called. "We've got to go down for dinner!"

"Yeah, just a minute."

I hurriedly rubbed conditioner into my hair and scrubbed hard at my skin. It didn't remove the feeling of Ru's touch on my body. Or help me forget how much I liked it.

~*~

The breeze from the city below hit my face as I pushed the window open. I knew I shouldn't smoke in the hotel room, but I really couldn't be bothered to make my way downstairs. That would involve getting dressed again with me all sweaty! Besides, I didn't want Ru to wake up and think I'd abandoned him.

I leaned out of the window as best I could, lighting my cigarette. I inhaled deeply, overwhelmed by so many things as I opened my diary.

Ru and I made love.

I shivered, quickly scratching the sentence out, deciding the wording was far too flowery. My hand hovered above the paper, telling myself to write 'had sex'. That didn't feel right to me, either. It was too blunt and too clinical. I shook myself off, carrying on next to the scribble, leaving things as they were.

It was honestly wonderful. It was so different from anything else I've experienced before.

It's strange, I don't think I find any men attractive other than him. Then again, why would I? Girls are amazing! They're clean; they're pretty! Men just straight up aren't. Every guy at our school is just a loud moron. It doesn't make sense.

When I'm with Ru, I just want to hold him and squeeze him! (He is still a loud moron though...!) Being with him was so intense. Every time he looked at me, I felt like I was going to melt inside.

I bit my lip.

It hurts because I don't know how much longer I can pretend to be a boy. It's getting harder to pretend. I'm realising that my life wouldn't be worth living if I had to carry on this way.

I promised Ru on his birthday that I would talk to him when I'm ready, but I honestly don't know how to even begin discussing the topic with him. Do I just walk up to him and tell him: "Guess what, I'm a girl now"?

My pen froze. I couldn't write anymore. Not after what my boyfriend and I had just shared.

~*~

"You've said that already!"

I sat on the stairs as I listened to Theo arguing on the phone yet again. I swallowed, hugging my knees.

Theo had been incredibly efficient since he'd found my diary. There had been so many phone calls, to the school, to helplines and doctors. He had booked an appointment with a

GP who we'd gone to see together and had got me a referral to a private gender clinic.

I winced when I remembered the price of just the initial appointment. Theo had said he was willing to do anything necessary to make things work, but I couldn't stop the guilt over the amount of money he was spending on me. Theo had already done so much before this, paying for my education and lifestyle. I didn't think I'd ever be able to pay him back, monetarily or otherwise.

I'd wanted to tell him that I didn't need him to pay for it. Before I remembered the public clinic telling us over the phone that the waitlist, just for a first assessment, would be over a year. Then I could start 'living in the role', as they called it, making it two years before they considered me for any kind of treatment. I didn't think I could handle that much waiting, not after pushing myself to the limit trying to pretend.

"Look, my daughter is over sixteen, so there is no legal reason for her to be excluded from the girl's dorm..." Theo huffed audibly. I peeked through the banister railings to see my guardian rubbing his brow.

"Alright, fine... Oh really? It's just more convenient to put her in her own room? Well, as luck would have it, I know Ocean asked for her own dorm at the beginning of the school year and you told her single dorms were only given out in 'special circumstances'. Are these the 'special circumstances' you were thinking of back then?"

I shut my eyes, playing with the globe around my neck. I remembered being told quite plainly and clearly that there were no available single dorms. I'd even been scolded for daring to ask; Mrs Tempest asking me why I thought I 'was so special'. Now that I was considered 'special', I really didn't want to be.

There were certainly aspects of having my own room that still appealed to me. Such as being able to walk about in a towel or dancing around to my music without anyone watching, or not having my things moved around 'for a laugh'.

I could also imagine the whispers behind the closed door as I sat on my bed, isolated and alone. As if I were standing shivering on the outside of a tight-knit huddle.

Then again, I might not have friends when I returned to school, anyway.

Right on cue, my phone buzzed in my pocket. I pulled it out. It was another text from Freja, this one asking why I hadn't joined our remote pizza night and if I was okay. I cringed, dropping my phone face down on the windowsill.

"Good!" Theo snapped, pulling my attention back to him. "And have your school's doctor call me back as soon as possible! Thank you. Yes, I'll discuss this with her."

I felt myself welling up again. Quickly, I rubbed my eyes with my sleeve. I'd been crying so much this past year, I couldn't imagine how much more emotional I'd get when I actually did start hormone therapy! I'd stayed up all night reading stories and blogs from other transgender women; one of whom talked about how three years after starting her hormones, she still felt like crying all the time. I seemed to be years away from starting hormones, even with the private clinic, but I already felt like crying all the time. It was at a point where I was starting to wonder if the Auntie at the foster home had known about me the entire time.

I jumped up quickly, clutching the banister, when I heard Theo draw closer. I tried to look at him nonchalantly, but one look from my guardian told me that he knew I'd been eavesdropping.

"I'm sorry about this," Theo said, rubbing his wrinkled brow. "They're not exactly cooperating. The Head is going to call me tomorrow, but if I'm honest, I'm not holding my breath." He threw his phone down on the end table in the hall. "Maybe we should find you a different school."

"No!" I hurried down the stairs. As terrified as I was of how my friends might react when they saw me as a girl for the first time, it didn't come close to the fear of never seeing them again. "I can't. I just... I can't."

Theo shrugged dejectedly and collapsed in his chair. His knees clicked as he placed his feet on his coffee table, wiggling his toes in his thick wool socks. His head tilted back with a long sigh, his neck resting on the back of the chair.

"Would you like me to make dinner?" I asked, tugging on a loose thread on the sleeve of my navy-blue jumper.

Theo looked me up and down. He focused on my tatty old jumper. I'd had it for years. It stretched a little every time it was washed and had almost grown with me. I pulled harder on the thread, watching it unravel around the cuff. I twisted it around my finger, admiring the shimmering blue nail polish I'd painted on that afternoon. I'd felt bold afterwards, so had paired it with a thin layer of eyeliner and a lip balm with a slight pink tint. Theo had undoubtedly noticed given how he was staring at me, but he didn't mention it.

"No," Theo said simply. "Let's go out to dinner."

"Really?" I looked at him, confused. "Where?"

"Wherever you want." Theo gripped the arms of his chair and hauled himself up with a groan. "Maybe we could go shopping first. They're open late tonight, aren't they?"

"Shopping? For what?"

He grunted, waving his hand at me. "I thought maybe you'd like some more... girly shit." He gritted his teeth. "I don't know about brands or anything of the sort, so you'll have to pick out what you want."

I made a noise like a cornered animal, covering my mouth with my frayed sleeve. "I can't..." I whispered.

"Well, you'll have to. I don't know what shit you girls like!" Theo stopped himself, brushing his moustache. "Sorry... that's not very PC. I just thought if you want skirts or makeup – things like that." Theo wandered into the hallway to grab our coats from their pegs. "Come on."

I stood paralysed in the doorway. I cautiously took the coat from him, holding it at arm's length as if it were a vomiting infant.

Theo's hand hovered before patting my head like a well-behaved dog's. "Are you ready? Come on, let's go." He squeezed my shoulder before stepping away, opening the front door for me.

~*~

Theo walked slowly behind me as we navigated our way around the huge clothing store. I could tell he was trying to ignore the anxiety that was seeping from every pore in my body. I knew he wanted to throw his debit card at me and go sit in a coffee shop until I was done, but ever since he found my diary, he'd been hesitant to leave me alone. Instead, he stood and watched while I flicked through a row of dresses. I picked up one with blue lace and long sleeves.

"That looks nice," Theo said, gesturing to it awkwardly. "That colour would, um... match your eyes."

"My eyes aren't azure," I teased. I turned around, holding the dress against me as I looked into the mirror. I glanced at Theo.

"You don't need my approval, Seahorse," Theo said. "Just get whatever you want."

"Whatever I want?" I gave him a cheeky smile.

"Within reason!" He snapped back good-naturedly. He rubbed his thighs, not missing the way my eyes narrowed in concern.

"I'll go sit down for a bit," Theo mumbled, no doubt wanting to suggest it before I did. "I'll just be in that seating area in the corner. You pick out what you want and then come find me. Okay?"

I smiled gratefully. "Okay, old man. Don't fall asleep!"

"Don't give me lip, brat!" He bared his teeth at me playfully, giving both his legs a little shake before walking away.

I watched him waddle over to the arrangement of large, squishy sofas. He sat down, his grateful sigh clear as he made himself comfortable. His doctor had recommended he start using a cane if he was going to be up and about for long periods of time, but he had angrily refused, declaring that he would not start descending that slippery slope just yet. He knew one day he would need one, but if he started too soon, he feared he would be stuck in a chair before he knew it. He shut his eyes, letting himself rest while I picked out my new clothes.

Walking through the store by myself felt like walking into the belly of the beast. Rationally, I knew there was nothing I needed to fear; I'd been through this store many times before. Only now everyone's eyes seemed to be burning into me. Every time I heard a hushed whisper, goosebumps rose on my skin. I'd turn around- only to see two or more people having their own conversations during their normal day.

My palms were trembling so much I was scared to touch the clothes, lest I accidentally rip them. It wasn't a matter of finding something I wanted. I was actually trying to restrain myself from grabbing everything that caught my eye! I was finally in a clothing store and didn't have to overthink every single piece I picked out. If something was 'too androgynous' or 'not boyish enough' or some other pathetic excuse my thoughts gave, there was no reason why I couldn't consider it.

There was just one major thing left in the way.

"Theo."

Theo sniffed, opening his crinkled eyes slowly.

"Are you finished?" He mumbled. I heard his stomach rumble impatiently.

"Sort of, but..." I held my selections a little closer. I had several dresses over my arm, including the blue dress from earlier, along with a couple of new tops, two pairs of slim jeans and a pair of high-heeled black suede boots.

"What else is there, Seahorse?" Theo glared at me.

My eyes flicked towards the changing rooms and the small, purple cut out of a 'woman.' It was a 1920s flapper caricature, flicking one foot out with her arms up as she danced the Charleston. A group of tween girls giggled to themselves as they walked out, handing rejected clothes to the smiling attendant.

"Ah. I see." Theo hauled himself up. He took me by the shoulder and led me to the changing room.

My arms tightened so hard around the clothes I felt like a child in a playground holding a comfort toy, worried another kid would run over and snatch it from their arms. More blood drained from my face as I approached the flapper woman, as if she were the guardian at the gates of hell.

"You shouldn't worry about that sort of thing," Theo said, shaking his head dismissively. "You've always looked a bit..." He swayed back and forth, looking for the right euphemism. "Soft, especially in the face area. I'm sure no one will question you."

I looked at him, mortified. "What the hell, Theo!"

"What, it's true! Don't worry, if anyone gives you shit, I'll deal with it."

Theo led me right to the dressing room entrance. He kept his hand on my shoulder, guiding me all the way. I walked obediently, my heart beating so hard I could feel it in my ears. My boots scraped across the floor, my legs suddenly unwilling to walk properly.

The attendant straightened up as we approached, pasting her customer service smile on her face. Her brow creased when she got a good look at me.

"Sorry, sir," she said, still smiling, "this is the ladies' fitting room."

I looked at my shoes, needing to tell myself that the employee was talking to Theo and Theo alone.

"It's alright," Theo replied, "my daughter just needs to try on a few things." He flicked my back. "Go on. I'll be right out here."

The attendant looked at me, my long hair falling over my pale face. "Alright, how many pieces do you have?"

I mumbled my reply, frantically counting the clothes in my hand.

"Alright then." The attendant didn't say more than that. She just took the numbered token and handed it to me. I snatched it and rushed into the cubicle.

True to his word, Theo stood right outside, grounded like a tree while I tried on my new outfits. I ended up taking almost everything, just putting back a pair of jeans that weren't quite long enough. Theo nodded at the attendant as she took them from me, ushering me away with a hand on my back.

He turned his eyes again when I dashed off to grab a few bras. I wasn't confident enough to dare try those on yet, but it wasn't like I had anything to fill them with. At least I knew my measurements. I shoved two underneath my pile of clothes, squeezing them beneath my arm.

Finally, we paid and left the store. I carried two shopping bags filled with clothes and one bag of makeup. I wasn't very confident with makeup yet, not having experimented with anything beyond eyeliner, nail polish, and tinted lip balm. I'd watched enough tutorials online to know what basics I needed and had gone with the brands I'd seen Freja use. If it was good enough for Freja, it was good enough for me.

Theo found his strength again when we got to the restaurant, settling us in a quiet corner of the heated terrace.

Mealtimes were usually a silent affair in our family. Theo had spent his entire life devoted to cooking and improving food. He liked to take his time to appreciate his meal and talking too much over dinner gave him indigestion. To him, dinner was a time to recharge and process the day while enjoying your food, rather than forcing idle chit-chat.

After the anxiety-filled trip to the mall, I didn't feel much like eating or talking. Instead, I twirled my spaghetti around my fork and pushed it around my plate, letting it fall in a pile on one side.

"Stop playing with your food!" Theo barked. "I didn't take you to dinner so you could fiddle with it. Eat the damn stuff!"

I slipped a few strands of spaghetti between my lips, shuddering as if they were live worms. Theo just stared at me in disbelief.

"Not like you to take an order without a fuss," he said, amused. "Are you going to tell me what's on your mind, or am I going to have to strangle it out of you?"

I put my fork down, bringing my hand to my lips to chew on my fingernails. "Why are you being so casual about all this?"

"I'm sorry?" Theo's face twisted into a frown.

I stared at him, both confused and oddly scared. "You're fighting with the school, you're making doctors' appointments, and you're taking me shopping." I gestured to the bags. "Why are you doing this?"

Theo straightened himself up. "Isn't that what I'm supposed to do? We looked it up; we need to see doctors and let the school know."

"Yes, but," I grabbed the collar of my jumper, rubbing it against my face, "I didn't think you'd... I thought you'd be mad."

"Why would I be mad?" Theo cut into his steak, acting deliberately casual.

"Because it's... well, I just thought you'd be!" I pressed on, "I thought you'd... give me up."

Theo put down his cutlery with a clatter. He leaned forward, looking at me intensely.

"I'll admit I don't understand this. I've never had to do anything like this before," he said, his voice a low rumble, "but that's not what's important. That important thing is that you're mine. I can't give you up and I never would. You told me how things are. We looked up what we need to do, and that's what we're going to do." Theo tapped his finger on the side of his water goblet, breathing heavily. "Look, as much as I hate to bring this up again, and yes, I know you deserve privacy and all that, I need to make myself clear."

He swallowed his half glass of water in one mouthful. I could tell he was regretting driving here, his lips smacking in desperation for something stronger.

"In your funny little book, you wrote about how it was getting harder to keep this to yourself. That you were sure you're a girl and how you were just pretending to be a boy." He reached across the table to grab my chin, forcing my head up. "Is that true?"

I hesitated. I nodded at my guardian.

"Then you're a girl. If you say you're a girl, I'm not going to argue with you. If you say that this will make you happy, I believe that you've thought this through. Nothing's going to change what I think about you, and I'd rather have you safe and alive than anything else. Got that, Seahorse?"

I stared blankly at him for a few moments.

I slapped his hand away suddenly and got up from the table, running around and throwing my arms around him in a hug. "Thank you, Theo!" I said, squeezing him tight.

"Yes, yes," Theo grumbled back, balancing his glass on the edge of the table so he could pat my shoulder affectionately. "Don't you dare start crying again! I've had enough of the waterworks from you. Sit back down and finish your damn dinner!"

"Yes, sir." I rubbed my hands on my jumper, trying not to sniff.

I did as I was told. My distressed expression had now been replaced with a small, content smile. The smile remained on my face as I picked up my fork and ate a proper mouthful of pasta.

It was Theo's turn to ignore his meal as he watched me, but I decided to ignore him. He had *that* face on. The one he had when he was playing our story over in his mind.

I knew our story as well as he did; he'd told it to me enough times. The social workers hadn't approved, but he'd insisted he wouldn't hide secrets about me from me. Theo often got his own way like that. It made the fact that he'd taken me in all the stranger.

He'd told me all about the first time he saw me. I was part of a group of rambunctious children from the local foster home. The others had decided the best way to spend their afternoons was by glaring at Theo's chefs through the kitchen windows of his restaurant, flipping them off and making stupid faces at them. They learned that they were all quick to anger and would start shouting and cussing in no time at all.

Theo would also find us rummaging through the waste bins, looking for rotten produce to use for pranks on other kids, teachers or care workers back at the home. The chefs would start yelling out of the back door, threatening to call the police. Theo never let them. He could tell the kids were just bored. He had admitted that he never particularly liked or understood children, but he recognised when someone was frustrated.

Children hold that same heaviness of stress and exhaustion in their eyes as adults do, even if not all adults see it.

Theo noticed there was something that was always weighing heavily on a particular scrawny, blonde child – one who always looked like they were starved half to death and hadn't slept since they were a baby. His words, not mine.

I'd been ten years old when Theo first met me. When he contacted the authorities to look into taking me in, they'd wasted no time filling him in on my tragic backstory.

My family had moved to France from Iceland when I was maybe six, but hadn't made much of an effort to integrate or start new lives there. It had barely been a few months before everything went wrong. My parents had been found dead from a drug overdose and their small child was found to be living on her own, feeding, dressing, bathing, and getting herself to school without any fuss. The social work file claimed that several days had passed since both parents had died, but she either hadn't noticed or didn't think it was worth mentioning to any of her teachers.

That was what the social workers decided had happened. One even noted that I may have seen the signs of an overdose and decided to ignore them. The social workers claimed that

I likely repressed the incident since I'd never made any claim to this story or have any memory of it at all.

Theo doubted the story very much. To him, the whole story had sounded like a twisted fantasy. He believed it was a concocted horror story designed to scare him away from me. Every time he spoke to the social workers, there was some new problem or some theory about what had happened. Some new trauma I was recovering from and more speculation about what he should be prepared for. It had even been suggested to him that my parents were running away from some dodgy deals back home- which was perhaps the most fantastical assumption they had come up with. When he pointed out there was no way they could possibly know that, they'd just raised their eyebrows and asked him to take a good long think about what he wanted for his future.

Theo understood why he was under a microscope. He remembered the disdain when he had told them he was alone, had always been alone and didn't have any intention of finding a partner. While they said it was all fine and legal for a single person to take on the responsibility of fostering, there had been the occasional passing comment about how I should have a proper family and that maybe one still might come along for me. Theo was sure a couple, maybe twenty years younger and preferably heterosexual, wouldn't have been told so many fantastical stories, asked as many intrusive questions and been put under such scrutiny. He'd admitted to wondering if things would have been at all easier if he'd been a single woman but hadn't let himself dwell on that.

What had really bothered him was that he was not convinced that the same concern and tireless checks had been done on me. The more time he spent with me, it became clear to him that they didn't know who I was at all.

His blood still visibly boiled when he talked about the social workers telling him I was shy and quiet, that I was so shaken up by everything that I could barely say a word to them- when in actuality I was only able to speak about ten words of French or English!

The more time Theo and I spent together, the clearer it was that I was supposed to be with him. The first passion we seemed to share was a love for old books, so for our first few weekends together, he'd take me to look around book fairs. Our tastes were very different. I preferred to dig out mystery books or period romances, whereas Theo would come out with a box full of old war novels. He would make sure we'd read them together anyhow, alternating whose turn it was to choose, and my language skills greatly improved within a matter of weeks.

Theo also took note of my love for music. I had found some old cassette tapes from jazz concerts in the glove box of Theo's car once, and listened to them the whole drive home, then asked to play them again during dinner that evening.

By our next weekend, Theo had tuned the old piano in his dining room and hired an instructor.

Not everything had gone smoothly during my transition into his life. Theo had already guessed that I would have a hard time at school. He'd tried his best to feed me well after I'd come to live with him. As much as he loved food, Theo had never really cooked outside of his restaurant, not seeing the point when it was just him. His diet before me had consisted mostly of toast, fried meats, and green salads. Sometimes at the end of the week, he would just fry up all the leftovers from the restaurant and freeze it for the next few nights. All of a sudden, with me at the table, he found himself compelled to make elaborate roasts, served with new potatoes and steamed vegetables, always followed with a proper dessert such as trifle or layer cake.

Despite his best efforts, I remained skinny and short for my age. More often than not, I would come home with a bloody nose, torn clothes, and bruises all over my body. Theo did his best to get the school to take things seriously, but all the teachers seemed to think it was just a matter of 'boys playing too rough.' One even had the gall to suggest that I should toughen up a bit and that perhaps I should stop making myself such an easy target.

Theo took the matter into his own hands after that and had asked me straight out if I wanted to learn to fight properly. He knew a martial art or fighting sport wouldn't be the ultimate end-all solution to the problem, but he thought that perhaps it would give me confidence and allow me to see off a few attackers.

I was rather enthusiastic about the idea. I'd looked through books at the library and started to read up on the various fighting styles and techniques the world had to offer. Finally, I settled on Savate, coming to the very logical conclusion that, while I had stick-thin arms, my long legs could perhaps give quick, sharp kicks. Theo had agreed and signed me up for some beginner classes.

As suspected, it didn't stop the bullying completely, but I was certainly surer of myself and wouldn't come home shaken up and bloody quite so often.

It was after that Theo learned just how talented and clever I was; his words again, of course. Several years after I'd started living with him, I could speak and read French perfectly, as well as being top of my English and German classes. I struggled a little with maths as I always have and probably always will, having little interest in the subject, but I applied myself in most other aspects of school. I thrived in history, much to

Theo's delight. He often helped me with projects and research for essays, his stacks of boxes of books from years of book fairs coming in handy. Even when I realised all the information was available and up to date on the internet, I never stopped him. He seemed to get a lot of joy shifting through pile after pile of dusty books with their earthy-vanilla scent in order to find one that might help.

Theo was convinced that I was: 'an exceptional child who deserved a bright future.' Again, his words.

The social workers hadn't been happy about his proposal to send me to school abroad. Nevertheless, he was determined that Averesch would be a good fit. It was an international school that would cater to my talent for languages. There was a taekwondo club where I could improve my martial art skills and it had a great reputation for safeguarding students. With me willing to go and Theo willing to pay, our small family had won the battle and the social workers had finally backed off.

There were still some things that we didn't talk about. While the social workers had tried to get me to remember my last few days with my parents, it was something Theo had never asked about. He'd always lived with the philosophy that if I wanted to talk about it, I'd say something. He didn't want to force me to tell him anything I didn't want to – even if he had accidentally read my diary. Similarly, I never asked why he never married or why he seemed to lack any romantic history.

It wasn't any of my business, although it was something I'd started thinking more about the past year. The chefs at the restaurant would say that Theo 'wasn't the marrying kind,' which, according to my old romance books, meant 'gay.' While I couldn't say for sure that Theo wasn't gay, or that he was straight, or if he'd ever had a relationship or even a one-night stand, I was entirely certain that Theo wasn't lonely. I never saw myself as a shining light who came in and brightened his miserable, solitary life. Theo certainly didn't! Before and after me, he was content to be by himself and preferred it. That was just how he was wired. It was just who he was, just as I was a girl.

The word 'aromantic' cropped up in some of the books I read. It seemed apt for Theo, but I didn't think he needed or wanted new labels at his time of life. I tried to imagine never needing or wanting a girlfriend, boyfriend or any partner. Something about it made my heart sink. I didn't think I could ever live my life alone as Theo had, but then he probably couldn't imagine transitioning into a woman. People at school often asked me what happened to 'my granny,' but I'd just shrug and say I didn't know.

We did look strangely alike, so much so that he was often mistaken for my biological grandfather. We were both blonde, though my hair was a light baby blonde, and his was much darker and didn't have my natural curls. Both of us had blue eyes, but his were more of a grey-blue, missing the tint of sea-green that mine had.

He'd once claimed that it was another sign that we were meant to find each other. A reminder that even in times like this, it was his job to stick by me no matter what.

"So, Seahorse," Theo said, breaking the silence, "do I call you something else now?"

I gave him a petulant look. "Other than 'Seahorse?'" I cringed exaggeratedly at the light tap to my shin under the table. Theo just mocked my 'ow' back at me. "No, I don't see the point in that. 'Ocean' isn't really a man's name anyway, right?"

"Don't ask me," Theo replied with a long shrug. "I thought anybody could be called anything these days."

"True," I conceded, "but it's enough of a struggle to get people to use 'Noyer' as my surname instead of that shitty *other* name." I shuddered, as if cold slime had dripped down the back of my neck. "Maybe we could change that? You know, legally?"

Theo looked at me with pride. It had been three years since I had started insisting on using Theo's surname, rather than my birth one. It always made him smile.

"Whatever you want," he said. "Whatever you need." He refilled both our water glasses, letting the moment settle. "Seahorse, I hate to bring this back up..."

"Yes?" I didn't look up from my plate. I'd stopped feeling nervous about what he had to say. Although perhaps this time I should have been.

"You mentioned in your diary—"

"Don't you *dare*, you stupid old man!" I snapped at him, my eyes catching fire.

"I know, I know," he said, holding his hands up in surrender. "It's none of my business. However, as your guardian, I have a right to be worried about you."

I huffed, slamming back in my chair and folding my arms across my chest. "What do you want?"

Theo didn't back down from my defiant stance. "In your diary," he said again firmly, "you mentioned that you have a boyfriend."

My cheeks flushed red in half a second.

"Well?"

"What?"

It was Theo's turn to huff. "Do you have a boyfriend?"

I cringed, burying my face in my hands. "I don't know!" I whined. "We've been dating for a couple of months. It's been great. Really great! He's rather annoying, a bit of a dorky muscle head. But there's just something about him that draws me to him. We're so different, but so similar in some ways.

He's the only person I've ever met who's as stubborn as me. I kind of like that in a bizarre way."

Theo raised his eyebrows. "He sounds interesting," he said. "I'd quite like to meet him one day."

"Well, that's unlikely." I deflated, flicking a tomato with my fork. "I don't think he'll be interested in me anymore. And even if he is... I don't know." I dropped my fork and pulled my sleeves down over my hands. "He's, you know..."

"No, I don't."

I glared at him again. "He's gay."

The cogs in Theo's brain started up again. "I see," he said slowly. "So, you're worried that when he finds out you're not a boy, he won't be interested in you anymore?"

"Yes."

"Huh." Theo took a bite of his steak. "That's stupid."

"What?"

"He's attracted to you now, right? At least based on what you wrote in your diary." Theo said it with pride this time, solely to make me whine in further embarrassment. "He's not going to suddenly stop loving you now that you're a girl. That's not how that shit works."

"No one said this was love," I insisted. "I'll get over it. *He'll* get over it."

Theo, thankfully, seemed too tired to push me further on the matter. He'd never approved of my previous relationships, mostly because he thought my girlfriends took advantage of me or pushed me around. I suspected he thought things would be the same when it came to boys.

"I'm sure you know better," Theo conceded. "Just promise me one thing?"

I'd taken a bite just as he'd asked the question, which he took as permission to continue.

"Don't let this kind of thing weigh on you, alright? Don't look at this like it's some shameful secret. Be upfront with people about it. I'm not saying you have to blurt it out the moment you meet someone you like. Just that there's no point in hiding it. And not because of their feelings; because of yours." Theo put on his best 'serious father' face. "Anyone who has a problem with this, for whatever reason, isn't someone worth your time. You don't want to waste time with someone who doesn't value you, right? Stay sensible, keep your head on your shoulders and don't treat this like it's a curse. Got that, Seahorse?"

I didn't know whether to laugh or cry. I wasn't completely sure Theo wasn't joking. Even if he was, I could at least appreciate the wisdom behind his words.

"Thanks," I said. "I understand."

"Good." Theo nodded firmly. "I'm not having you losing confidence in yourself. You won't be able to run the restaurant properly if you do."

I let out a long, exasperated groan. "I'm not going to run the restaurant!" I said, frustrated. "I've told you."

"Well, what are you going to do?"

"I don't know! Fashion or something. I'm not moving back here after graduation just to work with you. Why would you spend all this money on my school just to have me work in your restaurant?"

"Don't talk about my business like that," Theo snapped, although he didn't sound all that hurt. "You need to be smart and have a good education to keep any business alive, especially in something as competitive as the restaurant industry."

"What are you going to do about it if I don't take it over?" I teased. "Surely at that point, you won't be in a position to protest."

"I'll come back to haunt you if you're not running it properly."

"And I'll just pay for an exorcist with the money I get from selling it!"

Theo prodded my shin under the table. "Stop messing around and finish your dinner! I've told you enough times!" He scolded, although he smiled a little when he saw me laughing at my own joke.

"It's good to see you laugh again, Seahorse."

Chapter Eleven

Ru

The rain hammered heavily on the roof of the car. I stared out of the misty window, my head leaning against the glass.

"We can go if you want," I mumbled.

"We're not going anywhere in this," Yan said, checking his watch. "I won't be able to see a thing if we drive back now, so we might as well wait for it to stop." He looked at me.

I was still scrunched up in a ball, my legs resting on the dashboard.

It was obvious Yan thought he should probably say something, but he'd never been good at that. Instead, he adjusted his car seat, lowering it so he could nap until the rain stopped.

"Wait!" I said quickly. I reached into the footwell behind Yan's seat, shoving the two bouquets to the other side so they wouldn't get crushed. I ended up squashing a few flowers in the process, but it got them out of Yan's way.

Yan sat still, waiting for me to finish before he silently flattened the back of his seat and raised his legs to rest his feet on either side of the steering wheel.

"Who are we going to see first, then?" Yan mumbled, his eyes already closed.

"You can decide," I said bluntly. I hated it when Yan spoke to me like I was a child. I turned up the collar of my coat and pulled my phone out.

I shifted to give Yan as much of my back as I could, shielding the screen.

"Everything alright, Mamoru?" Yan finally asked.

"Everything is fine," I said automatically, slipping my phone back into my pocket. I continued to stare at the rain, tapping my fingers on the dashboard.

Yan shut his eyes tight and took a few moments to accept that his nap was officially ruined. He pulled himself back up, returning his seat to its upright position.

"What is it? Do you miss—" Yan trailed off, spinning his wrist, "you know, your girlfriend from school?"

I snapped back around. "My what?"

"The freckled girl," Yan said. "The one you brought over during the summer."

I dug my fist into my thigh to stop myself from punching him in the jaw. "That's Freja! She's not my girlfriend. She's a friend."

"Don't get so dramatic about it," Yan said, sighing heavily. "You went everywhere together."

"Because I wanted to show her around," I insisted. "You know, like you would do if a friend from out of town came to visit."

"I see." Yan shook his head, deciding this was an entirely pointless argument, despite being the one who started it. He looked at the slightly wilted bouquet of poppies on the backseat.

"You know," Yan said carefully, "you can talk about your new girlfriend here. I'm sure Mio would understand."

My clenched fist began to tremble. These were the moments I found it hardest to contain myself. If I were at school and a member of our group was pissing me off, I could just turn to them and tell them to shut up. I could head outside and break things or go attack the punching bag at the gym. I could start a full-on public fight with Ocean. When I was at home, I knew I had to keep my frustration under control or risk another lecture from Yan about how he 'didn't like what that school did to me.'

"First of all," I hissed, "Mio wasn't my girlfriend. She was a friend. As I've told you a hundred times a year for the past seven years!"

Yan just nodded, something he did when he didn't have the energy to argue.

"Secondly, I just told you, just now, that Freja is a friend. I introduced her to you as my 'friend, Freja'. When I told you she was coming, I said I was 'bringing a friend'."

"I was young once," Yan said in his defence, "I know what 'bringing a friend' means. Especially when that friend turns up, and she's a lovely, pretty girl. What else was I supposed to think?"

I threw my arms in the air. "You weren't supposed to think anything!" I snapped. "Freja likes girls!"

Yan recoiled in his seat.

My brain told me to shut up and stop there, but my mouth was apparently running the show. "Yeah? See, not all girls like guys. And guess what else? Not all guys like girls!"

The realisation of what I had inadvertently revealed hit me. I turned to give Yan my back, curling one of my legs underneath me to sit sideways in the car seat. I could feel the tension crashing down on us, more deafening than the sound of the rain beating on the roof of the car.

The moment the clouds parted and the rain cleared, I grabbed the poppies from the back seat and jumped out, slamming the door behind me.

"Hey!" Yan called. "Mamoru, let's go see your mother."

"I'm good," I called back, without turning around. "Tell her I said hi!"

I walked as fast as I dared through the large graveyard, sticking to the designated path, grateful for the first time that Mio's grave was so far away from my mother's. I ran up the stone steps, my boots squishing in the mud. The final drops of rain soaked me so thoroughly my shirt clung to me within minutes. I looked awful by the time I finally found Mio's grave. My boots were entirely coated in mud, along with half my trousers. I looked at the sparkling clean gravestone. Deciding I didn't have anything to lose, I sat down right on the footpath, my butt squishing in the mud.

"Hey." I shuffled forward.

A large bouquet of chrysanthemums already took up most of the metal vase joined by the grey stone. The engraved text was polished clean, and the granite shone brightly, despite the wet weather. I guessed her father must have come to visit her recently.

I squished my poppies in beside the chrysanthemums, frowning at the white and gold ribbon holding them together. I pulled the ribbon free, crumpling it up in my palm.

Mio had hated anything white.

"Hey," I mumbled again to the gravestone.

I rocked awkwardly, staring at the bold black lettering spelling out my old best friend's name. Years later, it still seemed so clear and fresh compared to the other faded names on the family stone. I grabbed my folded feet.

When I was younger, I'd often sit here chatting casually to the stone, telling Mio everything that came to mind. Telling her all about school, the teachers I hated the most, and the work I was struggling with. I'd told her all about my friends, mainly Enzo and Freja, but I'd mention the others too – how

Violet was the youngest but more mature than any of us, how Cam was an idiot, but could be funny and how much Mio would have liked them.

I'd told her about Ocean too. How he was annoying and how Mio would have hated him as much as I did. The update on our relationship balanced on my tongue as I sank further into the mud.

I couldn't bring myself to pretend that Mio was listening this time. I just sat there on the wet grass, staring at the lettering until I couldn't bear the cold anymore.

Yan was waiting for me in the car by the time I got back. His hair was a little damp and the medium-sized bouquet of white, pink and red flowers was gone from the car. This reassured me that Yan had at least stopped by at my mother's grave. He noticed the mud that caked my trousers, including the large unmissable butt-stain from where I'd sat on the ground, but he didn't say anything. I didn't bother to speak either, pretending to look out of the window again.

When we arrived back home, I stormed out of the car and ran inside the house, heading straight for the bathroom.

Twenty minutes later, I had showered and thrown on some loose sweatpants. I made my way up the stairs to my attic bedroom, bumping my head as I had done every time since I was fourteen years old.

Yan had built the room for me when I was five and already too big for the pull-out bed he'd set up in the living room. The room was pretty poor, still having the distinct look of a storage space, with bleach stains on the walls and splatters of paint across the wooden floor. It was cosy all the same, with enough room for a bed in one corner, a set of drawers against the far wall, and a bulky television on the floor.

The television was an awkward thing from the early noughties, something one of Yan's friends had given him after their daughter had gone to college. It was grey and square, with a heavy back and a DVD player built in. Half the buttons on the remote had been chewed off by someone's pet hamster, but it still worked perfectly fine if you pushed hard enough. My old game consoles sat tangled up next to it, wires in a big heap and games stacked up in a wonky tower leading up to the ceiling.

I collapsed on the bed, lying down being the only way I could be in the room without having to crouch under the low, angled ceiling. I wriggled my bare toes as I settled down, propping a pillow behind me before opening my laptop to type a message to Freja. I relaxed, interlacing my fingers against my stomach, tapping my thumbs together as I stared at the ceiling.

Almost immediately after I had been given the bedroom, I'd started decorating the ceiling with cut-outs from comic books and game manuals, along with stupid pictures of my friends. I looked at the photos of people I hadn't spoken to in years, faces I probably wouldn't even recognise if I passed them in the street. I'd considered taking them down, but I didn't want to ruin the mural or risk damaging the more meaningful pictures.

I looked at a picture of Mio sitting on a swing-set, her tongue poking out at the camera. Next to it was a large rectangular picture of my current friend group. Violet had given the photos to everybody as a gift at our end-of-school party last year. It was taken on a school trip to an amusement park. Everyone was grinning, with their arms around each other, except for Cam and Enzo, who were holding huge sticks of candyfloss.

Ocean stood between Cam and Noah, grinning wildly, head resting on Cam's shoulder. He was wearing a purple flowery button-up shirt with the collar open and sleeves rolled up to the elbows, even if it was still tucked firmly into too-tight blue denim jeans.

We'd been on so many rides, Enzo whizzing us around to one thing after the other that Ocean's straightened hair had frizzed after the first hour. For once it didn't seem to be bothering him. His bangs were wild and covered the whole top half of his face, a smile shining out underneath. Ocean's teeth always looked white and clean, even though he smoked and ate just as much junk as the rest of us. My tongue poked at the fillings at the back of my mouth.

I shut my eyes, not wanting to think about Ocean anymore. It had now been four days since I'd last heard from him. Sure, it was the Christmas season. Everyone was busy. Ocean was probably working at Theo's restaurant and had shopping to do; he'd told me so during our last phone call.

He had also ended the call with the whispered words: *"Sleep tight, Ru. I miss you; I'll talk to you soon."*

I huffed, pinching the bridge of my nose. I ran my fingers through my hair. The turquoise-blue dye I'd put in before the holidays had faded, leaving my hair mostly azure with patches of navy. I couldn't be bothered to do anything about it now. It didn't matter, nobody but Yan would see it, anyway.

I looked away from the amusement park picture and focused on the one photograph I had of my mother. She was sitting on a blanket outside, holding a two-year-old me in her lap. Both of us were giggling and waving at the camera; my tiny hand moving so fast it was blurred.

When I was younger, I'd fall asleep staring at the picture. I had a few memories of my mother buried in my brain, but nowadays they were all so blurry. Like a VHS tape that had been played so many times, the colour had faded and the picture was fuzzy. When I was a child, I'd make up memories about her – mostly with things I saw or heard other children do with their mothers. I'd talk to the picture about the wonderful time we'd had at the petting zoo together, laughing about a llama we'd seen spit at some stupid kids who had been warned repeatedly to stop jostling it. It wasn't like the conversations I had with Mio where I caught her up on what was going on in life. I played pretend with my mother, as if we were still sharing time together.

Since every story was based on something I'd seen or been told, it seemed real. At least to me.

When I got older, I realised the game had kind of ruined the real memory of my mother. I'd imagined her so much, her laughing with me, her mannerisms, and the way her voice would change when she was excited, that now she felt like a fictional character – someone I had made up in such detail that there was no way she could be a real person.

I sat up when my computer bleeped. I pushed the call button without reading Freja's message.

"Hey!" I said, seeing Freja's smiling face on the screen.

"Hey yourself," Freja said, her voice tired as she settled in on her bed.

I looked her over. At school, Freja always looked so carefree and loose. Even after one of Mrs Tempest's uniform inspections, when her tie was done up properly and her shirt was tucked in, strands of her hair would still be sticking out from her ponytail and her fingers would be stained with ink. She always looked ready to jump around, flip her hair back and scream at everyone to shut up and listen.

Now, she was dressed in a thick white turtleneck jumper with her hair tied up in a slick, tight bun.

"You look sophisticated," I teased, putting on a fruity voice. I stretched my arms over my head, shifting down until the laptop rested on my hips.

"Shut up!" Freja snapped. "We have to visit my stupid aunt again." She shivered in disgust. "We already went last week. It was mental! I had to endure two hours in the car with my parents arguing about the traffic – the freaking traffic! As if one of them called ahead to make sure the road was packed? Then of course there were four hours of fake grins and strangers telling me 'how pretty I'd be if I smiled more', followed by another two hours of screams, getting my seat kicked, and my parents pointedly ignoring each other. Such a stupid waste of time!"

I looked at her sympathetically.

Out of all our friend group, Freja and Noah were the only members who still had two parents who were healthy, alive, and still together. And Noah was the only one who was at all happy about that.

When first asked, Freja had described her parents as mental, bitter, middle-aged freaks who looked for reasons to get angry and didn't know how condoms worked. Sure enough, my view of Freja was soon obscured when the chubby face of one of her younger sisters, Aino, if I remembered rightly, was shoved right up against the webcam, giving me a close-up of her wide eyes and squashed up nostrils.

Freja went red. She flipped into a tirade, screeching a long stream of Swedish swear words. I watched her grab Aino by her pudgy arm and pull her out of the way. A door slammed, followed by the muffled sounds of Aino throwing a tantrum; which was soon followed by their mother banging on the locked door, shouting angrily.

Freja just untangled her headphones and sat back down on the bed. "So, how was your day?" She asked casually, as if she hadn't just had an Olympic-level screaming match with her sister.

I tilted my head, tugging on the faded tips of my hair. "Shut up," I mumbled, suddenly very tired. I shuddered, again looking over the pictures of Mio, my mother, and finally Ocean.

"Shit." Freja scooted forward on her bed, tilting her laptop screen. "Did you go see your mum?"

"No," I admitted. "I kind of got into a fight with Yan, so I just went to visit Mio's grave."

"Ru..." Freja raised the corner of her upper lip. "Are you okay? You look weird. What happened with Yan?"

I wanted to get angry at Freja for pushing things when I was fully prepared to shove my conversation with Yan deep down into my internal folder marked 'Never to be Mentioned Again'. I was about to tell her so, before remembering the role Freja had played in the awkward encounter. I smirked.

"I'm sorry, Freja," I said, "I accidentally outed you to my father!"

Freja gasped exaggeratedly, clutching her heart. "Well, I suppose it all had to come out sometime," she sighed dramatically, swooning onto her bed. "How on earth did this come up?"

"He referred to you as my girlfriend and wouldn't listen when I said you weren't," I explained. "So, I snapped and told him everything."

"Hey!" Freja pouted. "Why are you so offended by the idea of having me as a girlfriend?"

"I am not having this conversation with you again!" I groaned, lightly banging the back of my head against the wall.

I ignored Freja's cackles, letting her have her moment while I internally built myself up for the question I needed to ask.

"So," I said, as casually as I possibly could, "have you heard from Ocean at all?"

"Ocean?" Freja shook her head. "Not since our hang out call last week. Why?"

"No reason," I said quickly, jerking my shoulders. "He was supposed to join Enzo and me last night for *Overwatch*, but he never showed up."

I linked my fingers together below the camera, squeezing until my knuckles went white. As unusual as it was for Ocean to ignore texts, it was outright unheard of for him to do something as rude as not show up for something he'd agreed to show up to. Especially after Ocean had been the one to navigate the time zones. It had been almost midnight for me when the game started. Enzo had signed off at three, but I'd stayed online until five in the morning, just in case Ocean was running late.

"Huh. Maybe he's got a family thing?"

Before I could answer, I heard Yan running up the creaky wooden staircase that led to my bedroom. My bedroom didn't have a door as such. There was a door at the bottom of the staircase, but at the top there was just an open hatch in the ceiling. Yan never knocked on the door, but always gave a little courtesy knock on the edge of the hatch. Before coming in anyway.

"Yeah?" I called as Yan's head poked through the hatch.

"Are you coming to eat?" He asked.

"Okay, fine. I'll come down."

My dad turned and made his way back down the stairs, leaving the door at the bottom open.

"I've got to go," I said.

"Yeah, me too," Freja mumbled angrily. She glared at her door, clutching her headphones to her ears. "I'll talk to you tomorrow, right? Pizza party?"

"Right, pizza party." I nodded. I didn't have to worry about anything. I'd see Ocean tomorrow at our long-distance pizza party.

I shut my laptop, grabbing a shirt from my drawer and pulling it on as I made my way downstairs.

I wasn't surprised when I saw Yan already at the dinner table, sipping on a beer. He stared at me until I shuffled forward, taking my place at the table next to him.

"Thanks for dinner," I said under my breath.

I didn't bother to say anything more than that, focusing on getting the food into my mouth. I wanted to be done as soon as possible and get as far away as I could. Even if that likely just meant my attic bedroom.

Finally, halfway through the dinner, Yan sighed exasperatedly, placing his beer bottle on the table with a clunk. "For God's sake, Mamoru," he said in a long exhale. "Don't sulk about this!"

I raised my eyebrow. "I'm sorry?"

Yan just looked at me, unimpressed. "This isn't a big deal, so stop acting like it is," he said plainly, his expression softening. "I'm fine with this and if your mother were here, she would be too. Okay? Stop pouting and act like an adult!"

I resisted the urge to scowl. I wanted to snap at Yan for turning things around on me- just like he always did! But I was too tired to fight again. Besides, I always knew when Yan was trying.

I'd felt a little jealous when Ocean had told me about his foster father and how they'd found each other. It was cute how Theo had chosen to welcome Ocean into his life. I knew I wasn't exactly 'welcome' where I was at the moment.

Yan had romanticised this idea of taking in his son after his ex's death, wanting to be the hero and raise their child alone. Without realising that he'd actually have to *raise the child*. He'd never explicitly told me this, but I knew anyway. He'd made it obvious enough. Yan was terrible at being a parent; always forgetting to pay school fees on time, missing events or appointments, and regularly falling asleep drunk on the sofa. I knew that mum's inheritance money, while not being a 'vast fortune,' covered things like school fees and living expenses, but Yan had still waited until I was literally spilling out of the temporary bed in the living room before converting the attic. Yan insisted that mum had wanted me to go to school abroad, but I knew every time I was dropped off at the airport that Yan was relieved to see the back of me. If I got suspended from school, he'd let the host family deal with it, and asked at the beginning of every school break if I had a friend I could stay with if I didn't want to stay at school, arguing it would be less hassle than dealing with the jetlag of coming all the way back to his house.

However, despite all that, I still appreciated it when Yan tried. He'd pay the school fees when he got the late notice, sending an apology with them. When I was a little kid, Yan would take me out to get sweets or ice cream whenever he missed one of my tournaments, even if it came with the empty promise to go to the next one. Yan didn't drink too much at home. He was always out with his friends, so I never saw him drunk. He would collapse straight onto the sofa as soon as he came through the door. If I got up during the night and found Yan there, I'd always throw a blanket over his corpse and leave a cup of water beside him for the morning.

Yan had let me invite Freja to come stay with us for two weeks during the summer after I'd spent the spring holiday with her and her family. When it was time for me to go back to school, Yan would make sure I was all packed up and would drive me straight to the airport, walking me to the security gate to make sure I got through safely.

No matter how useless he was, Yan tried. And I knew he was trying right now.

"Okay, cool," I said. "Thanks."

"You're welcome." Yan picked up his bottle, draining the rest of his beer. "So... Do you have a boyfriend?"

"Yes," I said bluntly. Ocean might be ignoring me, but until he told me it was over, it wasn't over.

"Good." Yan took a steadying breath. "You should invite him to visit during the summer."

I finally felt a smile at the corners of my lips.

"Yeah. I might."

I imagined just casually hanging out with Ocean here at Yan's house. Watching movies with him on the sofa, Ocean maybe falling asleep on my shoulder. Playing all my old console games – Ocean would probably kick my ass with his nimble fingers, but I wouldn't let him have the victory easily!

I couldn't imagine doing all the touristy things I'd done with Freja, and I wasn't sure Yan was ready to let Ocean sleep with me in my room, even if we did share a dorm back at school. It didn't matter, so long as we could just spend time together – alone.

I spent the rest of the evening fantasising about Ocean coming back with me. I didn't pay any attention to the film Yan had picked out. I just stared out of the window, imagining walking down the garden path as I held Ocean's hand.

It wasn't until I was back in bed that night, staring at the picture of my friends at the amusement park, that reality caught up with me. I saw the group together again, smiling and laughing. I remembered that Ocean might not ever reply to me. It seemed the people that meant the most to me in my life were destined to suddenly disappear from it.

Mio's dad had taken us both on a fun weekend holiday at the seaside, only for us to get into a car crash on the journey back. My mother had just gone to the doctor for some tests and a year later, I was at her funeral.

I felt dread gathering in my stomach, pushing me down like a lead weight. I closed my eyes as tightly as I could, trying my best to block out the dark thoughts that were spreading like spilled oil throughout my mind.

~*~

I was starting to wonder if the crack in the top left corner of the dorm ceiling was getting bigger. I thought about telling maintenance about it, but then I would have to admit I'd noticed something small and stupid like that.

I realised bitterly that I should have prepared for this. Ocean had been my first real relationship, and we had shared a lot of 'firsts' in the three months we'd dated.

So, of course, the break-up was a different new experience that would logically follow all the others. This emptiness – knowing I'd just lost something I really wanted –was just another bitter part of life.

I wasn't sure how to act around Ocean anymore. After everything we'd shared over the past few months, I didn't think we could ever go back to being just friends, or even bitter rivals.

We were 'exes' now.

I'd told Freja that I'd broken up with my secret boyfriend. She'd pressed me for details, but I hadn't given anything away. I was paranoid that if I said literally anything, she'd figure out who I was talking about, so I thought it best to say nothing at all.

It also didn't help that Freja wouldn't shut up about Ocean; talking about how happy she was for her and how wonderful it was to have her as a roommate. As cool as I thought it was that Freja was taking this so well, it didn't stop the dagger that went through my heart every time she mentioned Ocean.

I looked at Ocean's empty bed – still made up as neat and smooth as it could possibly be. I quickly checked on my remaining roommates, making sure they were both still and sleeping, before I slipped slowly out of bed and walked across the room. I peeled back Ocean's stiff covers, carefully climbed inside, and pulled the white sheet over my head.

I groaned bitterly when I realised that the bed didn't smell like her anymore. It didn't even have the essence or aura of Ocean. I didn't know what I had expected to feel. Now I just felt like a lunatic, lying in the darkness in an unclaimed bed!

"Ru?"

I swore internally at Enzo's voice, pulling the covers tighter around me just in case he hadn't spotted me yet.

It didn't work. Enzo's bare feet padded across the floor before he roughly yanked the sheet away from my face. His amber eyes stared down at me like beacons.

"What are you doing in Ocean's bed?" Enzo asked. "Did you wet yours or something?"

I kicked him from under the covers, getting him in the thigh. "Of course not, you simple fuck!" I hissed, glancing at the still sleeping Noah. "I just..."

I trailed off, my mouth gaping open and closed like a goldfish. I realised too late that I probably should have just let Enzo think I'd wet my bed since it was decidedly less embarrassing than: *I wondered if this bed still smells like my ex.*

"Hm, I get it," Enzo said.

I furrowed my brow. Before I could say anything, Enzo had crawled into the bed. He wrapped his long arms around me and pulled me against him.

"What are you doing?" I dared to ask, even if the action was fairly self-explanatory.

"It's okay," Enzo whispered into the crook of my neck. "I miss Ocean too."

"What the hell are you talking about?" I scoffed.

Enzo didn't let go.

"I miss having her here, too. Even if she's happy with the girls. We can be happy that she's happy and still miss her, right?"

I didn't know what to say to that. I wanted Ocean to be happy, but more than that, I wanted her to be happy with *me*. Almost as if I hoped Ocean was miserable in the girl's dorm room. Not that I could say anything like that to Enzo. Instead, I just stiffened in the bed, letting Enzo hang off me.

"Are you sure you want to do that, Enzo?" I said in a hushed tone. "Noah will probably freak out if he wakes up and sees you nuzzling me like that."

"Let him freak out," Enzo said casually, pressing his cheek against my chest. "Your tits are comfier than my pillow, so why does it matter?" I relented, too tired to protest. "Noah already thinks I'm gay, anyway."

I arched my eyebrow.

"Really? Why do you think that?"

Enzo just shrugged before squeezing me a little tighter.

"All the guys think I'm gay, even Violet," Enzo explained, "because I like to hug you so much."

"'Because you like to hug me?'" I repeated, sounding out each word. "I don't think I get it."

Now that I was thinking about it, as anyone would have, I couldn't pinpoint a time when I thought my best friend might have been into me in that way. Sure, Enzo jumped on my back sometimes in the field or charged into me in the hallway, but piggybacks and tackling weren't exactly 'gay'. Not all the time, anyway. I'd always just thought Enzo was being clingy in general.

"I don't either," Enzo said. "Just so you know, it's not like that. You're just nice to hug because you're so big and squishy!"

"Thanks?"

"It doesn't matter. I don't care if they think I'm into you." Enzo rested his chin on my chest. "I'm not completely sure I feel that way about anyone, anyway. At least not... like that."

My brow furrowed. "What are you talking about?"

"I'm not sure I'm, you know..." Enzo smacked his lips. Something he did when he was either stuck on an English word or if his thoughts had halted in general. "Sexual. In that way. Or any way."

I didn't flinch. I continued to stare at Enzo, completely dumbfounded.

"Is that why you broke up with Marie last year?" I asked eventually.

"No, that just wasn't fun anymore," Enzo admitted, shrugging. "Although she does think I've taken some sort of religious vow of abstinence. I didn't tell her that. That's just what she assumed. And it was easier to let her think that was true." Our eyes met and we shared a forced laugh. The more we laughed, the lighter we both felt.

Enzo eventually rolled onto his side, still pressed up close to me, resting his head on the pillow with his huge grin. "I've not really talked about this with anyone yet. I want a girlfriend. Hell, I'm open to it being a boyfriend. Or an any-friend! I like the whole dating thing and spending time with someone. I just don't want to do some of the other stuff."

I hummed, counting the cracks in the ceiling above Ocean's bed.

"You sure you're just not ready for sex?" I asked bluntly.

"You sure you're just not ready for sex with girls?"

I winced at Enzo's retort, but understood what he was going for. "You've got me there." I smirked. "Still, you never want to have sex? Like, ever?"

Enzo looked at me quizzically. "Dude, aren't you a virgin?"

My cheeks prickled. "Yeah, sure. Sorry, I'll stop asking about it." I closed my eyes, ready to pretend to sleep.

"Hey." Enzo suddenly rolled over, pushing against my chest with open palms. "Is this why you're being so weird about Ocean? Because you have a crush on her?"

That caught my attention. I jolted upwards with such force I propelled Enzo out of bed. He crashed to the floor, vibrating what felt like the entire building. We both whipped round to check on Noah. He turned over in bed and continued snoring.

"A 'crush'?" I hissed at Enzo. "What the hell! Why would you—?"

"Because you do." Enzo stuck his tongue out at me before he jumped up to climb back into Ocean's bed. "That's why you always tried to annoy her before and start fights. You'd always get this strange, giddy look whenever you're about to throw down. If we were ten years younger, you'd be pulling her pigtails and tripping her over."

I wanted to protest. I wanted to tell Enzo that he was being a complete moron and that I wished I'd buried Ocean when I'd had the chance. Except I was too tired to pretend anymore. I groaned, rolling over in the bed and rubbing my head into the pillow.

"It's okay," Enzo said. "You can still like her, even if she's a girl." He wrapped his arms around me again to resume his clinging. "We don't have to worry about her anymore. We know she's here and she's okay."

"Yeah." I nodded into the pillow.

I couldn't ask for Ocean to get back together with me, I knew that. The only thing I could do was let myself take comfort in Enzo's words of wisdom and just be happy she was alive.

"Hey, Ru?"

"Hum?"

"Were you pissed off with me after your birthday?"

I frowned.

"No, why?"

"Because I did pretty much 'out' you, dude," Enzo said. "It's okay if you're mad at me, I understand. It was a dick move. I was kind of drunk and it just slipped out."

"Oh, that." I snaked an arm around Enzo. "No, you're fine. You didn't out me to the whole school and I could have laughed it off if I didn't want to say anything."

"You sure?" Enzo prompted. "You acted kind of weird after that. Like you've been ignoring me."

I cringed. "I'm sorry, man. I promise it's not about you." I rolled my thumbs together, trying to think of how to explain things. "It's a 'me' thing. Not a 'you' thing."

"You sure?"

"Yes!" I grabbed Enzo by his shirt when he tried to sit up. "Now shut up and sleep."

Enzo smiled. He laid down beside me and settled his head back on my shoulder.

"Alright then," he mumbled sleepily. "Platonic bro cuddle time!"

"Yep. Goodnight."

"Goodnight."

Enzo was asleep within minutes, leaving me to continue my sulking.

It had taken me a long time to come to terms with Mio's death, not wanting to accept that she just wouldn't be around anymore. I couldn't imagine doing that with Ocean. Remembering every day that I would never hear her voice again.

Expecting to see her in the kitchen or sitting on the field, only to realise her face was gone forever. I just couldn't picture talking about my goings-on in front of a gravestone with her name on it, or fabricating memories while I stared at a photo like I did with my mother. All I would be left with was the aching, painful heavy lump of lead inside me, dragging me down.

If Ocean had died over Christmas, then I would never have known who she really was, and would have lived with a false image of her for the rest of my life. Just the thought of that made me feel uncomfortable, like my skin had suddenly been swarmed with every small, wriggly bug I could think of. I tried to fall asleep with the thought that at least I had seen the real Ocean and could live knowing that she was alive and happy.

Chapter Twelve

Ocean

"Oh my God, did you only bring black stuff?" Freja said, making a loud tutting noise. She pulled the various garments out of my duffle bag, throwing them onto the bed. "You've always been a bit Emo, but are you going full on Goth now?"

"Not intentionally," I said, pulling at my sleeves. I was wearing my long black jumper with the decorative rips again, thinking it covered enough of my body to warrant going out in public. I inspected the hem, tugging it down further. In my mind the old sweater turned neon pink, flowers blooming between the wool. I shuddered. "I don't want everyone staring."

"Where is the fun in worrying about something like that?" Violet said, giggling. "Oh, can I do your makeup?" She dropped onto my bed, bouncing next to me.

"It's okay," I said hurriedly. "I don't need you to do that."

"What's wrong, Ocean?" Cam joined us on the bed, brushing a hand down my back. "Is it the name? Do you want us to call you something different?"

"No, nothing like that," I said. "It's..."

I sighed, rubbing my face on my sleeve- having forgotten that I was already wearing my eye makeup. I winced, seeing the end of the black trail on the edge of my palm. I leaned forward so my fringe covered my eyes.

"Are we making you feel a bit like a doll?" Violet asked bluntly. She knelt in front of me, giving me a comforting smile. "You can say if we are. If we ever go too far, just say so. Okay?"

I felt my eyes go watery. I didn't want to cry in front of my girlfriends, but every day seemed to be sending me through a stream of emotions. Strangely, I was finding it hard to handle the kindness from my friends. The dirty looks I got from some of my peers had been expected, along with the huddled whispers, when I walked down the hall. It was easy to ignore the cautious stares from Mrs Tempest and how most of my teachers were avoiding the use of pronouns. The overwhelming support from my friend group, however, was making me feel uneasy. As if I were afraid that it was all an act and that one day they would turn around to reveal that they weren't okay with it at all.

"I will," I promised. I bit the skin of my thumb. "You know, if you have any questions, it's okay to ask. Right? I'm not going to be upset if you just ask."

"What's there to ask?" Freja knelt by the duffle bag, rifling through the rest of my clothes. My blood turned to ice when she came close to the stack of underwear tucked away in a pocket at the bottom. Luckily, Freja's attention was diverted by a large, black makeup bag. She grinned widely, zipping it open.

"Aren't you at all curious?" I pressed on. "Don't you want to know what happened?"

"Not really." Freja carried the makeup bag to her bed, casually tipping out the contents. "Surely you know what's best for you. Oh, can I borrow this?" She held up my vial of shimmering blue nail polish, bringing her free hand beside it to compare the colour.

"But..." I lifted the neck-hole of my jumper and buried my face into it.

"Ocean," Violet sat beside me and draped an arm over my shoulders, "do *you* need to talk about it?"

I closed my eyes. I counted backwards from ten in my head before taking a deep breath. In for five, hold for five, then out for five. I felt the anxiety ease, even if it still churned slightly in my stomach.

"I just want to know why you're all okay with this," I finally admitted. "I mean, I don't want to pretend I've never said anything that might make this awkward." I had been looking at Cam, cringing as I thought about asking her out when she had been trying to focus on her French homework; but Freja spoke up first.

"Is this about the time you tried to kiss me at the New Year's party?"

I blushed furiously. As much as I would have adored denying the accusation, I knew exactly what Freja was referring to. An eventful evening last year shortly after we had returned from Christmas break. The group had almost all told tragic New Year's stories. Freja had been dressed up in a puffy pink dress better suited to a six-year-old and passed around various stuck up relatives, Enzo had been babysitting all twelve children of his extended family, I had been working at Theo's restaurant and, most tragically, Noah had been sent to bed at ten thirty. Ru had the only slightly pleasant story, having been left entirely to his own devices while Yan travelled to spend the holiday with some old friends.

Cam had whined about how annoying it was that we were never together for new years and thoroughly insisted that we had to have our own New Year's Eve party that Friday night. More than a few bottles of wine had been sneaked into the dorms and I had got more than a little tipsy. Resulting in me becoming a little too affectionate with Freja.

Even if it was something only my friends had seen, I'd cringed hard in the morning when I'd reflected on the moment. I'd buried my face into my pillow and begged God to pull my bed to the centre of the earth.

I shivered, wincing as I remembered it clearly. It had been such a strange time. I had vaguely known what was wrong, but was still firmly in a place of denial and had been doing everything I could to push it away. Including trying to kiss my friend!

"Aren't you bothered by this at all?" I tried to be blunt, not wanting to dance around the subject.

"No," Cam said simply. "I told you before, you're an amazing friend. If you're still Ocean, then you're still an amazing friend. That's not something that's going to change." Cam threw her arms around me, holding me in a sudden, tight hug.

"Seconded," Violet agreed, hugging me from the other side. "If this is who you are, then this is who you are."

"Right. Now," Freja approached us, effectively ruining the moment, holding out the bottle of nail polish, "can I borrow this?"

Laughter rose up from deep inside me, my arms looping around Violet and Cam.

Cam smiled against my shoulder. I could already feel the difference. There was less tension, less fear of being close. It made me unbelievably happy.

"Of course!" I said, grinning. "You're welcome to borrow anything you like."

"Cool." Freja threw the nail polish onto her bed, immediately grabbing a blue sundress from the pile of clothes she'd created. "In that case, I'm wearing this into town."

My eyes widened, despite my previous words. "Wait, you can't wear that!" I said quickly.

Freja paused on her way to the bathroom. "Why?" She held the dress out. "Are you going to wear it?"

"Not today," I confessed, "but... it won't fit you right. I'm so much taller and I don't have your—" I cut myself off, coughing into my sleeve.

"Boobs?" Freja finished for me, grinning cheekily. "They're called boobs, Ocean. You've never been embarrassed about saying 'boobs' before!" She jutted her hip out, throwing the dress over her shoulder. "I'm going to try it on," she stated simply. "If I stretch it out and ruin it, you can break something of mine."

Freja darted into the bathroom before I had the chance to protest further. The lock clicked loudly behind her, declaring the matter solved.

"Don't worry about that," Violet said. "She does that sort of thing all the time. You'll get used to it."

I nodded in defeat, rummaging through the pile of my clothes. I settled on wearing my grey jeans and kept my black, loose jumper, deciding that if the outfit had been good enough for my first date with Ru, it would be good enough for our first trip out as roommates.

I looked at the corner where Ru's bed would have been.

The girls' room could have been a copy pasted version of my old dorm. It was arranged differently, the beds and drawers having been moved to the corners to open up the space, rather than staying in the military order my last roommates had left them in, but the actual room itself was eerily similar. The white paint was still peeling off the walls, black mould still framed the windows and faded grey cushions padded the deep windowsill. There were even marks and scuffs on the skirting board that could have mirrored the ones in my old room.

When I looked at Cam's bed and turned it in my mind so it was vertical, with the headboard against the wall, I could almost see Ru sitting there and waiting for me.

"Won't you be hot?" Cam asked. I turned to see her pointing at the bright sky outside the window. She was dressed in a pair of green cargo shorts and a tight blue t-shirt with lighter blue stars along the collar, her pink flannel shirt pulled on loosely over the top.

I looked out of the window. I recoiled, blinking, having accidentally looked directly into the sun. Psychedelic splodges appeared behind my eyelids. It certainly did seem to be a very warm day for early spring.

"Maybe, but I'll be okay." I forced myself to stop picking at my jumper, the fraying on the sleeves already worse than it had been when I'd put it on.

Discussions of the weather were cut off the moment Freja stepped out of the bathroom. My heart sank to my knees. I was barely able to look at her. The dress, which had been light and flowing on me, looked very different on Freja. Her body filled out the loose garment, showing off her curves, the neckline dipping down below her cleavage. It was like a completely new dress.

"That looks great on you," I whispered, omitting to tell Freja that she could keep it. I could tell her later. I stepped past Freja into the bathroom to change into my grey jeans.

~*~

I straightened my tie and tightened it around my collar. My blouse was pulled in tight around my waist and the skirt fluttered around my knees. I could see every bruise and scar on my legs. My knees looked pale and pasty in the unflattering light of the bathroom.

I shuddered, unbuttoning the side of my skirt and stepping out of it. I threw it against the sink, quickly grabbing the formal trousers from my boy's uniform.

Cam jumped off the bed the moment I came in. "You ready now?" Her eyes went wide when she looked at my legs. "You're allowed to wear trousers!"

I bit down hard on my nail, wincing when almost a third of it snapped off, leaving my fingertip pink and exposed. "No, not really," I said. "I'm just not used to the skirt yet."

My heart started thudding dangerously hard. Just the thought of stepping outside of my dorm caused me so much anxiety these days. I was certainly more comfortable wearing trousers, but there was a fear that I was just making myself more obvious. The last thing I needed now was to stand out even more!

"Hey," Cam said, "come on, what's up with you?"

"I'm sorry. I'm just—" I went to rub my eyes, but this time managed to remember my eyeliner at the last second. "I want to do this right. I know I'm a girl. But…"

"Hey!" Cam squeezed me so hard I winced. "Don't think so much about it. Girls wear trousers, right? And boots and ties. And flannel! I mean, I do. So why can't you?"

I understood Cam's logic. I looked at Cam's short haircut. She wasn't wearing an ounce of makeup and I couldn't recall a time when I'd seen Cam wearing any outside of the occasional vibrant green nail polish. I'd learnt that nail polish hardly counted as make up in our circle- Enzo wore nail polish most of the time these days, scarlet red being his favourite. Even Ru wore it on occasion. When we shared a dorm, he'd borrow my black nail polish, often without asking, if he was going to a metal concert. He looked rather dangerous with his nails painted black, even if they were always chipped within a few hours.

"Don't try and box yourself in, okay?" Cam said when I didn't respond, shaking me playfully. "You already did the hard part and came out. Don't make yourself into someone else you're not after all your effort." She patted my cheek, laughing at my bewildered expression. "I'll wear trousers too!" She ran to open her own drawers. "I hate these fecking skirts. You just wait and I'll walk you to class. Got it?"

I didn't feel like I had a choice. I stepped back into the bathroom, shutting the door to let Cam change in peace.

~*~

My cheeks burned as I avoided the stares. During the first few days back at school, I'd mostly only noticed it in the common rooms or in class. Now I could tell that word was spreading throughout the school, beyond the students who already knew me. A second-year whispered to her friend as I walked past, pointing in my direction without any subtlety. The girl stared at me before turning back to her friend mouthing: *'No way!'*

"Miss Doyle."

My stomach tightened at the familiar voice of Mrs Tempest, even if it was Cam's name on her lips. Sure enough, the teacher was standing behind us with her arms folded over her long maroon cardigan. Her brow was creased in that familiar way it was when she was about to give someone a proud, stern lecture.

Cam squeezed my hand. "Yes, miss?"

"That's 'Mrs Tempest'," The teacher said firmly. "Although that's hardly the point right now." She let out an exasperated sigh. "Miss Doyle, surely you've been here long enough to know our uniform standards."

"Yeah," Cam replied dumbly, her eyes wide in mock innocence.

Mrs Tempest just tutted, pointing her bony manicured finger at the lower half of Cam's body.

"Those are not part of the standard uniform," she said. "Go back to your dorm and get changed this instant."

"They *are* uniform, though," Cam said proudly. "They're school trousers from the uniform shop."

That much was true. She'd gotten them from Enzo last year, after he became too tall for them.

Mrs Tempest didn't budge.

"For boys, Miss Doyle." Mrs Tempest ground her teeth, getting ever closer to her limit. "The girl's uniform is a knee-length, pleated skirt."

"But—"

"No buts, Miss Doyle! I don't make the rules and you, as a student, don't get to choose which rules you want to follow. I expect this kind of defiance from the boys, but I expected better from a young lady such as yourself!"

"It's okay," I said. I stepped in front, putting myself between Cam and Mrs Tempest. "We're sorry, Mrs Tempest. We'll go get changed."

I walked briskly back the way we came, not wanting to see the expression on the teacher's face. I pulled Cam gently behind me, past the group of boys wolf-whistling at us. One of them made a V-shape in front of his mouth, wriggling his tongue around between his fingers in a disgusting manner.

I shut my ears off before I could hear whatever it was they shouted. It wouldn't be anything new at that point.

"Ocean? Come on!" Cam whined. "We don't have to do what that old bag says."

"I know, we shouldn't. It's bullshit." I kept my eyes forward, directing my focus on getting back to the dorm. "Mrs Tempest is an uptight bitch who takes her failed dreams out on us. I'm sorry, I just really don't want to cause a fuss right now."

"Why not?"

I licked my sore nail. As much as I greatly admired Cam's attitude, I wasn't willing to rock the boat. Theo had argued with the school authorities until he was blue in the face to make sure I would be welcomed back. I already knew I was skating on thin ice and I didn't want to risk letting Theo down.

I scratched at the stump of my ruined nail; the pain causing a tremble in my hand. The dark voice in the back of my mind reminded me that I wasn't the one who had just been reprimanded. It was such a stupid thing to get upset about and I hated myself for it, which made me want to cry even more.

"This is total bullshit," Cam huffed again once we were back in our dorm, grabbing her school skirt off the floor. She turned, catching me heading back into the bathroom, clutching my own skirt. "Hey, Lady Tempest didn't say *you* had to change."

"I know, but it wouldn't be fair to you if I didn't," I said with some level of confidence.

Cam still looked very confused, but gave me an encouraging nod as I disappeared into the bathroom.

~*~

"Ocean, dear?"

I flinched at the sound of my name, my hands jumping on the black and white keys. I looked at the tall, stick-thin man leaning against the piano, his fingers tapping against the shining wood while his other hand patted his afro. He quirked an eyebrow at me.

"I'm sorry, Mr Smets," I mumbled, looking back down at the keys.

Mr Smets sighed, shaking his head playfully. He gently tapped my shoulder, encouraging me to budge along on the piano stool so he could sit down next to me.

"I take it you haven't been practising since you've been away, Ocean, dear."

I blushed at being called out. "I'm so sorry, Sir. I was distracted."

"That's completely understandable, my dear." Mr Smets licked the pad of his finger and flicked the pages of the music book back to the starting sheet. "Now then, start again."

I looked down, my hands shaking above the keys.

"Sweetheart," Mr Smets said in an annoyingly casual voice. "I take it that adapting hasn't been going all that well."

I bit my lip. "It's been so weird," I admitted. "For the most part, my friends have been very encouraging about it. Especially Freja and Violet."

"Well, that sounds wonderful." My piano teacher smiled at me, waiting for me to continue.

"But there have been some shitty... shitheads."

To my annoyance, my teacher's musical laugh shot straight into my ear.

"There will always be 'shitty shitheads', Ocean," he whispered. "It shouldn't stop you from being proud of yourself. You should be so proud of yourself. You're happy, aren't you?"

I had been asked that so much in recent months. No matter what kind of day I'd been having, the answer was simple enough. I was sure the high would crash eventually, but it didn't mean I couldn't ride it while I could.

"Yeah." I relented, giving my teacher a wide smile. "I'm so fucking happy. I mean just, so very happy."

Mr Smets laughed again.

"Well, good. That's the only important thing, right?"

One of the teacher's long fingers reached down, hooking the silver chain around my neck.

"What the—?" I jolted back slightly in surprise.

Mr Smets ignored me. He picked up the chain, rolling the shimmering ball around in his fingers. "This is rather beautiful, Ocean," Mr Smets said, humming. "I take it whoever gave it to you made you very happy, didn't they?"

I sat stiffly, almost slapping his hand away in shock. Mr Smets let go, the globe bouncing against my collar.

"Now then." He tapped the book. "Let's try it again."

~*~

It was the afternoon I had been dreading ever since I returned to school. I'd seen the damning words on my new timetable and had averted my eyes every time.

Wednesday 13:30 – PE – Mr Fan

I shuddered the moment I stepped out of the cafeteria, wondering if I could just wander off and not bother going to PE at all. It was tempting, especially since the consequences of doing so were unclear. Mr Fan might become concerned that I wasn't there and file a report over it, or he'd might just shrug it off, assuming that I had transferred to a different class.

I didn't know Mr Fan well enough to know which path he'd go down. Ms Khil oversaw the taekwondo club, and that was the only sport I took recreationally. I'd barely said anything to Mr Fan in the years I'd been at this school. I felt the urge to throw up, realising he'd probably already been 'briefed' on my 'condition'. Since returning, I had learned a bitter lesson – that teachers had absolutely no sense of confidentiality.

Without thinking, I reached into my pocket and pulled out my phone. My thumb hovered over the screen. I thought that Ru must know Mr Fan as he oversaw boxing and rock climbing, Ru's trademark sports. Or athletic activities. I didn't know if punching people or climbing stuff really counted as 'sport'. Regardless, I figured that Ru could tell me what to expect from the teacher. He'd probably go with me if I asked.

I scrolled through my contacts, bringing up the number for 'Shithead Barbarian'. I stared at the screen, trying to build up my courage.

"Hey girl!"

I jumped, nearly dropping my phone as Freja pounced on my back. The phone flew up in the air, Freja laughing as I juggled with it frantically.

"Sorry, sorry," I said quickly, slipping the phone back into my bag. "I was miles away."

"Oh, stop apologising," Violet said with a little bounce on her sandals. She jabbed my foot with her cane.

"Yeah! You've said sorry at least fifty times a day since you've been back and it's annoying." Freja grabbed my chin, staring wickedly into my eyes. "From now on, every time you apologise, I'm going to fine you ten euros. Got it?"

I nodded, not feeling in the mood to argue, especially not with Freja.

"Sure, okay. I'm—" I stopped myself, clamping my mouth shut.

"There's a good girl." Freja patted my cheek. She linked her arm through mine and took Violet's hand. "Now come on, Mr Fan will make us run laps if we're late."

I couldn't stop myself from squirming. My hand slipped into my blazer pocket to squeeze my packet of cigarettes. The tingling feeling from nicotine withdrawal was encouraging me to make a run for it, knowing that even if the equipment cabin would be too risky right now, no teachers would check the bushes behind the dorm buildings at this time of day. I could sneak off and have a few cigarettes before going to the library to read. Or I could take myself into town to try and find some new tights before treating myself to a much deserved hazelnut latte.

As glorious as the thought of running away was becoming, Freja seemed to be persistent. She pulled me out of the main building towards the sports hall. One glance told me that making a run for it would be a fool's errand. Freja could read all of us like we were bold text, step-by-step instruction manuals.

"We're going to gym class," Freja said firmly. "You can cut class now, but you know someone will catch up with you at some point, and then you'll have to go."

"Not necessarily," I protested. "I'm in my final year. I've got, what? Six months left. What are they going to do about it?"

"Yes, but do you really want to kick up a fuss so close to the end?"

I stamped my foot as defeat washed over me. I knew Freja was right. It was better to bite the bullet and go to PE now rather than putting things off. The last thing Theo needed was an angry letter about me missing classes.

"Alright," I said with a steadying breath. "Let's do this."

"Good girl."

~*~

Mr Fan wasn't exactly how I'd remembered him. I'd been picturing a muscular, intimidating brick wall of a person, with a drill-sergeant snarl and a sadistic PE-teacher grin. Instead, a rather scrawny looking man stood in front of the changing room door, wearing a baggy forest green tracksuit; the cuffs of which were so faded they were almost mint. He had a short bowl cut with a messy fringe that he had to flick away from his face every few minutes. He looked at each pupil with weary, age-withered eyes, yet he still had a splatter of acne on his left cheek and a few stray spots on his nose.

I practically sighed in relief when I saw him. Even so, I kept my head down as I stepped into the changing room alongside Freja.

"Come along, ladies," Mr Fan barked. His voice was loud and clear, despite carrying a rather shrill squeak. "Basketball today. Get yourselves changed into your indoor kits."

"But sir," someone whined, "we do swimming on Thursdays."

"Well, this Thursday we're playing basketball. You're welcome to join the swim team for practice tomorrow evening if you want to swim so badly." His eyes swivelled across the line of girls. "Excuse me."

I froze, clutching my messenger bag to my chest. I just knew Mr Fan was talking to me. A hand came to rest on my shoulder, keeping me in place while the rest of the class filed in.

"I'm sorry. Ocean, is it?"

He held open the door to his office. I hurried inside, trying not to draw attention to myself.

"Take a seat," Mr Fan said, gesturing to the worn-out chair opposite his desk. He brushed aside some pamphlets so he could sit down in front of me, the wobbly desk creaking. He gave me an equally wobbly smile when he saw the obvious anxiety in my eyes. "Don't panic, you're not in trouble," he insisted. "I just wanted to let you know, if you don't want to take class with us, today or any other day, I won't make you."

I blinked at him in surprise.

"I trust that you are getting sufficient physical exercise. Sticking with taekwondo is good," Mr Fan explained. "If the thought of being in my class is making you uncomfortable, then I won't hold it against you. I'll write you a note and you can go study in the library."

I clutched the edge of the seat, unsure how I felt. I knew some of my friends, especially Noah, would give anything to get out of PE class. I would have liked to have got out of various PE lessons when I was in the boys' class. Like when we had to run along the pitch immediately after it had been raining. Even I, as one of the better runners, would always end up slipping in the mud and twisting my ankle.

I didn't hate *all* PE lessons. I didn't mind football so much. I was good at it, even if I didn't quite understand the 'offside rule'. I smiled to myself, remembering the smug grin I would always give Ru when I was one of the first picked for a team. Ru was strong, but he was clumsy and bulky, so was always one of the last chosen for football.

After that, the entire lesson would turn into a new game of getting one over on the other. Even when we were on the same side, we would try to tackle each other. No matter how many lectures we got about 'working as a team', it didn't stop us. Being better than Ru was more important than a group victory.

I laughed softly, forgetting that I was in Mr Fan's office, as I remembered the games of dodgeball I'd enjoyed on rainy days.

Ru and I were never placed on the same team for dodgeball since it would always end up with someone having a bloody nose, which seemed less disturbing when we were playing against each other. The hour-long lesson would melt into minutes as I threw the rubber balls at Ru's face like it was my only goal in life.

"Ocean?" Mr Fan prompted after a few moments. "Do you need more time to think about it?"

I looked up at the teacher. He was staring at me with a calm, patient expression.

"No," I said quickly. "I don't want to be an exception."

"Alright then." Mr Fan reached into his drawer, pulling out a small key with a round, grubby wooden ball keychain attached to it. "Here. There are some cubicles at the back of the locker room. We don't give keys to everyone, mostly just if someone has some sort of religious or cultural reason why they don't want to change in front of others. I'm not telling you that you *have* to get changed in a cubicle, but if it would make you more comfortable, you can. Understood?"

I pressed my knees together to stop them from shaking. "Yes, sir."

"Good girl." Mr Fan stood up, throwing the key towards me. He nodded his head in praise when I caught it with one hand. "Well done. Now, hurry up and get changed."

I headed into the locker room, not surprised to see that most of the other girls were already changed and filing their way into the sports hall in their little groups. I spotted Freja and Violet waiting for me, sitting side by side on a wooden bench.

"Sorry, guys," I said, throwing my bag down beside them. "I'll be quick."

Freja smirked at me, victorious. "That's ten euros! Thanks!"

I made a face, unbuttoning my blouse. "Yeah, yeah. Just shut up!"

I turned to face the wall as I undressed. I felt the key burning a hole in my blazer pocket, but for now, it was just Freja and Violet with me. None of the other girls seemed to be paying me any mind. I knew I couldn't hide away forever, and getting changed in the locker room was a challenge I had to overcome if I ever wanted to be seen as a normal student again.

My eyes stayed fixed on the wall, not looking around at the other girls in case they thought I was leering. I whipped off my blouse, pulling my white t-shirt on in less than a millisecond.

I kicked off my shoes and stepped into my shorts underneath my skirt.

"Dude! We're not in a hurry," Freja snorted, leaning back with her arms folded behind her head.

I didn't say anything, too scared I would accidentally apologise again, as I whipped my skirt off and shoved my clothes into my locker. Freja and Violet stood up, ready to go when I was.

"Okay, let's…" Freja paused. She frowned, spotting Janie hurrying off into the sports hall as she tagged along behind another group of girls.

~*~

Violet insisted we got ice cream together after PE. She claimed it was something they always did and while I wasn't convinced that was true, it did feel good to be included in a routine. We walked across the road to a small kiosk opposite the school. I giggled as I sat on the wall with my two friends, licking on a strawberry cone drizzled with blueberry sauce and sour drops, swinging my legs joyfully.

"You seem to have cheered up," Freja teased, nudging me with her elbow.

"Hey!" Violet pointed at the school gate.

I closed my mouth, spotting Janie heading down the path.

Before Violet could question why Janie hadn't joined us, Freja had shoved her chocolate cone into her hands. She jumped off the wall, storming towards Janie.

"Hey!" she cried out. "Oi, Janie!"

The hairs on the back of my neck stood up.

Janie continued walking forward, pretending she hadn't heard.

"I said 'hey!'" Freja grabbed Janie's wrist, tugging her around to face her, fire burning in her eyes. "Don't you run away from me! Tell me what's going on."

Janie cringed, her legs pressed together nervously. "Not a lot," she said nonchalantly. "How about—"

"No!" Freja glared hard at her. "Do you have a problem with Ocean?"

Janie sagged. "No."

"Really? Because it seems like you do!" Freja took a step back, trying in vain to control her anger. "You're happy to eat her pizza and cakes, but you don't want to talk to her anymore? You avoided her like hell during gym class. What the hell did you run away from us for?" She folded her arms, clearly proud of herself for asking the question outright.

Janie's face went bright red.

"Well, are *you* okay with it?" Janie hissed. "Ocean has literally tried to kiss you before."

She glanced at me. I looked at my cone, pretending I wasn't in earshot.

"That was ages ago!" Freja scoffed. "You weren't even there!"

"It still happened! And from what I've heard, Ocean seemed serious." Janie shivered vigorously, as if she'd stepped in something disgusting. "And what about earlier *this year* when Ocean told Noah that Cam was... That she was apparently Ocean's girlfriend? Cam didn't know about any of that! It was really creepy; she was really upset! Then Ocean had the nerve to have a panic attack about it! Just stealing sympathy and taking all the attention. Ocean didn't even apologise properly, from what I heard."

Freja rolled her tongue in her mouth, replaying Janie's words. Each word was said carefully and slowly, as if she were considering every single one before daring to let them escape.

Both Freja and I could tell why. She was obviously trying to avoid using pronouns as much as she could, which, on some level, I respected. On another, I wanted to curl up in a ball on the pavement until I was left alone in the dark.

Based on the thunder in her face, Janie's choice of speaking seemed to make Freja want to rip every one of her pretty hairs from her large head. She flicked her hair over her shoulder, her hands resting on her hips as she switched tactics.

"You know I like girls, right?" Freja said, smiling smugly, thinking she had caught Janie in the perfect trap. "I want to watch girls change! And kiss them! And do *so* much more than that."

"No, you don't," Janie said, rolling her eyes. "Don't make this about that."

"Why not? It's the same, isn't it?" Freja had to take a small break, forcing herself to breathe and remain as calm as possible. "Ocean didn't mean it. She was drunk when she tried to kiss me; you know how much of a light-weight she is. I was the one she tried to kiss, so I can tell you it wasn't serious. And she didn't look anywhere but at the wall today in the locker room, so she clearly doesn't want to watch you!"

"Oh, please!" Janie scoffed. Her eyes narrowed as all pretence was dropped. "He used to be obsessed with me. Remember that time he ran off after my hat?"

"Don't flatter yourself!" Freja's voice went high as she finally snapped. "Ocean is like that with everyone. She did the same thing when some guys ran off with Noah's English textbook that same week, and she didn't tackle anyone to get your fucking hat back! How can you talk about her like that? Why are you focusing on the stupid things she did after everything she's done for you and the rest of us?"

That seemed to silence Janie, at least for a little while. She dug the sole of her shoe into the ground, focusing on the sound it made on the gravel. "It's not just me," Janie admitted. "Noah doesn't want me to get changed in front of Ocean, either."

Freja's eye twitched.

"Putting aside everything else that's messed up about what you said," Freja bit back, "are you just planning on doing everything your boyfriend tells you?"

Janie edged away from Freja. She tried her best to keep her composure. "I'm transferring to a different gym class," she said. "So we won't have to worry about any of this again, okay?"

"No, it's not okay!" Freja yelled. "If you and Noah have a problem with Ocean, you can both fuck off! Got it?"

Janie didn't say anything more. She just turned on her heels and walked away down the path. She sighed in relief when Freja didn't follow her.

I flinched as Violet placed a well-intentioned hand on my back.

"Ocean," she whispered, "your ice cream is melting."

I looked down. Sure enough, half my ice cream had melted and was dripping down my wrist. I clenched my fist, crushing what was left of the cone.

~*~

Freja made it clear to the friend group that Noah and Janie wouldn't be joining us for our weekly movie night. She had made the announcement sternly, being so forceful that even Enzo hadn't attempted to argue. She didn't give a reason and, after a quick discussion when she went to the bathroom, the group agreed not to ask her for one. The others assumed Freja was probably punishing them for something and would forgive them next week. It had happened before to all of us at least once.

I decided not to say anything. The rock inside me finally dropped, splashing into the angry waves that crashed through every part of my soul. My meeting with Mr Fan had gone so well that a downfall elsewhere had felt positively inevitable. I just nodded along with the delicate discussion before slipping outside at the first opportunity. I crossed the field, planning to slip behind the cabin for a cigarette- until my heart clenched with the memory of Ru's heartbroken face when I had officially ended things between us.

A sob rose in my throat before I could stop it. I blinked rapidly. My head went dizzy. My chest tightened. I tried to make myself take five deep breaths, but found I couldn't even take one.

I turned on the path, sprinting as fast as I could across the field. I jumped over the small fence next to the chapel, running into the forest beside the school. My heart was hammering and my body was burning up, but I didn't feel tired. I quickly lit up a cigarette, hoping it would calm my nerves. Even if my breathing was still painfully shallow. I pulled my phone out of my boot, cursing the limited pockets in the girl's uniform.

"Seahorse?"

"Theo." I wheezed desperately as I tried to think of what to say.

"What's wrong?" Theo asked immediately. *"Do you need me to come to get you?"*

"Calm your tits!" I snapped back. I leaned my head against a tree. My eyelids felt so heavy. "You don't need to come to get me. But can I come down? Just for the weekend? I can take the train."

Theo paused. I could tell he was at work, the clatter and screams from the kitchen muffled in the background, even while Theo was shut up in his office. I heard his heavy feet shuffling against the floor before he collapsed in his desk chair.

"Of course, Seahorse."

Chapter Thirteen

Ru

"Hey! Ru!"

I blinked suddenly, my brain skidding to a halt. Blake grabbed my wrist, holding me in a vice-like grip. It was only then I noticed that I was half an inch away from slicing the tip of my thumb off. I looked up, alarmed to see my teacher almost in tears from worry.

"Shit... Sorry, Blake," I quickly let go of the piece of wood, moving my hands away.

Blake turned the power saw off before lifting my hand to inspect my fingers. He sighed in relief, seeing they were all intact.

"Wait outside," he said, pointing at the door.

"Ha! Ru's in trouble!" Three other boys chorused, jeering and openly flipping me off.

"No, no one is in trouble," Blake reassured the class, going into a rare 'Mr Miller' moment. "I just think Ru needs some air. Go on, get!" He waved me away.

I didn't argue. I just grabbed my coat and bag before heading out the door. I rested against the brick wall, my eyes fixed straight ahead.

Eventually, the door opened, and the large figure of Mr Miller approached me. He'd taken off his work apron, the bright colours of his Hawaiian shirt almost blinding me. He lifted his thick-rimmed glasses off his eyes, staring at me, both concerned and mildly flustered.

"You okay, Ru?" Blake asked.

"Fine." I slipped my hands into my pockets, turning away to look back into the distance.

"Kid, listen." Blake looked behind him. He took me by my shoulder, pulling me away from the windows where the other students were starting to gawp. "I get it. I don't want to lecture you about being safe in my classroom because I know you don't need it. But you're not usually one to be away with the fairies. So what's up? Is something bothering you?"

I rubbed my face roughly with both hands, growling into my palms.

"Is it something personal?" Blake prompted, his face now disturbingly serious. "Trouble at home?"

"No."

"Finals?"

"No."

"Relationship trouble?"

"Kind of." I squirmed in embarrassment. "It's super complicated."

"Okay, well, let's talk about it." Blake went back inside, leading me into his office.

Blake's office was filled with various colourful projects in different states of completion, including some that looked like they could be used to take over the world! There were strange orbs and machines with cogs that would be better suited to a late-night sci-fi show than a design teacher's office. He lifted a stack of folders from the chair opposite his desk and swept away some loose nuts and bolts with his large, hairy forearm.

The only 'normal' thing I could see in the office was a framed photo of Blake and Ms Khil on a beach. I didn't want to pry, but I couldn't help but glance at it curiously. Ms Khil was wearing a white swimsuit with an elegant golden sarong around her waist. Mr Miller was standing next to her, flexing his muscles, dressed in a colourful pair of Hawaiian shorts with oversized pink flowers. The matching shirt was completely open, his large, furry beer belly on proud display.

He had one arm wrapped around Ms Khil's waist, while she had her free hand curled around his bicep, the other cradling a large margarita glass. His wide grin and hands the size of dinner plates made Blake look like an oversized teddy bear. Ms Khil looked like a little pixie standing next to him.

I smirked, always amazed that Blake could be married to someone who looked and acted like his polar opposite. Not that I could judge.

Blake placed a full glass of water in front of me. I wasn't particularly thirsty but took it anyway, figuring I wouldn't have to explain myself if my mouth was full.

"Okay, Ru." Blake leaned forward, trying to put on a serious face. "What's going on?"

I swallowed several mouthfuls of the water at once, gasping when I pulled away.

"It's complicated." I cringed again at how whiney I sounded.

Truthfully, I didn't want to talk about this with a teacher, but I also couldn't think of anyone else to talk to. At least no one who wouldn't immediately figure out I was talking about Ocean.

"Okay." I took a very deep breath, deciding to start as close to the beginning as I dared. "So, I told everyone I was gay before Christmas break."

"Ah." Blake nodded. "Have stupid kids been giving you a hard time?"

"Not at all," I answered honestly. Truthfully, the reception to my coming out had only been supportive. It probably helped that I was huge and captain of the boxing team, as well as someone who already had a bit of a reputation for getting into fights. No one picked on someone like me. At least not to my face.

"Alright, so are you having boy trouble, then?"

I cringed again. "No." I leaned back in my chair. "I honestly thought I was gay. But now... there's this girl." My heart ached when I thought about Ocean. "She's so pretty and special. I... I can't stop thinking about her."

I screamed in frustration. I was furious at myself for how lame and sappy I sounded!

"Do you think she might like you back?" Blake asked.

I grunted. My fingers curled in my hair.

I remembered the look on Ocean's face when I gave her that tiny ocean globe. She looked so touched, like the globe was the most beautiful thing she'd ever seen. Like no one had ever given her something so special- although I knew that last bit was probably wishful thinking.

I thought about holding her in the hotel room later that night.

After I'd found Ocean on the windowsill clutching her diary, I'd picked her up and carried her to the bed. She'd looked so nervous but had let me lay her down on the soft covers. We hadn't said anything more after that. Ocean wrapped herself around me and kissed me hard. I had felt so touched by the trust she had shown me that night. She had laid herself bare, wanting to feel me in the same intimate way I'd felt her. It had felt so amazing I was convinced I was going to die! Every time Ocean touched me with those soft fingers or kissed me anywhere on my body, my nerves would light up. My mind spun as if every second that passed was more amazing than the last, repeating over and over until I was a sweaty, broken mess.

I didn't think I'd ever forget it. I thought about waking up beside her the next morning. It had been the most peaceful morning I'd ever experienced in my eighteen years. Ocean breathed lightly with my head pressed against her chest, one hand wrapped around my shoulders while the other nested in my hair.

I must have fallen back to sleep because when I opened my eyes again I saw Ocean's face smiling at me as she leaned over to kiss me awake. It was the only time in my life I had been met with an image that literally took my breath away.

After we were both up, I'd washed and dressed as quickly as I could, knowing we had to check out by twelve. Ocean had been surprisingly calm about the whole thing. She'd already tidied the room and gathered our things, sitting patiently on the bed with her legs crossed and hands folded in her lap. She even held my hand again when we walked back to the train station. If she had been worried about someone seeing us, she hadn't shown it. She leant against me the moment we'd sat down on the train, closing her eyes to catch a little more sleep.

She had looked so small and peaceful. I hadn't thought she could look so calm. It was such a contrast to the scared person I'd seen sitting on the windowsill ten hours earlier. There wasn't a trace of anxiety or fear on her sleeping face. The thought that I was responsible for that made my heart twitch.

Despite everything that had happened between us since, with Ocean abandoning me and breaking my heart, I knew what I had felt that day.

"I think she does. Sometimes." I tightened my grip around Blake's glass. It cracked suddenly—water rapidly trickling down my hand and over the desk.

"Jesus, kid!" Blake shook his head and reached for a box of tissues. He wadded some up and took my hand, again checking it for cuts. "Then just tell her what you think. Tell her you were wrong about being gay." He shrugged, dropping my miraculously still unharmed hand. "Or maybe you're not wrong, just that you like her. Sexuality is a spectrum, you know? You don't need to focus on picking a side or letting a label stop you from pursuing someone you like."

Blake dried his hands on his shirt before pulling a booklet from his cluttered shelf. I raised my eyebrow. The thin cover had a rainbow flag with various symbols drawn in amongst the stripes. Some I recognised as the basic 'sex symbols'. Some stood alone or interlocked, some overlapping, some looking like a combination of both. Smaller versions framed the title, which was printed in the middle in bold lettering: *The ABCs of LGBT.*

"Huh..."

"Right." Blake squeezed my shoulder. "Just think about things. But for the love of any God you want, pay attention in my class!"

"Yeah. Thanks, Blake."

"Anytime." The weird teacher patted my shoulder one more time, before making his way out of the door. He shut it behind him to give me a moment to myself.

~*~

"Oi, Ocean!"

I halted, my gym bag slung over my shoulder. A strange sensation burst in my stomach, making me feel both sick and excited.

I turned to see my ex walking quickly through the corridor. She held her head high. Her hair was in bunches, the tips bouncing against her shoulders. A group of boys called after her with stupid grins fixed on their faces.

"Hey, Ocean, we're talking to you!" One boy called. "Come show us your pink bits!"

Ocean ignore them completely, turning to head down the staircase. I wavered at the side, wondering if I should interfere or not.

An empty soda can flew across the hallway, hitting Ocean hard in the back of her head. She stumbled, grabbing the banister to steady herself as the group of boys burst out laughing.

It was enough to help me make a decision.

"What the fuck do you think you're doing?" I stormed towards the group.

They looked at me. For a brief moment, they looked like they were about to pee themselves! To his credit, the leader of the gang straightened up, shrugging his shoulders heavily.

"Relax, Ru. The he-she's fine." He smirked. "You protective of it? Maybe you'd be into it. You know it has a dick?"

I grabbed his shirt and yanked him forward.

"Let go, Barbarian."

I turned to see Ocean clutching her messenger bag to her chest, staring at me.

"Frizzy."

"*Let go.*"

I glared at the slightly trembling boy. His gang members stared gormlessly, wondering what would happen next. A couple of them scoffed and puffed their chests out as if they were planning to interfere, even if they kept themselves at a safe distance. I huffed, reluctantly letting go of the gang leader's shirt. The kid stumbled backwards but kept his glare focused on me, even if my attention was already elsewhere. I watched Ocean as if waiting for further instructions. She nodded sharply before hurrying down the hall.

The moment she was gone, I stepped close to the leader until I felt his breath on my face. "If you ever bother her again, I'll kill you all. I'll kill you dead. I'll kill you, hide your bodies, and no one will ever find you." I bared my teeth. "And if anyone did find you, no one would recognise you."

I spat at their feet before running after Ocean. I turned a corner, seeing her speed-walking away.

"Frizzy!"

Ocean turned around slowly, heels clicking. "I have a piano lesson," she said bluntly.

"Wait," I stumbled. "I wanted to say... um, something."

I rolled my tongue around in my closed mouth, trying to catch the words. I thought about the booklet that Mr Miller had given me.

Ocean continued to stare at me, her fingers drumming against her bag. She waited patiently in silence for one minute. "I have a piano lesson." She turned her back on me, walking down the corridor.

~*~

I flipped through the pages of Blake's booklet as I lounged on the grass. I hadn't moved for at least an hour, but I was completely and utterly exhausted. My eyes stung as they dragged over the pages yet again, trying to take in every word. It was clear Blake had been right about sexuality being a spectrum—gender, too. There was a whole world of terms I had never even heard of before. Yet the more I read, the more interested I got. I made a mental note to lend it to Enzo when I was done with it.

"Hey, Ru!"

I quickly closed the book when I heard Freja's voice, shoving it deep into my backpack. I kept my hands inside, pretending to be rummaging through it. Freja didn't seem to have noticed anything, or at least dismissed my clumsiness, sitting down on the grass beside me.

"Whatcha doing?"

"None of your business."

"Oh, cranky Ru! Fun." Freja batted my backpack away like a cat taking a swipe with its paw. She cackled, settling her head in my lap and looking up at me. "Do you want to come out with me tonight?"

"Tonight?" I frowned. "What about pizza night?"

"It's not happening this week."

"What, why?" I shoved her off my lap. "Is this because of that thing with Noah and Janie?"

"No," Freja said firmly. "Ocean's going home, so she won't be here to make pizza. Obviously, Enzo still wants pizza, so he wants us to go out and get some. I thought since we're all going to the city anyway, you and I could go for a drink afterwards."

My heart skipped a beat. "What? Why is Ocean going home?"

"For the weekend," she said, deliberately slowly. "Calm your tits!"

"Oh." I dug my hand into the grass, feeling the mud gathering under my nails. Freja flicked my face with her forefinger.

"Anyway," she said, "come out with me. There's someone I want you to meet."

My throat dried up like a worm in the sun. I suddenly found myself in desperate need of a strong drink. "You want me to meet someone?"

"Yes."

"You mean like...?" I waved my hand awkwardly, hoping that would substitute for a euphemism.

"Yes." Freja grabbed my tie, pulling me down to her level. "I'm sick of you moping around about your mysterious ex. Tonight you're coming out with me and Violet to meet our friend. Got it?"

I grabbed her hand, forcing it away from me. I knew with absolute certainty that I wasn't ready to meet anyone else. Despite the part of me that wondered if it would be good for me. I didn't like the person I was becoming—drifting off, moping around, and reminiscing in front of my teachers. Surely one person couldn't be enough to break me completely, even if that person was Ocean.

All of that aside, I knew there was no point arguing with Freja.

"Fine," I said to the grass, "I'll go."

"Good! Wear something nice."

"Define 'something nice'."

"You'll figure it out."

Back in the dorm room, I decided that 'something nice' could translate to jeans and a plain black t-shirt. I stared at myself in the mirror, ruffling my hair. I hadn't re-dyed it, deciding it wasn't worth the effort. Most of the blue had faded out completely, leaving an ugly spinach-coloured sheen in my black hair that was only visible in the right light.

"What are you doing?" Noah asked, pulling his earbud out and looking up from his tablet.

"Nothing." I shrugged, deciding I was as 'ready to go' as I was going to get. "Aren't you coming?"

"Don't you remember?" Noah mumbled. "I'm banned."

"Oh yeah." I paused on my way to the door. "Why?"

"Don't worry about it. It's Freja being a bitch."

My fist clenched around the door handle. I wanted to defend Freja, but I was still a bit mad at her for forcing me to go on this blind date. Besides, without even knowing what the fight between them was about, I couldn't really take sides.

"Alright then." I walked into the hall, kicking the door shut behind me.

~*~

It became very obvious soon after ordering that Enzo had picked the restaurant purely based on cheapness and closeness. The pizza served was ridiculously greasy; the cheese slipping off and dripping onto the plate with a wet smack before I'd even had the chance to bite it. I stared at it for a millisecond before scooping it up with my fork and shoving it into my mouth. I grimaced as the grease coated my tongue.

I'd ordered a large cheese pizza to share with Freja and Violet, wanting to save money for the bar. The pizzeria's saving grace was its large portions, the three pizzas we'd ordered barely fitting on the table. The one cheese pizza seemed to be enough for the three of us, even with the two slices Cam had stolen. I'd taken a plate of nachos from the complimentary salad bar and shoved a handful of them into my mouth to take away the bitterness of the oil.

"Fuck's sake, Ru." Freja leaned over, brushing the crumbs off my shirt with a napkin.

"Shut up!" I nudged her away. "Why do you care so much, anyway?"

"You shut up, that's why."

There was a clattering at the head of the table. We looked at Enzo, who was flicking his empty plate.

"Do you want the rest of mine?" Violet asked, holding out her plate. "I'm full."

"Thanks, but no." Enzo shook his head, putting his elbows on the table. "This just isn't as nice as Ocean's pizza."

"We could have gone somewhere else," Cam pointed out. She'd only eaten one small piece of her vegetarian pizza, the one with suspicious circles as if pepperoni had been picked off at the last minute.

"Nowhere makes better pizza than Ocean!" Enzo whined, leaning back in his chair. "This isn't fair! She missed the Friday before Christmas to go to that dumb book fair. Then she missed a bunch of Fridays afterwards." He picked up a piece of Violet's offered pizza, watching as the cheese slid onto his plate with a plop, in an almost exact replay of mine. "She's coming back this time, right?"

"Yes, she's coming back," Freja said, exasperated. "She said she was coming back."

"Freja," Violet picked up her chair, edging it closer to her girlfriend, "she said that last time."

There was an awkward silence. Everyone jumped when I stood up. The table shook as my chair fell backwards. "And she did come back," I said plainly. "Eventually at least."

I snatched my bowl and turned towards the salad bar, leaving my friends staring at their plates.

Chapter Fourteen

Ru

I dug my fingers into my jeans in a hopeless attempt to stop my knee from jiggling. I was starting to realise I should have prepared better – not that looking up 'how to behave on a blind date' would have got me anywhere. Any answer I found would have just had me rolling my eyes.

The build up to this had gone by so quickly. Now that the date was minutes away, I couldn't think of what to do other than sit there, bouncing nervously.

"Here." Freja shoved a half pint of jet-black stout at me.

I took it without question, draining half the glass in one swallow. Freja slapped my chest.

"What the hell? This is craft beer! You can't just down it like the crap you drink in the dorm." Freja reclined on the sofa next to me, wrapping an arm around Violet as she sipped her beer delicately.

"Well, thanks, I guess," I muttered, placing the remainder of my drink on the wooden table in front of me.

The bar was rather comfortable, with leather sofas and wood-panelled walls, clearly an attempt at a rustic look. Although most of the walls were covered in fading posters for shows and performances, some from two years ago. It was very dark despite it still being sunny outside. The lightbulbs hanging above us were painted black, except for small heart-shapes left at the tips.

"Why here?" I asked.

"This is Noël's favourite place," Violet said. "He's performed here a few times."

"Really?" I looked at the small stage in one corner of the bar. It was made out of several bulky drama blocks pushed together with a single microphone stand in the centre. "What does he do?"

"He's a drummer in a band," Freja said, grinning, raising her eyebrows exaggeratedly. "They mostly do classic rock covers, but they've started writing more of their own stuff recently."

"Okay, cool." I shrugged, taking another large swig of my beer. "What's the band called?"

"They keep changing their name," Violet said, giggling. I stared blankly, wondering what was so funny. "There's been a bit of a drama."

"Alright then." I sat back on the sofa, folding one of my legs to rest my ankle on my thigh. I looked at the peeling posters that covered the ceiling. I wondered if one would land smack bang on my face before the evening was over.

I wasn't sure how long we waited. Violet occasionally tried to tell me something else about Noël. It seemed Noël and I were expected to have some kind of musical connection, so I at least had to concede that point to Freja, but I let most of what Violet was telling me go in one ear and out the other.

Finally, after Freja had angrily checked her phone for the fifth time, Violet waved crazily towards the open doors. I braced myself, standing up hesitantly.

Noël gave Violet a half-smile as he entered the bar. He was lithe and slender, so much so it made my stomach clench.

Rather luckily, his hair seemed to be a stark contrast to anything warmly familiar. It was sticking up at various angles, back-combed far too much and dyed jet black – recently if the grubby marks on his fingertips were anything to go by. He wasn't wearing too much makeup, but even I noticed the foundation powder dusted over his stubble was a little too light for his skin tone. His eyeliner was a deep charcoal, and a little smudged, as if he'd applied it on the bus. Or perhaps he thought it looked edgy like that.

He strode over to our sofa with a somewhat uncharacteristically bouncy gait, leaning in to kiss Violet on both cheeks.

"Hey, Freja," Noël said. His voice was slow and breathy. "How's it going?"

My eyes glossed over as they made small talk, staring mournfully at my empty beer glass.

"So, this is Ru."

I flinched at the sound of my name, looking up to see all three of them staring at me. I rubbed my hand on my jeans, standing up to extend it to Noël. "Ru," I said flatly.

Noël offered me one of his half-smiles and shook my hand. I tried not to wince at how calloused and straw-like it felt.

"Noël," he said. He looked again at Freja and Violet before turning back to me. "Do you want a drink?"

"Yes, please!" I said. Freja poked my arm sharply.

I followed Noël to the bar, my date immediately ordering us two more 'craft beers'. I'd hoped we would go back to sit with Freja and Violet, but Noël took me over to another corner of the bar. I decided not to say anything, still struggling with blind date etiquette.

"So," Noël said, throwing himself on a leather sofa identical to the one I had been sitting on before, "you go to Freja's school?"

"Yeah." I reached for one of the beers, looking at Noël. When he nodded I quickly picked it up, before remembering what Freja had told me about drinking slowly. I sipped it, smacking my lips at the sharp aftertaste. It reminded me a little of forest berries.

"Sorry, just to check; you're a senior, right?" Noël asked. His brow furrowed. "Although, you kind of look like you're twenty-eight!"

I snorted. "Yeah, I get that a lot," I admitted, gesturing to my bulky body. "I'm eighteen, I swear. Freja's in my history class."

"Cool." Noël stretched out his legs before crossing them slowly. "What else do you study, then?"

"High school shit," I answered casually. "You studying?"

"Music tech," Noël said.

"Oh, yeah? Freja said you were in a band."

"Yep. You should come to see us sometime!"

"Yeah, sure. We can do that."

I scratched my jeans again, chipping my black nail polish. I hated this intense pressure to say *something*. My head practically throbbed as I tried to think of any question to ask that didn't seem generic or pointless.

"Hey," Noël said, "relax a little, yeah?" He smiled smugly. "Freja said you weren't all that experienced."

His patronising tone was anything but reassuring. I clenched my fist around my glass, making a mental note to 'accidentally' spill coffee over Freja's homework during breakfast tomorrow.

"I've dated," I said, trying not to sound like a bratty kid. "Sorry if I'm a little... It's just that I broke up with my girlfriend kind of recently."

"Huh?" Noël frowned. "Freja said you were gay."

I bristled, even if Noël hadn't said anything actually 'wrong.' "I am... I think." I tried not to wince at how uncertain I sounded.

"I'll tell you what." Noël reached over, nudging the base of my glass to encourage it up to my mouth. "How about we have a few more drinks? See if that loosens you up any."

I shrugged, downing my beer in three mouthfuls. "Can't hurt."

We managed to sit together for over an hour, draining a few shots and several more beers. I answered Noël's questions. It turned out we did indeed share several favourite bands. Noël was the first person I'd met who already knew who Korpiklaani were! Even if he could only name two of their songs. He tried to ask about Yan and my hometown, Freja having apparently also filled him in on my backstory. I started getting a little annoyed when Noël didn't catch the hints I dropped literally all over the place, trying to steer the conversation in a different direction—*any* different direction I could think of. I tried turning things back to music, bringing up Korpiklaani's YouTube channel so we could watch their videos, even if we couldn't hear the music over the bar. At one point I asked if he thought blueberries were blue or purple! I tried to appreciate the interest Noël was taking in me, but my fists clenched harder with every probing question. I forced a smile when Noël asked what Yan did for a living before quickly downing my drink.

After that, I stared past Noël, focusing instead on one of the posters. It was a poster for a 'dark comedy double act'. Someone with a wide grin, clutching several skull-shaped candles, stared at me. The other member of the duo stuck their tongue out and made random gestures with their hands. I nodded along, giving short basic answers to continue the conversation with as little effort as possible.

I didn't break away from the poster until Noël excused himself to use the bathroom. I looked across the bar, trying to find Freja and Violet again. I had been ignoring them when I first sat with Noël, Freja making a crude kissy-face at me every time our eyes met, while Violet giggled. I squinted, trying to spot them, expecting them to still be making fun of me from a distance.

I cringed when I finally found them. They were as close as they could possibly be without melting into one twisted mutant blob, their faces crushed together. I bit down on the rim of my glass.

"Oh my God!" Noël collapsed on the sofa, giggling at the ceiling. "You must have a bladder of steel!"

I shrugged, not sure how to respond. I prepared to fix my attention back onto the poster- only to freeze when a hand clutched my thigh. I looked up slowly. Noël's face was now right next to me.

"Um... hi?"

"Hi."

The next second, Noël's lips were on mine. Two hands grabbed my shoulders and a slimy tongue entered my mouth. I winced but played along, gingerly rubbing my tongue against Noël's. A weird feeling grew inside me. It wasn't a nauseous feeling, just a strange sensation of dread. As if I had just stepped into an uncovered manhole and didn't know how far I'd fall. It started in my stomach, spreading further throughout my body with every lick from Noël until the tips of my fingers tingled. Weirdly, I couldn't close my eyes. I was stuck staring at the powdered skin a millimetre away as Noël pawed at me.

The hand on my thigh slowly crept upwards and inwards. I slammed my hand on top of Noël's, only for him to interlace our fingers.

Noël pulled away, grinning slyly. "Want to get out of here?"

I stared straight into his coal-covered eyes. "Um... sure."

~*~

I looked curiously around Noël's flat. The atmosphere was similar to the bar, only with Ikea furniture. It was a ground floor studio with a microwave, a box fridge with mismatched magnets stuck to it, a dirty kitchen sink, a door leading into a bathroom the size of a cupboard, a gritty carpet with books and clothes covering half of it, and finally, a rickety-looking single bed in the corner.

I hung my jacket on an over-crowded peg by the door and kicked my shoes off.

"You don't have to do that," Noël said, pulling two more beers out of the fridge. "Make yourself at home."

"I will."

I didn't bother with putting my shoes back on. Instead, I took two small steps into the student flat, looking for somewhere to sit. Noticing there weren't any chairs, I sat down on the bed, bracing myself when it creaked. A second later, the bed creaked again; only much louder this time.

Noël pushed his tongue back inside his mouth. His dirty fingernails dug into my cheeks as he straddled me, pushing me down against the thin mattress. I bounced stiffly onto the bed, watching in shock as Noël reached under my t-shirt in an attempt to tug it off.

"Wait!" I said firmly. I shot up, hands gripping Noël's waist as he stared at me, confused. "Look, I'm sorry. I don't know why I came here. I guess I was just going along with things. I don't actually think I like you that way."

Noël just scoffed. "We're still getting to know each other." He slipped his hands back underneath my shirt, dragging a fingernail around my nipple. "This will help, I promise."

A wet, slobbering mouth latched onto my neck. It felt like a pond leech was hanging off me. I tried my best not to recoil. My nipples were stiff from the draft pushing its way through the thin window, which Noël seemed to take as a good thing. He smirked in triumph, scratching the sensitive skin until I winced. I wriggled even more when I remembered how dirty Noël's hands had seemed. Again, Noël seemed to take this the wrong way, his hips starting a fast, grinding rhythm against my thigh.

"Hey." I nudged his shoulder. "I'm sorry, but I don't think I want to do this."

Noël cupped my pecs, squeezing them roughly. His hips ground a little harder against me- until I placed both hands on his shoulders and gave him a sharp, hard shove.

Noël shrieked, his shoulder hitting the wall as he was propelled off me. He rubbed it, finally noticing my serious face. He looked at me pityingly, as if I were a dog begging at the dinner table.

"You're right, you shouldn't have come back here," he spat. "What's the big deal? If you don't want to date me, then fine, but we're both guys! You really don't want to just do stuff for fun?"

"I think we have a different definition of fun," I mumbled, pulling my t-shirt down as I stood up. I walked away to grab my jacket, toeing my feet back into my shoes.

"You sure you're not straight?" Noël called after me.

He was at least a little drunk, his voice slurred, but I knew his words were meant to be insulting. I didn't turn back. Instead, I zipped my leather jacket up, catching a glimpse of how ruffled my hair was in the fingerprint-smeared mirror hanging by the door.

"Yeah, maybe I am."

I swung the door open and stepped back out into the street.

I didn't remember the way back to the bar. I relied on my legs to carry me there, hoping that if I kept walking around, I'd eventually spot it. It was only a few streets down and I kept my eyes open for any familiar landmarks. I sighed in relief when I turned into the side street, seeing the black heart on the kitschy, pseudo-Edwardian sign hanging outside the bar.

Freja and Violet walked out of the arched entrance, leaning in close to one another. I whistled, running down the street towards them.

They both turned, startled.

"What the hell?" Freja called. "I thought you went back with Noël."

"I did." I shrugged. "And now I came back. You guys heading back to school?"

Violet and Freja shared a look.

"You going to tell us how you fucked everything up?" Freja asked bluntly.

I rubbed my brow. My eyes were sore and heavy underneath my lids. I certainly didn't feel drunk, despite having had more beers than I could count. Rather, my body felt weighed down by everything that had happened over the last two hours. I felt so utterly and completely drained I didn't think I could formulate more than two words at a time, let alone explain the situation with Noël.

"Tomorrow," I said, "I'll... tomorrow."

Violet detached herself from her girlfriend to give my arm a sympathetic pat. "Tomorrow it is," she said. "Let's go back now."

It was an hour before the last train of the night was due to leave, but we still walked briskly, the night air biting at our faces and keeping us awake. We all collapsed in our seats at the back of the train, Freja immediately spreading her arms and legs out, her head lolling on the window.

"I can't wait to hear what your problem with Noël was," Freja said, yawning. "He seemed to like you enough."

Before I could say anything, Freja's phone chirped in her bag. She immediately scrambled for it and I mouthed a silent 'thanks' to no one in particular before attempting to take a half-nap against the window.

"Oh, for shit's sake..." Freja whispered, frantically thrusting her middle finger up at her phone.

Violet nodded sympathetically, wrapping her hand around Freja's to squeeze the offending finger. "Noah again?"

"Yes." Freja dropped her phone into the bag. "Apparently I'm still 'not being fair' and 'taking this too seriously.' Oh, and 'not looking at this from their perspective.'"

"They'll calm down," Violet tried to reason.

"And if they don't?" Freja spat, glaring at the opening in her handbag as her phone continued to buzz. "They're being freaking ridiculous!"

I opened my eyes, tiredness giving way to curiosity. "What's this about?"

~*~

"You bastard!"

I stormed into the room, my eyes burning with fury. Noah barely had time to register what was happening before I ripped him out of his bed, slamming him against the wall.

"What the fuck is wrong with you?" I growled menacingly. "I can't believe you'd dare – *you'd dare* – pull this shit after everything she's done for you!"

I could hear myself getting louder with every word, despite my ears ringing with anger.

"What?" Enzo finally climbed out of bed, still taking in the scene in front of him as he rubbed his eyes groggily. "What's wrong, Ru?"

"What the hell!" Noah finally screeched, reality crashing into him. His eyes came into focus, as if he'd suddenly realised that this wasn't a dream. "Dude! Calm down! Put me down."

I slammed Noah against the wall again. The room shook.

"Freja told me what you and Janie said about Ocean!" I screamed in his face. "Like, apparently, what she does with her life somehow involves you. Is that what you shitheads think?!"

"Okay, seriously, calm down!" Noah winced, as if knowing those words would make things worse. "Ah, okay. What I mean is, it's not like we have a problem with him—"

I cut him off. My fist landed square in Noah's jaw. His head bounced off the wall, his eyes spinning.

"Hey! Cut it out!"

Noah gasped in relief at Blake's voice. He clutched his jaw as I was pulled off him.

"He attacked me, Mr Miller!" Noah whined like a little brat.

"Fuck you!" I spat. "She's supposed to be your friend!"

"Why do you care?" Noah glared back at me, feeling a lot more confident with Blake intervening. "You hate Ocean."

I stiffened. I could feel my heartbeat pulsing in fists. My face felt hot with rage.

"It doesn't matter," I said, my voice now quiet and low. "I don't care what she does to you. I don't care if she burns down your home, if she breaks everything you ever care about, or if she does take a look at your girlfriend in the showers!"

Noah recoiled. I didn't look away.

"She's still Ocean, she's still 'she', and you have no right shit-talking about her. You know that!"

"Alright, come on, kid." Blake beckoned me towards the door. "Come sleep in the teacher's bunk for tonight, okay?"

I dug my nails into my palms, taking in the sight of Noah collapsed against the wall with sweat dripping down his face. Enzo was still staring in awe. I couldn't even bring myself to feel guilty for punching Noah. Not when Freja's story still buzzed in my brain.

"Let's just take a breather," Blake said. "Enzo, go back to bed. Noah, you OK?"

Noah rubbed his jaw again, but nodded. "Yeah, I'll be fine," he said reluctantly.

"Good. Wash up and get some sleep." Blake didn't dare say any more than that.

He placed his large hand on my back, guiding me towards the door. He braced himself when I stopped.

"The internet exists," I spat over my shoulder. "If she wanted to look at naked girls, she could do it on her phone."

I turned back to the door, letting Blake lead me away.

Chapter Fifteen

Ocean

"Seahorse?" Theo knocked on my door again. I heard the rattling sound of a tray being balanced before another, much louder knock. "I'm coming in, Seahorse," he said finally. He kicked the door open with his foot. His eyes swivelled across the room to see my bed pristinely made.

I was sitting on my bay windowsill. The window was wide open as I leaned against the wall with a cigarette in my hand. Theo sighed when he noticed I was wearing the same outfit I'd arrived in last night. My eyes were red and there was a grey tinge underneath them that I hoped Theo would think was smudged makeup. He walked into my room, placing the tray down on my bedside table and sitting down on the bed with a grunt.

He'd made my favourite breakfast—blueberry waffles with warmed raspberry syrup and a hot, fresh pot of Earl Grey tea. He'd even gone through the trouble of decorating the tray with a tiny water glass containing a bunch of lavender he'd plucked from the garden. It looked gorgeous and smelt even better, yet the breakfast felt like such a trivial thing. From his own tired expression, I could tell Theo knew this, which rather made me feel a little better.

"Are you going to tell me what happened, or do I have to shake it out of you?" Theo said firmly.

I saw the veins in his forehead twitch as I shook my head, bringing the cigarette to my lips to take a long, forlorn drag.

"Seahorse—"

"There's nothing to tell!" I snapped. "Why do you always assume something must have happened? Can't I just be fed up with it all?"

"You can," Theo said, surprising me with his compliance. "But you sounded pretty desperate on the phone the other day." He tapped his large hands on his knees before rubbing up and down his legs awkwardly. "Perhaps it was a mistake sending you back to school. You're almost finished there, anyway. I'll get you some home-schooling resources or a tutor and you can sit your exams locally."

I groaned at the thought of giving in, pressing my head against the window frame. I imagined the sneering faces of the boys in the corridor after learning they'd successfully chased me away. I saw Janie and Noah sighing in relief. I didn't know how to begin to explain the well of conflicting emotions inside me, so I decided to head down the practical path.

"What about the tuition fees? They're already paid."

"To hell with them!" Theo shrugged. "It doesn't matter at this point."

"Theo!" I whined. I took a final, long drag from my cigarette before stubbing it out on the windowpane. "Stop trying to make everything 'easier'."

Theo snorted. "What a stupid thing to say. You want things to be harder?"

"This is just hard!" I turned around. "It's just something that is hard and can't be made less hard!" I leaned forward, drawing my knees right up to trap my head snug between them. "I don't regret this, okay? I just thought I would be more prepared."

"Seahorse?" Theo held out his arms, beckoning me over.

I looked up, hesitating for a moment, before shuffling over to my bed. Theo took my arm as soon as I was close enough, pulling me down to sit beside him. He pulled me into his lap and wrapped his arms around me.

"How is all your taekwondo going?" Theo mumbled into my hair. "You'll never hurt anyone with these spindly, thin arms. These lanky things are clearly the better weapons." He tapped my legs, continuing to hold me. "I'm sorry, Seahorse."

"What? Why are you sorry?" I said petulantly.

Theo winced. "First of all, can you use your indoor voice while close to my ear, please?" He scolded. "Second of all, I have good reason to be sorry." He took a moment, letting his tone come down to a softer level. "I've been looking at this too practically. I wasn't thinking about your insides."

I jolted back. Theo rolled his eyes at the fear on my face. "Not what I mean, Seahorse!" He said, disgruntled. "I'm not going to make you be a boy again. I just mean that I didn't think about how tough the actual switch would be for your head. Goodness knows it's not going to get any better when you finally get your next appointment with that specialist and start those blockers."

He ran a hand down my back. "I think you need to speak to someone," he said bluntly. "I can sort you out with something. I think the school has a programme for that. Of course, if you'd rather have someone with experience of your thing, we could probably find them."

I wriggled off his lap. I sat beside him, straightening out my shirt and flicking my hair back. "I'm not seeing another therapist," I said stubbornly. "I've talked about all I want to talk about."

"Yes, when you were a kid," Theo said cautiously.

He knew why I was hesitant. I'd been seen by many child psychologists when I was younger. They all probed me with the intention of getting me to open up about my birth parents, but none had any real interest in listening to me or making me feel safe. All of their notes had gone straight into my file without any sense of confidentiality.

"It doesn't have to be just talking," Theo explained. "We could try art therapy or writing therapy. Something creative like that? We'll look it up and see. I won't force you, alright? Just think about it." He wrapped his arm back around me. "Either way, I want you to know I'm proud of you. But more importantly, you should be proud of yourself."

My whole body shook as I chuckled lightly. "You're the second person this week to say that to me, old man."

"Well, I'm the second person to mean it."

~*~

I felt incredibly drained as I stepped off the train. The journey hadn't been entirely unpleasant. There hadn't been any delays, and I'd had enough time to get a hazelnut latte from the station cafe. There was just something about long journeys that always made me feel sweaty and gross. I sniffed as I pulled my suitcase down onto the platform, casually wiping my nose on my black sleeve.

"Ocean!"

I froze in place at the familiar voice. I looked down at my body. Through the smudges on my glasses, I could see the small stains on my jumper and the grubby marks on my jeans. I had splashes of mud up my boots and calves from dragging my suitcase and the general grime from the journey all over me.

I looked up cautiously. Sure enough, Violet was heading towards me, waving excitedly.

"Hi, Violet," I said nervously, bracing myself as my roommate flew into my arms with a tight hug. "What are you doing here?"

"I figured you'd be coming back this evening, so I checked the train times."

I wriggled at the confession, finding it both flattering and unsettling. "You didn't have to meet me, Vi," I tried to insist. "I'm just going straight back to school. Don't you have swim practice today?"

Violet looked back at me, eyes twinkling. "This was more important." She reached over, taking the handle for my suitcase.

"Hey, Violet! You don't—"

"Yes, yes, I don't have to." Violet winked at me. "You should know by now, Ocean. You can't make me do anything I don't want to do. You don't have that much power over me."

I gaped at her, my hand hovering in the air above where the luggage had been. Violet walked towards the lobby of the train station, dragging the suitcase behind her, walking smoothly despite her cane in her other hand. I reached into my pocket to flick open the lid of my cigarette packet, my stomach twisting itself back into knots as I watched Violet walk ahead. I had no choice but to hurry after her, gently taking my suitcase back and following her the rest of the way down the platform.

A yawn crept up from inside me, slipping out before I had fully prepared for it. I wasn't sure why, but I could feel a thickness in the air. Something unusual was weighing down between us, like a heavy rock gradually pressing a little harder with every moment, crushing us slowly.

"Violet."

"Yes, Ocean?"

"Why are you here?"

Violet stopped. She looked away, her thick hair smacking the side of her face.

"Ocean, let's talk."

I kept quiet as Violet dragged me over to the train station coffee shop, letting her place me at a corner table with my suitcase. It was surprisingly empty for a Sunday afternoon. I could spot various people being greeted as they came off their trains. One man in a suit dropped his bag and briefcase, letting two small children run into his arms. I smiled as he lifted them in the air, kissing them both over and over before he kissed their mother tenderly on the lips.

The clatter of a tray brought my attention back to Violet. My friend presented me with another hazelnut latte and a cappuccino for herself. I took it with a grateful smile, even if the thought of having another sweet drink made my teeth throb. Violet took the seat opposite, holding up a hand to stop me when I moved to get up and pull her chair out for her.

"Ocean," Violet said, before taking a sip of her coffee. She licked the white foam away from her trembling lips. Her whole face seemed to twitch as she looked across the table. She kept glancing back down at her coffee as if she was forcing herself to look at me. "I did a bad thing."

"Oh." I shuffled on my chair. "What kind of thing?"

"I read something I shouldn't have," Violet admitted. "When you came back to school, I was still really worried about you. We all were! You have to expect that thing if you disappear. Even since you've been back, you've been so twitchy! So, I...," she cringed again, "went through your things."

My hand clenched around the coffee mug until my knuckles went white. "What did you find?"

Violet sighed. "Your diary? The pretty black and gold thing."

I couldn't stop the scream of frustration that escaped my mouth. My face fell into my hands as I internally scolded myself. I had always thought I was careful with my things, but apparently, my diary was becoming common reading material.

"I'm so, so sorry!" Violet said quickly, somewhat panicked by my reaction. "I won't say I didn't mean to. I was just so scared for you, Ocean!"

Violet stood up so hard the table screeched against the floor, both our drinks spilling. She dragged her chair closer and sat down flush against me.

"Ocean," she said bluntly, "some of the things you wrote in there scared me. The way you saw yourself; the way you *thought* of yourself! You're an amazing woman. You want to make everyone happy and you're so considerate of everyone's feelings. More so than you think or realise you are. I need to know that you know how loved you are. That you're a wonderful person who deserves to live! We want you to live! We need you!"

I felt guilt rise inside me. It was so bitter I felt like I'd swallowed a mouthful of charcoal. I didn't know what Violet had read exactly, but I knew my diary well enough to know there were quite a few entries that could have given her cause for alarm.

"Violet." I put my arm around her, my eyes never leaving hers. "You don't need to worry. I understand why some of the things I wrote could scare you. But I promise you, I was never going to hurt myself."

Violet let out a heavy sigh of relief. She linked her arm through mine before leaning her head on my shoulder. "Really?"

"Yes, Vi," I said. "I promise. I was just being dramatic. It was my diary, I needed to be! I didn't know what to do or how to tell you all. It was just getting on top of me. Sometimes it just felt like there was no way out without hurting everybody."

"You could never hurt us by being yourself, Ocean," Violet reassured me. "We're your friends."

"I know that," I said gently. "I promise, I've never tried to stop being myself around you." I cringed, trying to find the right words. "It's easy to be around you guys. And not just for me. Remember what Freja said? You know, like when she's around older people, they expect her to be more mature because she's so advanced at school."

"Right." Violet nodded quickly. "But when she's with us, she doesn't feel like she has to pretend."

"Exactly!" I snapped my fingers. "I don't feel like you guys are ever going to judge me for what I want to wear or how I want to act." I leaned back in my chair, Violet still clinging to me stubbornly. "I appreciate it. I mean… I'm hardly a girl, really!"

Violet didn't seem to take my words as a joke, squeezing my waist tighter.

"Of course you're a girl!" She declared.

I petted her shoulder gratefully, despite the turned heads from the neighbouring tables.

"I know I am," I said. "It's just weird that I'm this way sometimes. I tried wearing dresses but they just make me uncomfortable. I guess I like pink? But my favourite colour is still blue. And I like sports."

"I like sports," Violet said firmly. "And Cam doesn't like makeup or skirts. I like blue and so does Freja. She doesn't like pink all that much either. Besides, did you know that before the 20th century, pink was the 'boy's' colour? It was considered the masculine, stronger colour. Whereas girls were dressed in blue because it was considered daintier. Then at some point it was swapped round! Now every shop has a stupid section decked out in pink and glitter because girls apparently innately love that shit! Sometime in the future it'll probably flip again and boys will be expected to be into mahogany and girls will be told they have to have things in lime green! So you might as well just like what you like. There is no one way to be a girl."

I sat dumbfounded for a few moments, the speech settling in.

"Yeah," I agreed eventually. "That's sort of why it's complicated to explain what makes me a girl."

I was still learning how to explain everything. It was the strangest feeling inside me; certainty that I was a woman battling with not wanting to do 'women's' things. I rarely found a girl like me on TV or in books. Then whenever I did, they always wore skirts and make-up, had girlish hobbies and generally seemed very femme. I'd never played with dolls as a child. Then again, I never really played with anything. I'd never taken much of an interest in any toys, preferring to read if I wanted to use my imagination. I knew the concept of femininity wasn't one exclusive to women or girls. Men could like nail polish and heeled boots. Women could like sports and blue. I hadn't realised who I was through a need for femininity. Only a burning, throbbing, avoidable desire to be seen as I really was.

"You don't have to explain." Violet interrupted my reverie with a poke to my cheek. "You never have to explain yourself to us."

A warm feeling erupted inside my chest, briefly washing away the confusion. I let it comfort me. We were just two girls chuckling together in a cafe, even if it was out of relief more than amusement.

"I know," I admitted. "I appreciate that. And I promise you," I looked directly into Violet's eyes again, making sure I had her full attention, "if I didn't feel safe or if I wanted to hurt myself, I would have told you." I bowed my head in shame. "On reflection, I probably should have told you all a lot sooner. It would have made things easier on everyone. I'm sorry I didn't have more faith in you."

"Its fine," Violet said sincerely. "I understand. I mean, I still haven't told my parents about Freja."

"It'll come," I reassured her. "I know it's an awful feeling. Still, they might surprise you. I never thought Theo would react the way he did." I leaned in, pressing my forehead against Violet's. "And if they don't, we'll sort something out between us."

Violet winced, giving me a grimacing smile.

"I know," I said sympathetically. "I thought about all that, too. That Theo could cut me off or hand me back into care. I mean, if you're really scared about that, you can wait until after you graduate. But if you decide the time is right before then, don't worry. We'll all take care of you."

Violet nodded in agreement. "I know you all will," she said. "And we'll take care of you..."

I hesitated, but upon seeing Violet's face, I quickly recovered. "Yes, Violet," I said. "I absolutely completely promise, I'm not going to do anything to myself." I took Violet's hand. "I value my life. Especially now."

I caught my reflection in the window. I still looked awful. My hair was in desperate need of brushing, sticking up and frizzier than it had been in months, and my eyes looked almost as grey as Tempest's. I still smiled, happy to see the person that looked back at me.

"I have everything I never thought I'd have," I confessed. "I can't wait to see what else comes."

"You deserve it." Violet reached up to pat my wild hair back into place as best she could. "You deserve all the happiness in the world."

"So do you."

I chuckled, brushing my fingertips over the globe hanging from my neck.

Chapter Sixteen

Ru

"Hey, Ru!"

I reluctantly opened my eyes. Freja was walking towards me, her familiar yellow tote bag swinging. I blinked in surprise when she pulled out a bottle of Havn rum.

"What?" I sat up, catching the bottle against my chest. I looked at it, frowning. "I'm eighteen now. I'm not paying you to buy drinks for me."

"I know." Freja sat down opposite me, pushing her straw inside her usual carton of rosé. "It's a present."

I looked at her like her hair had suddenly turned bright pink.

"Why would you get me a present?" I twisted the cap from the bottle anyway, taking a large swallow before she could change her mind. I regretted it immediately. I'd skipped dinner, needing to lie down outside in the field and be with my thoughts, occasionally flipping through Blake's book. My stomach churned and protested the lack of food, threatening to hurl the alcohol back up. I swallowed a mouthful of saliva, turning away from Freja to take deep breaths until the queasy feeling died down.

She scooted forward on the grass.

"Because I'm worried about you," she admitted. "What's been up with you lately?"

I shivered, my stomach protesting again. I screwed the cap back on the rum and slipped it into my bag to share with Enzo later.

"It's nothing. Just finals."

"And Ocean?"

I gawped at Freja, unable to stop the giveaway expression. Not that lying would have got me anywhere.

"Bitch..."

Freja laid down beside me. "I kind of gathered she was the one you were obsessed with. It was one of the reasons I tried to set you up with Noël," she admitted. "I honestly felt stupid that I hadn't figured it out sooner, since you stopped talking about your secret lover after she disappeared. I then realised that you breaking up with them came immediately after Ocean returned. It properly clicked when I thought about how worried you were about her."

"Bitch," I said again, but I wasn't really angry. I looked over my shoulder. "You can't tell anyone!"

"You think I'm a moron!" Freja scoffed. "I get it. Besides, it's Ocean. She's hot!"

"Yeah." I spotted the rainbow cover of Blake's book inside my bag. I shuffled, sitting firmly on top of it before Freja could ask any questions. "She is." I stared at the clear sky. "She dumped me after she came back to school. Said she couldn't date the 'gay kid.'"

"Aw, Ru." Freja patted my knee sympathetically. "I'm sorry."

"No, I get it," I shrugged. "Everything with Noah and those guys that have been following her around – she's been having a hard enough time of it."

"My God!" Freja snapped at me. She shoved her straw right inside her carton and screwed the cap back on. In a split second, I was lying flat on the grass. Freja straddled me and pinned me down, her angry face staring at me. "Could you stop being understanding for five minutes?"

"Huh?"

"You really liked Ocean, right? And I know she didn't text you anything while she was AWOL, since you were asking us every day if we'd heard from her. You guys were supposed to be dating, even if you were keeping it a secret from us. It was really bitchy of her to not even tell you that she was going off the grid!"

"Freja—"

"No!" She dug her nails in deeper, daring me to try and escape. "You've been moping around ever since she came back. For as long as I've known you guys, you've been at each other's throats, even after you started screwing! You never missed a chance to throw a jibe at Ocean, comment on how you would have done something better or how she fucked something up. But now, you've barely looked her in the eye for days! I'm sick of your moping and so is everyone else."

"Everyone?" I panicked.

Freja loosened her grip but stayed on top of me.

"Don't worry, those idiots are too stupid to figure out what was going on between you two. Even Violet. That doesn't mean they haven't noticed how you've been acting, though." She let go of my shirt. "It sucks to have your heart broken, right?"

I couldn't do it. I couldn't hold it in any longer. I'd tried so hard to let out all of the pain the night Ocean had broken up with me, literally kicking and screaming into the dirt! It hadn't been enough.

"It does, Freja," I croaked, my voice breaking. "It hurts so fucking much!"

My eyes went fuzzy. I tried to wriggle away, but Freja pulled me into a tight hug. Water suddenly sprayed from my face like a burst water main! It streamed from my eyes, my nose, my mouth- I was pretty sure it was coming out of my ears at one point!

"I hate this!" I sobbed loudly into her shirt. "I want to take it all back, to go back to the time before! I knew she was hot back then. I knew I liked her. I just didn't know—" I hiccupped. It was like my soul was doing the talking. Saying all the things my brain hadn't processed yet.

"I didn't know how pretty her laugh was," I admitted. "I didn't know how peaceful she looked while she slept. Did you ever notice how she hides behind her cigarette smoke when she's not looking so great? Like when her hair starts to curl again after it gets wet. I did, and now every time I see her do it, it makes me want to kiss her face off!"

I rubbed my tears onto Freja, sniffing violently.

"I want to forget all of it and go back to the way things were. But I know I can't."

"Let it out," Freja whispered. "Let it all out, Ru. Then we're going to make this right."

"How?" I mumbled.

"You need to talk to Ocean."

"What?!" I looked up, horrified. "How can I speak to her? She doesn't want anything to do with me."

"Did she say that?"

I shivered on the grass, enduring the sickness to take another swallow from my rum bottle. I hiccupped, wiping my mouth and nose on my sleeve. When I was done, it looked like there'd been a snail race on my blazer.

I remembered running into Ocean last week when those assholes had been heckling her.

"Not directly," I admitted. "I've tried, but she won't talk to me."

"Then I'll talk to her."

"No, you can't. Then she'll know you know about us."

Freja folded her arms, sitting back on her heels. "Then find a way to talk to her, or I'll make you!"

She gave me that look that always made me want to run into the forest screaming. The look that said, 'I know what you're thinking better than you do, so shut up and listen'.

"When this all started, you didn't know what to do about any of it. You were just lying here whining about your kisses with your dumb crush. Then *I* told you to talk to her and low and behold, she went out with you!" Freja slapped my belly playfully. I tried to hide my wince as the rum continued to take its toll. "So now you need to talk to her and get everything out in the open so you can either get back together or move on. Got it?"

I stared at her blankly.

"I'm late for boxing practice," I said slowly before grabbing my bag and walking away, swaying just a little bit.

~*~

I slammed my locker door shut, the sound rattling in the empty changing room. I hated to admit that Freja had been right. Despite how obvious it was that Freja was definitely right.

Freja also knew perfectly well that there was no boxing training after dinner, but I figured I'd stay around and do my own training. It wasn't like I had anywhere else to be. I walked into the dimly lit gym, my brow furrowed in thought. I breathed into my hand. The smell of rum was certainly there, although it wasn't too strong. Then again, Mrs Tempest had a nose like a bloodhound.

I stopped at the water fountain and took a big gulp. I closed my eyes, water dribbling down my chin. Freja's speech played over and over in my mind. I hated that it made sense. My heart felt weird when I thought about Ocean. I wanted to be with her. I wanted her as my girlfriend. If she didn't want that, then we could at least be what we used to be. Rivals. Friends. Something in between. Whatever it was. It was the same conundrum I'd dealt with when deciding whether or not to ask her out in the first place, and, logically, it had the same conclusion. Just having Ocean close by would be better than nothing, even if it wasn't what I really wanted.

I wiped the water from my mouth, trying to think about where Ocean would most likely be.

"Hey, there it is!"

My eyes snapped open at the sudden shout. The words and voice sounded familiar. I swivelled around, hearing someone running outside the window. I peered into the darkness, squinting until I could just make out four boys running across the field. Two of them were part of the gang that had been tormenting Ocean before. The other two were on the boxing team.

"Shit."

I bolted across the gym. It was possible that they weren't after Ocean, but I couldn't take that risk and those idiots certainly didn't deserve the benefit of the doubt. I trampled over the workout mats the gymnastics club had left out everywhere. I skidded, crashing into the windowed doors that led to the playing field. I pulled back, shaking off any injuries, staring across the field and focusing on the dorm buildings at the very end. Lights switched on just in time to show a girl falling to the ground.

I tugged desperately at the locked door, swearing loudly. I saw red. Without any thought about potential consequences, I ran to pick up a large dumbbell resting beside the punch bags.

Chapter Seventeen

Ocean

"There it is!"

I cringed at the sharp words.

I took a deep breath and carried on walking down the path towards the dorms, letting the same mantra from the past few weeks run through my mind. I raised my head high and focused on getting inside, reminding myself that I didn't need to bother with whatever my tormentors wanted.

"Hey, he-she!"

My pace quickened. I felt the obvious urge to turn around and slap every one of the shitheads in their stupid faces, but I was determined to stay calm. I counted the remaining steps to the door, turning up the volume on my internal thoughts.

"Oi, we're talking to you!"

A sharp pain hit me in the back of my head. I fell forward, crashing onto the path. Lights from the dorms flickered through the windows as curtains were pushed open. I could just imagine the laughter as the people inside watched me fall on my face. I grimaced, looking at the dirt and grazes on my palms. The rock that had been thrown at me lay on the path beside me, mocking me.

I tried to stand up, only for someone to grab me by the back of my collar. I turned my head, staring into the eyes of one of my attackers. I was still reeling from the rock, still too shocked to run or get out of the way. The demented look in the boy's eyes urged me to brace myself.

A heavy fist fell against my face.

The rest of the gang jeered and laughed behind me as I moved my jaw carefully, spitting out a mouthful of blood. A second punch came down. It slammed into my nose. Blood trickled from both my nostrils.

My attackers didn't seem to notice me rolling my eyes as I was punched. My body lay splayed on the grass, waiting for it to be over. Students came running out of the dorms to watch the action – gasps and laughter ringing out into the evening air. I closed my eyes, letting the punches hit me. I had endured it before. I could endure it again. I was strong.

Another punch hit me in the gut. I tried to take a breath, but my stomach clenched, twisting with the impact. Dizziness from the lack of oxygen filled my head. I curled up, clutching myself from the pain. My skirt shifted against my legs, riding up.

"Oh my God, look! He's wearing panties!"

A foot slammed into my thighs as a hand lifted my skirt, revealing my blue cotton underwear to the crowd. I shivered, nausea taking over at the feeling of the unwanted hand on my skin. It felt slimy and gross. I coughed, blood and bile spilling from my mouth.

"Does it have a smooth crotch? I want to see!"

My vision faded as someone turned me over onto my back. A rough hand grabbed at my groin.

Rage rushed through me, my leg coming up on instinct to kick the bastard away. Someone caught my ankle, holding my leg open to keep me exposed.

"Get off of me!" I screamed around a cough, vomit spilling onto the grass.

My words only spurred my attackers on. They continued to grab at me, jeering. I kicked out again, striking the boy in his chest. He fell backwards, smacking his head on the ground. I jabbed my right elbow at one of the other boys holding me down as my leg came round to kick him in the side.

"Aw, you don't like us touching you there?" The last attacker cooed. "You a dyke as well as a trann—"

Silence filled the crowd as the boy was cut off. I blinked, trying to stop the spinning.

I spotted a flash of dark hair from the corner of my eye, followed by the sound of a fist landing straight in someone's throat. A pathetic gargling noise broke the eerie silence.

I pushed myself up, trying to see past the blood in my eyes.

Ru was looming over my attacker, the one who had grabbed my underwear. He was punching him repeatedly in the face.

His right hand was holding onto his collar, keeping him still and trapped. His left came down over and over. Hitting his jaw, eyes and nose. I could see his head shaking, his hands attempting to bat Ru's fist away. He wailed as Ru smacked into them, his fingers crushing against his own face. One of them bent right back with a sickening crunch. Ru didn't even flinch. His pupils were so wide they seemed to take over his entire eyeballs! More blood trickled from the attacker, mixing with the blood on Ru's knuckles.

His foot was pressed against the chest of the one I had elbowed. He was in tears, his face purple as he begged Ru to stop. He swayed back and forth like a turtle on its back, batting at Ru's ankle. Ru didn't even seem to be pressing too hard, although his heavy foot did bounce every time he punched the boy in his grip. The final attacker clutched at his throat.

His face was pale as he wheezed, doubled over. I couldn't find the fourth boy. He'd presumably run while he had a chance.

Tears filled my eyes at the sight. After everything I had done to Ru, he was here for me. I didn't deserve that. Ru was fighting with a fury and a passion I'd never seen before. I'd thought our fights were violent, but compared to this, they were just playful wrestling. Granted, this fight had none of the grace Ru had used with me. This just looked like pure bloodlust.

I blinked the tears away as the third boy lifted his head, glaring at Ru as he rubbed his throat. He ran towards him, preparing for an attack.

'*Sorry, Theo,*' I thought to myself.

I jumped up, propelling myself forward with my hands, landing gracefully on my feet. Instinct took over as I locked eyes with the enemy. I forgot that I was wearing a skirt. My leg flew upwards, my foot hitting the boy in his stomach.

He screamed, flying an impressive distance across the grass.

"That's enough!"

The familiar voice of Ms Khil sent both relief and terror through my body.

"Ms Khil...," I whispered. The thrill and shock had gone, leaving me with an aching gut and a sore jaw.

Ms Khil squeezed my shoulder before heading towards Ru and hauling him off the crying bullies. I noticed Ru looking into Ms Khil's eyes. I knew he could see the disappointment there.

"Ms Khil, wait!" I protested, trying to run, only to buckle as my stomach twisted.

Ms Khil sighed heavily, reaching out to take my hand. "I'm sorry," she said, "but we'll have to notify the headteacher about this."

I blinked, tears falling down my face. To me, the only thing worse than ending up in a fight and letting Theo down would be Ru ending up in a fight and finally getting expelled.

Other teachers finally arrived and stepped in to attend to Ru's victims. I watched as Mr Fan angrily held Ru's hands behind his back as if he was a criminal. I tried to call out to Ru as Ms Khil led me away, wanting to tell him that I was sorry. Only for blood and spittle to drip down my front, staining my white school shirt.

~*~

I was summoned to Tempest's office first thing the next morning after spending the night in the infirmary. I shuffled down the hall, finally dressed again in my old school trousers and long black jumper. My bag bumped against my thigh as I carried it in my hand, the strap having broken during the fight. Freja had brought the clothes down for me last night, but the night nurse hadn't let her in to see me, no matter how much she begged.

I winced when I caught sight of my reflection in one of the glass doors, gingerly petting the ugly bandage stuck over my swollen nose.

I hadn't sustained any serious injuries from the attack; just a busted nose, a chipped tooth and a black eye that I was able to cover with my fringe, anyway. The night nurse had called me lucky. I certainly didn't feel it. Every time I was left alone with my thoughts, I could hear the slurs the shitheads had thrown at me and the feeling of that disgusting hand under my skirt.

My fists rubbed hard at my eyes to push back the tears, wincing when I irritated the bruise there. I couldn't let Tempest see me cry.

I took a deep breath to ground myself, knocking on the door of the headteacher's office.

"Come in," Tempest's gruff voice called out.

I pushed the door open cautiously, preparing for the worst – to be told I couldn't stay at this school with my friends anymore and that I would be 'safer elsewhere'. It was one of the things someone had said to Theo on the phone before he had given them a barrage of abuse. I bit my lip, once again sending telepathic apologies to my guardian.

My good eye widened in shock when I saw Ru already sitting opposite the desk. He wasn't wearing his uniform. Instead, he was dressed in a white t-shirt and dark green jogging trousers. I cringed again, thinking he was about to be sent home, too.

"Take a seat please, Miss Jónsson," Tempest said ominously, sitting himself down at his desk.

I didn't even bother to correct my surname, carefully walking across the room to sit next to Ru. He turned towards me, his face unreadable.

The headteacher's gaze flicked between us, the tension in the room thick and heavy.

Tempest rubbed his brow.

"I've been up since five dealing with this mess," he mumbled, as if it was all our fault. He reached for one of his pre-rolled cigarettes, tapping the base of the filter with his thumb before placing it between his lips to light it.

"You might as well smoke too, Jónsson," Tempest suggested, noticing my eyes following the cigarette longingly. "Sorry, Noyer."

I was startled by this but was too anxious to question it. I immediately rummaged in my bag for my cigarettes.

"Now then." Tempest leaned back. "This is a complicated situation. Miss Noyer, I am terribly sorry that this happened to you on school grounds. Rest assured, your attackers have been named and action will be taken. The last thing I want is to retire from this school with the reputation of a headmaster who let his students feel unsafe."

I noted how Tempest worded his statement carefully. I knew he wouldn't say more than that, but I so wanted to know what would happen. The thought of running into those boys in the hallway after last night felt entirely unbearable. My stomach lurched, threatening to empty itself over Tempest's pokey office.

"We have called your foster father." Tempest held up a hand at the panicked look on my face. "We haven't detailed the attack yet. We just told him you were involved in an 'altercation' and that you'd talk to him. As you're not eighteen for another week, it is our policy to notify guardians. However, that also means that you'll have to talk to him if you want to press charges for the assault. Understand?"

I swallowed before inhaling deeply on my cigarette, nodding lightly.

"However..." Tempest visibly braced himself. He paused, taking long drags of his own cigarette. I didn't think it was possible for a teacher to look guilty, but that was the only way I could describe his expression. "We have been offered a compromise of sorts after speaking to the mother of... Well, she wants to press assault charges against Hamasaki."

My head spun around to face Ru. He just folded his arms, looking straight ahead.

"However, after discussing the witness accounts," Tempest continued, "she's willing to let it slide if no charges are pressed against her son."

"Yes."

Tempest furrowed his brow. I met his eyes, my face still and serious.

"I only ask you to consider your—"

"Yes," I said again. "I won't press charges. So long as Ru won't get expelled. Or arrested! He stopped it, after all."

"Fuck's sake," Ru said with a sigh. "I don't need your sympathy, Frizz Head!"

"Just be grateful that I'm helping you out, Barbarian-pig!"

"Enough!" Tempest slammed his palms down against the table. He stood up, tapping the half-smoked cigarette out in the ashtray, leaving it there for later. "I understand that this has been a trying few hours for you both, with many unfortunate incidents, including a broken window that I'm going to *assume* is not connected!" He glared at Ru. "But I'm telling you now that I am not in the mood to deal with the same old nonsense that you two stirred up before. Whatever is going on between the two of you, whatever has made you snap back into your old ways, you're going to deal with it now.

"I'm going to leave for an hour. Whatever is happening, fix it. Work it out! Understood?"

He didn't wait for an answer. He walked past us, closing his office door tight behind him.

I exhaled a long line of smoke. My legs jiggled as I sat cross-legged in the uncomfortable plastic chair, trying to ignore the feeling of déjà vu it gave me. I couldn't bear to look at Ru, feeling both angry and relieved at the same time.

Ru huffed petulantly. "That's so typical 'you'," he mumbled. "Throwing yourself under the bus before you even think of the freaking consequences."

"Don't you get snippy with me!" I hissed. I took a deep final drag of my cigarette, sucking the nicotine in desperation, before stubbing it out in Tempest's ashtray. "You should be thanking me."

"Whatever."

We sat in silence for five minutes of the hour.

"Why didn't you fight back?" Ru asked softly. "I know you could have got them off you. They weren't anything special. Why didn't you at least try?"

I rolled my eyes. I pulled my knees to my chest, hugging myself on the chair.

"I didn't want to get in trouble," I admitted. "I didn't want my name to be used in a fight. Theo fought really hard for me to come back here. I didn't want to give them a reason to kick me out."

Ru's jaw dropped.

"That's bullshit! You were the victim! What do you think would have happened?"

"You know that's not always how this works," I said calmly. "Besides, it wasn't anything I couldn't handle. It's not like I haven't been punched in the face before." My eyes sparkled as I looked at Ru, my heart fluttering at the now distant memories of battles between us. It made me feel strangely warm to think about it now. "You shouldn't have done that. Especially after I—"

"After you ghosted me for fucking weeks!" Ru snapped.

I winced, but knew I couldn't protest.

"I'm so sorry," I admitted. "I really couldn't... I just didn't know what to do. I was thinking for months about how to break this to everyone. More you than anybody else. Then, at the same time, I was trying so hard to deny it. I didn't want this for me, Barbarian." I scratched at the sleeve of my jumper, pulling on a thread. I stopped myself, reaching into my pocket for my glasses instead. I didn't put them on, but fiddling with the ends kept my hands busy. "Do you know the names of the guys who attacked me?"

Ru clicked his tongue.

"Rhod? I think? And the other guy was..." He trailed off.

"Exactly!" I turned to face him. "I have no idea who they are, and I doubt they know that much about me. I've been doing a pretty damn good job of being unnoteworthy up until recently. I worked hard in P.E so I wouldn't be the scrawny guy with the pretty hair. I knew that the moment I showed my real self, I couldn't just blend in anymore. I thought I'd feel better about myself when we got together. I thought acknowledging that I liked you would make things easier. And it felt so good to be with you! But it just wouldn't stop." I pressed my hand against my chest. "It was just this constant ache inside me. This feeling that I was standing on the outside of everybody else. No matter what I did, it just didn't seem to get any easier. Like this huge black mass weighing me down everywhere I went."

"You can't hide from stuff like this," Ru stated, still in his attack stance. "If you're a girl, it's because you're made that way. It's in your hormones or chromosomes or your brain structure. Something like that. Anyway, you can't change it even if you wanted to."

My face twisted in confusion. "What?"

Ru reached for his backpack, pulling out a brightly coloured booklet. He passed it to me. I took it, staring at it as if it was a rare, decorated geode.

"Blake lent it to me," Ru mumbled. "I needed to learn about a whole bunch of different sexuality terms, apparently."

"Really?" I looked at him, bewildered.

"Yeah." Ru scratched at the back of his head. "For example, I thought I was gay because I was more into guys than women, but now I think I'm more pansexual, maybe. And I'm for sure demisexual!"

"Demisexual?"

"It means I don't really feel any sexual attraction to someone until I feel…" Ru made a strange grinding noise in the back of his throat, "…some romantic or emotional connection."

"Oh?" I looked at the book, rubbing my thumb over the title.

"As for that invisible shit, I don't know what to tell you," Ru admitted. "Probably because I never had the option to be invisible."

"You make yourself stand out too much," I teased, attempting to break the tension. Ru just shrugged again.

"I make myself stand out because I already did," he explained. "I was chubby and weird looking before I started dying my hair or wearing piercings. I figured if people were going to stare, I might as well do what I want."

Ru's confession felt like a green light flashing beside me. I felt like throwing myself out of the window for being so stupid- even if being on the ground floor would make things less dramatic.

"I've always been so good at hiding," I confessed. "Slipping by without anyone noticing."

"Then maybe it's time you learned how to actually be a fucking human!" Ru said harshly. To his surprise, I nodded.

I slipped my glasses on, thumbing through a few pages of the book. I held it close to my face, my breath warm against my hand. Every instinct in my body was telling me to pull Ru into my arms and hold him tight. To kiss him until he passed out; to let his arms close around me and do whatever he pleased.

For the first time, I couldn't think of a reason not to.

I threw the booklet onto Tempest's desk, jumping out of my chair. I grabbed Ru's shoulders and pressed my lips against his.

Ru sat bewildered for a few seconds before his large hands reached up to cradle my face. My glasses clattered to the ground as he kissed me back with equal passion.

"I hate that you left," he mumbled against my lips, "but I love that you came back."

He pressed a hand against my chest, his fingertips tracing the shimmering globe as he felt my heartbeat.

"I'm sorry," I whispered. "I want to be with you. I don't want to give a shit about what anyone else thinks. All I want is you!"

Ru laughed loudly, squeezing my hips. "It gets easier," he said breathlessly. "I can teach you." He leaned in closer, embracing the warmth between us. "I want you too. You're my Ocean."

I whimpered, a tingling sensation shooting upward through my body at our closeness. Ru kissed me again, wrapping an arm around my waist.

His lips curled into a smile against mine.

"What?" I asked.

"I just," he pecked my lips, "love the thought that you're my girlfriend."

Girlfriend.

I gasped, shivering in his grip as my thumbs caressed the shells of his ears. I leant against him, climbing onto his lap, my thighs hanging on either side of his hips.

"You want to do it here?" Ru teased as I straddled him, "Right now, in Temp's office?"

"He told us to work things out," I said, smacking my lips, "So, let's!"

We kissed again. I felt my skin light up at the contact. I leaned back, taking in Ru's face. My thumbs ran over the underside of his jaw. I tilted my head, looking into his dark eyes. My fingers trailed up until they touched his hair, clean and fresh from being washed that morning.

"You're so beautiful, Ru," I whispered.

"What?" He looked at me, bemused. "*You're* beautiful. You're textbook beautiful!" He scoffed. "You got that soft hair, large eyes and perfectly symmetrical face!"

I giggled, Ru's hands squeezing my hips as I did so. Even with such high praise, Ru made the compliments sound like a spitfire. I didn't reply, my hands sliding down his face in a long, swooping caress.

"Beauty is subjective," I murmured, "and I think beauty is rebel hair, bewitching eyes, and dimpled, chubby cheeks!"

Ru's arms wrapped around me, still needing to keep me close. He gently kissed my cheekbone, my nose, and my temple.

"Well, to me," he said in a low, husky voice, "you're beautiful. Your face has always made me feel something. Since the day we met."

"Even when you wanted to punch it?" I asked playfully.

"Yeah. Even then."

Chapter Eighteen

Ru

"Oh my God, thank fuck!" Freja shot up from the table the second we walked into the common room. Both of us looked like crap, even if Ocean's injuries didn't look too bad anymore. The swelling had gone down rapidly over the past few hours, even if her glasses balanced askew on her plastered nose. I quickly shoved my bruised knuckles into my pockets before Freja could see.

She threw her arms around both of us, squeezing hard.

"Freja!" Ocean gasped, "I can't breathe!"

"As if I care!" She pulled away, squishing Ocean's face between her palms, forgetting to be mindful of her sore nose. "What the hell happened?"

"Nothing," Ocean said, gently taking Freja's hands away when she started to wince.

"Nothing?" Freja screeched. "You were attacked and assaulted. Ru literally knocked someone's teeth out. And you have the mother-freaking nerve to tell me it's—"

"It *is* nothing." Ocean spoke calmly, using a soothing, motherly voice. "I promise you, Tempest fixed everything. Ru isn't being excluded."

Freja's eyes went wide, her already pink cheeks going red. "I don't give a shit if Ru gets excluded!"

"Oh, thanks."

"Shut up, loser!" Freja snapped. She framed Ocean's face again with a much gentler touch. "What did they do to you? What's going to happen to those boys?"

"They didn't do anything to me," Ocean said with confidence. "I promise you. I don't know what's going to happen, but I'm not going to let them give me trouble like that again. Neither is Ru."

Ocean smiled at me. She held her hand out, wriggling her fingers.

I smiled back. I wrapped my rough fingers around Ocean's soft, slender hand.

"God, how did you even let them get that far?" Freja couldn't stop herself from asking. "You kicked that jerk's ass last year when he snapped Violet's bra open."

Ocean tensed. "I didn't want to cause a fuss," she admitted. "I didn't want the school to have an excuse to exclude me after Theo stuck his neck out to convince them to let me stay."

Our group surrounded her in an instant. Freja stood right in front of her, Violet and Enzo behind, with Cam at her side. Noah and Janie stood in the corner. All of them were giving her the same sickening expression of sympathy. The next second, multiple arms were encasing her. Cam clung to her waist while Enzo jumped on her back.

"Don't think like that, Ocean," Enzo declared, his voice a little too loud next to her ear. "We love you, you big, stupid idiot!"

"He's right," Violet said. "We want you to be safe. That's the most important thing."

Ocean paused before letting out a long, defeated breath. She let go of my hand, returning the hug as best she could, feeling the warmth of her friends all around her. Cam clung to her like a gibbon, giggling gleefully into her neck.

"I know," Ocean said. "I'm sorry. It won't happen again."

"Hey." Freja stuck her tongue out at her. "That's seventy euros you owe me this week! You want to spend all your allowance on pissing me off?"

Ocean snorted. "Yes... I'm s—" She cut herself off, backing up with Enzo, Violet and Cam still clinging to her. "Thank you, Freja."

Enzo chuckled, rubbing his cheek against hers, grinning. Ocean's face flushed. The declarations and touching seemed to be overwhelming her fast. She took another step back. My arms wrapped around her from behind.

"Right..." Ocean mumbled under her breath.

I ran a hand down her back, resting my chin on her shoulder and leading her in taking five deep breaths. She started the steady rhythm of breathing in for three counts, holding and releasing. Ocean relaxed, letting me ground her. I caught the glint of silver against her chest. The room fell silent as I lost myself, holding my girlfriend.

"Hang on," Cam said, narrowing her eyes suspiciously. "What... Why are you guys being so friendly to each other?"

I looked up to see our friends staring at us. I didn't let go of Ocean.

"Shit," Noah said, his voice going high. "Did you guys kill someone?"

"Of course, they didn't, you shithead!" Freja said.

"They might have!" Noah snapped back. "It could have been an accident, landing a punch in the wrong place and the school's trying to cover it up."

"That's very dramatic, Noah," Violet said calmly. She sat down on one of the rickety chairs, legs crossed and hands folded over her knee. She eyed Ocean, almost expectantly. "Do you have another announcement for us, Ocean?"

I wrapped one arm around Enzo, holding him for mutual comfort, keeping the other around Ocean's shoulders. I was ready to let go the moment she wanted me to, but she kept herself still and steady. She turned, looping her arm around my waist.

"Not really," she said simply. "Just that Ru and I are dating."

Freja looked at Ocean with intense pride. Silence passed over the group. Even Enzo looked speechless. He blinked at us dazed- before he jumped up, hugging both of us.

"That's awesome!" He cried. "Congratulations, you guys! Let's celebrate? Hey, Ocean? Will you make pizza?"

"It's Thursday, shithead."

"Yeah, but last pizza night sucked, so we should have two pizza nights this week!" Enzo nuzzled into her like a kitten, practically pleading.

"You're really dating?" Janie asked. "Really?"

"Of course they are!" Cam scoffed. "Oh my God, you're so cute together! This is fabulous!" She pinched my earlobe, squealing.

"Thanks," I muttered, wriggling away from Cam's hand.

"Congratulations," Violet said warmly. She stood back up, kissing us both on the cheek. "I'm happy for you."

Freja raised her brow, looking at me triumphantly. She couldn't resist mouthing the words: 'I told you so.'

"Hang on." Noah backed away, holding his hands up defensively. "So, you two are like a boyfriend-girlfriend kind of thing?"

"Yes," I said, pulling Enzo off said girlfriend.

"Huh." Noah looked at Janie, who seemed equally confused. "But aren't you like, gay, Ru? And Ocean aren't you supposed to be... I don't know... a lesbian?"

Ocean composed herself at Noah's question, but Freja jumped in before she could think. "She's not 'supposed' to be anything, jackass!" she barked. "And your shitty attitude is really starting to piss me off!"

Noah stared blankly.

"Starting?"

Freja lunged at him in a blind rage. Violet and Enzo immediately grabbed her arms to restrain her.

"I'm going to kill you, you dumb, shitty idiot!" Freja screamed.

Ocean watched it all, still leaning against me.

"Noah." Ocean stepped between her friends, looking straight into Noah's eyes. "Do you have a problem with me?"

The air around them was so tense it could have been cut with a knife. Enzo dug his nails into my arm, biting his lip hard. Noah didn't answer. Freja was still staring daggers at him.

Yet when I looked at Ocean, I only saw sincerity. The person we had known for so long. Who, despite having a temper sometimes, had never wanted to be the cause of any animosity, particularly between her friends. There was no anger there, just someone asking an honest question.

"It's not that I have a problem with you being..." Noah thankfully stopped himself from changing his tone or using air quotes, "...a girl. It's just, well, surely you understand that..."

"That you don't want me getting changed with your girlfriend," Ocean finished for him. Freja was grinding her teeth behind her, but Ocean remained calm. She looked at Janie. "How do you feel about it, Janie?"

Janie's lips flattened. "It's a little awkward for me," she admitted. "I've seen you as 'Ocean the boy' for so long. I'd never get changed in front of any of the boys. I can't make the switch just like that."

I held Enzo tighter, torn between my need to defend my girlfriend and letting her fight her own battles.

Ocean didn't flinch. She folded her hands together, smiling warmly. Janie relaxed a little. I hadn't seen Ocean look at her like that since before she went away.

"I understand and I appreciate your honesty," Ocean said. "I assure you, Janie, I don't want to make you feel uncomfortable."

"Thank you, Ocean," Janie said, trying to match her maturity.

Ocean reached for her bag. She rummaged through it, pulling out a small key attached to a wooden ball keychain.

"If you want to switch P.E classes I won't judge you," Ocean continued, holding the key up for all to see, "but please don't do it on my account. If you'd rather stay in the same class with Freja and Violet, then please do so. I won't get changed with you. I have a key for one of the private cubicles, so I'll get changed there and come out when you're all finished."

Janie stared at the key, looking surprisingly touched.

"No!" Freja suddenly grabbed the key from Ocean. She turned to Janie. "This isn't fair on Ocean. I want to be in a gym class with her and I don't want to wait outside until she's done changing! You can't expect her to just sit daintily in the cubicle until everyone else has left the locker room – all just because *you* are uncomfortable."

"Its fine, Freja," Ocean cut in.

"No!" Freja glared at each of us, commanding the room. Her eyes landed on Janie, holding the key out to her. "It's not fair to ask Ocean to hide away because you're the uncomfortable one. If you don't want to get changed with us, then you can get changed in the cubicle."

Janie and Noah hesitated.

"I think that's fair," Enzo said, his sore lip sticking out comically.

"No, Janie has the right to continue changing in the locker room as she always has," Ocean countered.

One look from Freja, however, told her that she would not be beaten in stubbornness.

"So what?" I spoke up. "It's not your problem. It's hers."

There was a long pause. I folded my arms, standing next to Freja. Finally, Janie nodded.

"Yes," she said plainly, "thank you."

She took the key from Freja and wrapped her hand around Noah's wrist, tugging him forward. "We're both sorry. We want to stay friends and we don't like the tension any more than you do. We'll work on things, we promise."

Ocean sighed in relief. She took a step closer to offer Noah and Janie a hug. Freja shoved her away gently, still glaring at Noah. He kicked the ground like a moody child, but still managed to look at Ocean with some sense of sincerity.

"I'm sorry too," he said sheepishly. "If you want to be a girl it's none of my business why. I hope we can stay friends."

Violet sighed in relief, spreading her arms wide.

"Good! Come on, everyone!"

"Yeah!" Enzo cheered. "Super best friend group hug time!"

Violet nodded in agreement as she pulled us all close in a large hug, Enzo giggling as we were squished together. Ocean was pressed in the centre of it all, smiling tranquilly, relieved to have made peace with all of her friends.

A sudden strangled noise from Cam had everyone jumping backwards. She looked wide-eyed between Ocean and me.

"So, wait. For real?" she cried. "You guys are dating?"

Ocean laughed freely. It was like a wave of relief crashing over me. My mouth fell open in a dumb smile as she inhaled like a choking donkey! The sound spread through the group. We all paused- before laughing just as loud!

"Yep! I know. Who would have thought this stupid barbarian would understand the complexities of a relationship?"

"Hey, you're the dumbass blonde, Frizz Head!"

Our eyes met, giving each other our familiar challenging scowls. My forehead pressed against Ocean's as she gripped my shoulders.

All six members of the group focused on our faces, seeing the same expressions they had seen a thousand times before—the fire and the anger—but for the first time, they saw the affection underneath it.

"You guys look so sweet together," Cam cooed.

"Yeah!" Enzo shouted. "We can have a pizza celebration!"

"Pizza night is tomorrow," Violet said firmly. "Let's go out to celebrate. Someplace nice."

"That sounds really good!" Freja turned to Noah. "Are you guys coming?"

Noah sighed in relief. "Yeah," he said, grinning. "I'd really like that."

"Me too," Janie said.

~*~

Later that night, we were all gathered at a tapas restaurant, shouting around a long table. We had sat in a far corner of the restaurant, hoping to cause as little disruption as possible to the other diners.

It didn't seem to be going too smoothly. Everyone had turned to stare at us at least once since we'd arrived. Even the ones who were trying their best to ignore the noise couldn't help giving us the occasional sideways glance. Ocean watched us through the window as she stood outside the restaurant with a cigarette.

I excused myself from the table, deciding to step outside and keep her company.

"Hey, Frizz?"

"Hey yourself, Barbarian."

We both laughed at the stupid nicknames which last year would have sent us into a murderous rage. Now, they felt like pet names.

I wrapped my arms around her from behind, kissing the back of her neck softly. Our cheeks pressed together as we watched the stars, occasionally looking through the window at our rowdy friends.

"Remind me to invite everyone down to visit over the summer and book us all a large table at Theo's restaurant," Ocean said playfully. "He needs to meet them all properly!"

We laughed together again. I shut my eyes to take in the perfect noise. A few months ago I was worried I'd never hear Ocean's stupid laugh again. Now, I'd heard it multiple times in one day!

I decided to push aside the thought of meeting Theo- that was something I could panic about later. There were other, louder things poking at my mind right then.

"Are you really okay with this?"

"With what, Barbarian?"

"You know exactly what, dumbass!"

Ocean rolled her eyes, even if she kept her fond smile. She flicked the butt of her cigarette into the ashtray as she turned around, her hand cupping my jaw.

"It was wrong of me to break up with you for being 'the gay kid'," she admitted. "And it was stupid of me to try and hide or give up something that made me happy." She snorted, shaking her head with an expression of disbelief and mild amusement.

"I spent the last few weeks keeping my head down and staying off everyone's radar, and it still got me attacked!"

I was quick to grab her by the shoulders, looking at her with what I hoped was a serious face. "Hey! You didn't 'get yourself' attacked. Nothing that happened was your fault."

Ocean scoffed and flicked my hands away. "I know that, you shit for brains! I just meant that..." she trailed off before closing the distance between us, pressing herself against my chest. "I managed to piss people off by being who I am, when I was trying my best not to. So, there's no point in making myself miserable because of what someone else might say. Even if people call us 'gay' when they learn we're together, I just need to learn to deal with it. Just accept that they're wrong and it doesn't matter if they don't know that. Because if I don't, I'm just going to lead a shitty life and it'll all be my fault." Ocean's boots clicked against the slightly damp cobbles. Her right leg was pressed against me as she gazed at me with a look that almost made my heart shatter for a second time.

Her thin lips were bright red, despite her lack of makeup, and her face was scrunched up, like a newborn about to have a fit.

"I'm sorry, Ru," she said. "I love you."

I swallowed the breath that had caught in my throat, quickly blinking back tears.

Pride still flared inside me, screaming that I shouldn't forgive Ocean so easily. Memories of lying in bed freaking out over what could have happened to her still felt so fresh- but right now, Ocean was here. She had said everything I needed to hear, and the last thing I wanted was more anger festering inside me.

Ocean was alive. Ocean was here. We could talk through all the negative things later; after I'd had a chance to hold her.

"I love you too," I said finally. "I've loved you for a while."

I dragged my fingers through her soft hair, inhaling her familiar scent of cigarettes and blueberries. I was here in the open, holding my girl. And it felt perfect!

Ocean was perfect.

There was a light in her eyes I thought I'd never see again. She stood tall with pride. Just like the person I'd developed a crush on a long time ago. She looked happy, and that was all I wanted from her.

I made a note to myself to take Ocean to a hotel at the weekend. I knew what she'd think about the suggestion, and yes, it was difficult to find time to be alone together while we were both still at school. The main reason, however, was that I just wanted to watch her sleep again. I knew she'd be curled up and peaceful, perhaps even fully relaxed. I could picture that sweet, beautiful smile on her face. I needed to see it. I'd borrow money from Freja if I had to!

"Thank you," Ocean whispered. "Are you sure? Will everything be okay?"

"Of course it will." I turned to kiss her tenderly. "It has to be. It's us."

I closed my eyes in relief when I felt the last of the tension leave her body. I smirked against her cheek, unable to resist muttering: "Buy me a drink and we'll call it even."

"You dick!"

Chapter Nineteen

Ocean

I hummed to myself as I picked up the kettle, filling the teapot. My heart fluttered when I heard the door to the common room open, followed by a familiar yawn.

"Oh! Hey!" Ru said in surprise.

I turned around. His face visibly lit up.

He crossed the room in several large steps to wrap his arms around me. "What's up, Barbarian?" I teased, putting the kettle down to return the hug. "You're not usually this affectionate."

"Want you," Ru mumbled, kissing my cheek.

He reached up, gently brushing his thumb over the fading remains of the green bruise underneath my eye. The sight of it still made him angry. Even when it faded completely, I was sure that his blood would boil every time we approached the dorm building. I was very glad the boys involved in the assault were never coming back, partially for their own sake. If Ru saw them again, I knew he'd have a hard time holding himself back. The school staff had not confirmed that the boys had been expelled. They probably weren't allowed to, but the rumours had spread like wildfire since none of them had been seen since.

Not only had their expulsion felt like a victory, it also seemed to have set a precedent for the rest of the school. The weird looks, whispers and crude comments hadn't gone completely, but they had massively reduced over the past few weeks. It was also possible that everyone had just moved on and found new things to be interested in. There was only so long 'that transgender girl' could be an interesting piece of gossip.

The latest rumours flying around about us were reasons why Ru hadn't been expelled too! Reasons spread from Ru's father having some connections to the mafia, to Ru threatening to murder Tempest. Truthfully, Ru had just been saved by the numerous eyewitnesses who said the other party had been the instigators and a final, and frankly long overdue demand, for Ru to see a counsellor for anger management twice a week.

He'd huffed and pouted when he'd told us, with Enzo teasing him relentlessly, of course, but Freja and I saw a strange shimmer in his eye. Something that could have been fear or possibly hope.

It had only been a few sessions so far, but I could already tell Ru was taking it seriously. I walked him to every appointment and waited outside the office for the whole forty-five minutes. Each time before he went in, he'd squeeze my hand tight and each time he came out he'd pull me in for a hug. A few times, he'd come out with bloodshot eyes. I never mentioned it, but I'd cup his face, gently caressing his earlobes with my fingertips while I kissed a trail up his cheeks to right underneath his eyes.

I was still expecting some kind of fallout from the revelation that Ru and I were dating. It became crystal clear to everyone a few days after the fight. Ru would always hold my hand when we walked across campus together. Sometimes, he would randomly kiss me in front of everyone or pull me into his lap. It was embarrassing, certainly, but it was also so sweet that I didn't want him to ever stop.

Part of me was sure the strange looks we got now were more related to the dramatic shift in our relationship than anything else. After all, those giving us the looks were the same people who used to gather around to watch us fight. Ru and I never said anything about it. We didn't even look at them. Whatever they were thinking didn't matter so long as they kept their thoughts to themselves.

Tempest had offered to do a 'special assembly' on gender identity, but I had asked him courteously yet firmly not to. I hadn't said why, although I could tell Ru and Freja had figured it out. There were only a few more months of school left, and I wanted to stay out of the spotlight as best I could. While I was glad I had sat down with Noah and Janie and explained everything properly, it had also been exhausting. I didn't want to spend my last term at school being an educator.

Ru understood and certainly had no intentions of pushing me. So long as I held his hand back, he was content.

I sighed in his arms, my right hand trailing up his back to ruffle his hair. I chuckled at the softness of it. Ru had decided a few days ago, since he couldn't be bothered to dye his hair for the moment, to have Violet cut the last of the colour out. For the first time since I had met him, it was sleek, jet black, the tufty ends sticking up like a bear cub's fluff. Something about it still felt unfamiliar, but I was growing to quite like it. It was like seeing a completely new, softer side to my boyfriend.

"Do you want some tea?" I asked.

"Sure. Thanks." Ru threw himself down on the sofa.

I handed him a mug of Earl Grey before sitting down next to him to snuggle into his side. He draped an arm over me, content to enjoy a rare moment of silence.

Ru looked up when we heard the wall clock chime as it met the hour.

"Hey, happy birthday, Frizzy!" He said, grinning.

"Oh yeah!" I smiled, not having paid the clock any attention until now. Today was officially April fifth. My birthday! I was now eighteen – officially an adult. "Thanks, Barbarian." I kissed his lips softly.

"Welcome to adulthood," Ru said.

"Thanks."

"You're a fully grown woman!"

"Shut up!" I rolled my eyes. "That just makes you seem creepy for dating me yesterday."

"Whatever," Ru mumbled against my collar, "want to go to a bar tonight since we're both of age?"

"What about the others? Won't they want to have a party?" I asked. "You know what Enzo's like."

Ru huffed, wrapping both arms around my waist to cling to me. "But..." he trailed off, knowing very well that he couldn't make demands on my birthday. Even if he'd had enough of parties and celebrations to last him right through university.

"We can go at the weekend. Just us two, okay?" I promised.

I placed my mug down on the coffee table and climbed over Ru, perching on his lap. The tips of his fingers brushed over my robe in gentle, calming strokes. Neither of us said anything for a while, taking a moment to enjoy the closeness.

"This feels good," I whispered.

Ru hummed in agreement. "Yeah. I've kind of missed having you in the bedroom, to be honest."

"Me too." I nuzzled my nose against his neck. "Don't get me wrong, the girls are great, but I liked having my barbarian nearby."

Ru noticed my blush even in the dim light, my hair falling over my suddenly shy face as I squirmed.

"Hey, what's up, Frizz?"

"Well, um." I coughed nervously, reaching for my tea. "I heard from Freja that you got that scholarship for Roxkarta. Congratulations, by the way!"

"Oh. Thanks." Ru shrugged. "What about it?"

"It's a good university," I continued, "and it's a good location. Lots of museums and shopping centres; plus it's only a two-hour train ride from Rotterdam. It's only an hour away from here on the train. Or an hour and a half on the bus."

"Yeah, that's what I thought," Ru said, "since we're all talking about meeting up in Antwerp on weekends to hang out."

We both sipped our tea to get rid of the bitter taste left in our mouths.

Our group had excitedly discussed getting together at least once a month after leaving school. It seemed to be a promise made with much sincerity. We'd spent almost every day together over the past few years. After everything we'd shared as a group, being apart didn't feel possible.

None of us wanted to be the one to address reality.

Freya and Violet would be travelling together for a year. Noah was going back to Cape Town for university and Enzo would be studying in Berlin. Nobody was ready to admit how tall of an order once a month seemed, especially not on my birthday.

"Great." I tugged on the thick sleeve of my bathrobe. "I was also thinking... Well, I'd like to take one of the vocational courses at the college there. Maybe fashion design or cosmetology? So maybe..."

Ru chuckled, no doubt about how shy I seemed. He wrapped an arm around my waist, pulling me in closer. "Don't worry, you'll get in," he teased. "I'm sure even dumb blondes can get onto vocational courses."

"Oh, fuck you!" I glared hard at him. "Maybe I'll have to rethink my position on Roxkarta being a good uni if *you* managed to get in! Maybe the anthropology department got some funding and decided to invest in a project on the failures of human evolution." I pressed my palms on either side of Ru's face to squish his cheeks together. "The long-term study of the dumbass barbarian man and his attempt at higher education!"

Ru slapped my hands away. Suddenly, he grabbed my hair to mash our lips together in a kiss. I shivered, cupping Ru's face in a much gentler fashion as our tongue tips flicked together. He gripped my thigh through my robe, feeling the firmness of the muscle there. His other hand ran smoothly up my arm, carefully caressing my neck before trailing down to cup my breast. Ru wriggled his thumbs beneath the padding of my bra, sighing in relief when he reached my soft flesh. I melted under his perfect touch, letting my body be worshipped.

"Do you want to live with me?" Ru mumbled against my lips.

I felt joy bubbling up inside me. I squealed, throwing my arms around Ru's shoulders to squeeze him tight.

"Hey! Easy!" Ru wriggled away, wheezing. I didn't let go, bumping our noses together.

"Yes, Ru!" I said through giggles, bouncing on his lap with excitement. "I'd love to live with you!"

I kissed him with all the passion I had. Ru buried a hand in my hair, both of us melting into this perfect moment. It was a moment I felt was well earned. After everything Ru and I had been through, I wanted these first few minutes of my eighteenth birthday just for us – to make a memory that would never leave us.

"I love you," I said, my voice as soft as velvet.

"I love you too," Ru growled inside my mouth. "Happy birthday, Frizzy."

"You already said that, Barbarian!"

"Well, I want to say it every day."

"You're an idiot."

"Shut up!"

I giggled as my boyfriend flipped me onto the sofa, trapping me firmly between his legs. He cut off whatever snarky comment was on my lips with another deep kiss.

"Ocean!"

Ru moaned in protest as the door slammed open. Enzo ran in and jumped on the sofa- right on top of Ru's back!

"Happy birthday, Ocean!" Enzo screamed, wriggling between us. "Happy birthday!"

"Thank you, sweetheart," I said, smiling fondly.

Ru tried to push Enzo away, but he just climbed on top of me, singing *happy birthday* loudly as the rest of our friends made their way into the common room.

"Happy birthday!" Violet said, hurrying in behind the others with a package in her hand.

My attention was diverted away from Enzo when Violet opened the box, revealing a beautiful, sweet smelling cheesecake, decorated with blueberries in the patterns of various seashells. I could tell Noah had decorated it by the way he looked up hopefully from behind his fingers.

"You don't always have to go with sea-themed stuff, you know?" Ru mumbled.

"Ignore him!" I hugged Noah, kissing his cheek. "Thank you, Noah. Violet. Everybody!"

"You're welcome," Noah said happily, hugging me back. "Happy birthday!"

Enzo cheered again, causing Ms Khil to peek her head around the door to warn us to keep it down or she'd have to escort us back to bed. She smiled anyway, also wishing me a happy birthday.

Violet placed some candles on the cake, Enzo insisting on snuggling into my side. Noah and Janie sat in front of us as Cam leaned over the back of the sofa. Freja brought over a fresh pot of tea, gathering everything together for our small midnight party.

Ru's large hand snaked past to reach the back of my neck. I turned to see my boyfriend crushed into the corner of the sofa. He still looked a little fed up from the interruption, but he offered me a smile. I wriggled through the sea of friendship to nuzzle my nose against his until he stopped scowling.

"Ew! Can you not with the PDA?" Cam whined, grabbing a squirming Enzo to cover his eyes.

Ru just ignored the fake retching noises, flipping Cam off as he kissed me with more vigour. I tapped him lightly on his head and ruffled his hair as our friends piled on top of us. I let the sound of laughter surround me, enjoying the ever-present company of my friends. I felt safe, loved, and entirely whole.

Ru

We both did.

A Note from the Author

I had considered writing an acknowledgement for the beginning of this book, however I realized there were too many people to thank. There have been so many people who have supported me and offered their encouragement, some of which may see their inspiration in this book. I offer my love to you all and thank each and every one of you. I would still like to thank my husband Ben for his love and support as well as our dog Vernon for making sure I took the necessary breaks to go outside and take a walk.

To any readers who are not trans or a sexual minority, (aka cisgender and or heterosexual readers) I'm pleased that you read this book and I hope you enjoyed it. Still, I worry that any story written by a queer author will be taken as an accurate and universal account of what it is like for all of us. While I did make sure to consult trans men, trans women, and non-binary people about this story, as well as using my own experience for inspiration, there are still things I may have gotten wrong. This, like any fiction book, is one story about queer characters. I have taken liberties in this story that may not have worked in real life- for example someone in foster care being allowed to go to boarding school abroad.

Some situations, such as Janie agreeing to get changed in the cubicle, worked for these characters, but other groups may have found different solutions. So long as everyone involved is happy, there is no right or wrong way to go about an issue that involves one specific group of friends.

Another reason for not writing an acknowledgement is because this book is for everyone who felt different or out of place, especially at school. Know that you are loved and anyone worth keeping around, while it may take them time to understand, will stick with you of their own accord. If you identify with any of the characters in this book, then I'm pleased. If not, that's okay. If you're a trans woman, a trans man, asexual, aromantic, demisexual, pansexual, genderqueer, gay, lesbian or any label that works for you, know that you are valid. It's okay to be masculine or feminine, either or a mix of the two. It's okay to be a trans man who wears skirts. It's okay to be a trans woman who wears trousers. It's okay to experiment with a new label or change labels many times in your life. There is no one way to be yourself. You are you and deserve to be respected as your authentic self.

There will be days that will be more difficult than others. There may be days when it feels the whole world is crushing you and your spirit, especially when reading the news. I have been there and felt this pain. Remember that you are perfect as you are. Things will get better.

Thank you for reading.

~Dougie K Powell

About the Author

Dougie K Powell is an author, journalist and stand-up comedian. They write LGBTQIA+ romance stories, mainly for a young adult audience. Their goal is to create stories that are both empowering and relatable to their audience.

"I want to write the books that I wanted as a teenager and a young adult. We live in a diverse world and it's important to reflect that in our work, particularly as queer authors. I feel Spectrum Books gets that."

They have also dabbled in the world of non-fiction, having published articles for several gaming websites, focusing on promoting positive LGBTQIA+ representation in gaming.

Dougie was born in Britain and currently lives in Helsinki, Finland with their husband, their dog Vernon and their terrorising bunny Iku-Turso.

Excellent LGBTQ+ fiction by unique, wonderful authors.
Thrillers
Mystery
Romance
Young Adult
& More

Join our mailing list here for news, offers and free books!

Visit our website for more Spectrum Books
www.spectrum-books.com

Or find us on Instagram
@spectrumbookpublisher

Printed in Great Britain
by Amazon